THE HAWK WHO WHO HATED WAR

HAWK KIEFER

ISBN 978-1-964462-27-1 (Paperback)
ISBN 978-1-964462-28-8 (Ebook)

Inquiries and Book Orders should be addressed to:

Leavitt Peak Press
17901 Pioneer Blvd Ste L #298, Artesia, California 90701
Phone #: 2092191548

CONTENTS

ABOUT THE AUTHOR

Hawk Kiefer graduated from West Point in 1952 and fought in Vietnam. He went to Saudi Arabia, Lebanon, and Jordan. Also, he commanded a nuclear unit in West Germany. Retired in 1977, he now lives in Florida with his wife of many years.

CHAPTER ONE

Lieutenant Hank Kean thanked God he was at Taif, rather than with headquarters on the Persian Gulf. Here, at three thousand feet in the hills above Mecca, the air was clear, cool, and fresh. Better than on the gulf, just a few feet above sea level. If guys there put on a fresh set of khakis and stepped out into the humidity, their uniforms melted onto their bodies like wet suits. He could have had it even worse. Could have been sent to Vietnam where President Kennedy had sent special forces paratroopers like Hank to swat red ants in hot, triple-canopy jungle. If the army had to send him away from his lovely wife Helen and year-old daughter, Faith, Taif was better than Vietnam.

Headquarters had sent him coordinates of a nomad winter camp in the barren hills north of Taif. Said Bin Laden was there holding a *medjlis*, a meeting which Hank could attend. But what good would coordinates and a map do in the midst of nothing but rocks, sand, and camel trails? His land rover was waiting with his Palestinian interpreter, Bashir. The guy knew where the nomad camps were. That was the good news. The bad was that neither Hank nor Bashir could carry a weapon, and the nomads had plenty. Did nomads like Americans? It really didn't make any difference. If he had to, he would knock some heads around, the way he had done so many times on so many football fields.

"Morning, boss," Bashir called, smiling, half waving, and bowing a greeting. "*Salaam*. You ready to walk in camel dung?"

"Does the little bear play in the woods?" Hank smiled. "Let's do it." While Bashir grinned and guided, Hank drove north out of Taif, following one twisting camel trail after another into the barren hills.

Barren was an understatement. Long ago, the goats had torn all bits of greenery away and left only dirty sand and black boulders.

"Magma" the books said. It looked like a giant hand had swept huge boulders from the Red Sea to his west and the sweltering sands to his east and then pushed them together to create these poor, rock-sand hills. He loved the grandeur and serenity of most mountains, but this worthless place was just plain ugly. Maybe the nomads loved these hills because nobody else could stand them and they could live alone there as they wanted.

"*Hemdu Allah*, sometime you sound almost al-Arab," Bashir said. "You know something, Bashir," Hank said. "My language ability's a gift from my mother. She's a school teacher and she always read to me the works of a poet she loved. I never really understood all the funny words he used, but I liked the sounds, rhythm, and flow. So when the army sent me to language school, it was almost the same. I couldn't understand all the words, but the rhythm and meter of Arabic were almost like that poetry. Made it easier."

"Holy Allah, the army sent you to schooling?"

"Yeah. I didn't have money for college, so I signed a long-term contract; they would pay for my education and I would stay in the army. That's how I ended up here. It looked like a good deal at the time, but I had no control over what I studied. I wanted to learn about finance and how to handle money, but they wanted me to study Arabic, the Middle East, and nuclear weapons. Can you imagine that? Study nukes and then come here. What for? They said Israel has them, Iran intends to build them, and Saudi Arabia wants them. So I signed their contract and came to Taif to find a rich guy named Mohammad bin Laden in the desolate hills of western Arabia above the holy city."

"Careful, boss," Bashir had said, "some of the people out here don't like to see you infidels this close to Mecca. Bad guys might shoot at us."

Ignoring the warning, Hank followed Bashir's directions for two more hours until he pulled the land rover over a low crest and stopped. A mountain valley full of low hills sprawled below, and hundreds of tethered camels were guarded by small boys. More than fifty black goatskin tents were widely scattered on the little hills, but he saw only a few people and no vehicles.

"Abandoned?" he asked Bashir.

"No. It be a *medjlis.* Everybody in tents. We okay. This be it. But look at those guys in front of that big tent. You can see their ankles. They *ikhwan,* (brothers). They *medgnun* (crazy) guards. Hate everything not Islamic. Hate even this truck. They shoot at us."

Sure enough, one of the guards raised his ancient musket and fired at the rover. He missed, and Hank went into reverse. Then, a Saudi officer emerged from the tent, wearing a modern uniform; brown Ike jacket, trousers tucked into combat boots, the insignia of a captain, and waving a pistol. He yelled at the *ikhwan* who lowered their weapons and backed off. He then signaled the rover to come forward. As the subdued guards glared, Hank saluted the officer and asked if Mohammed bin Laden was inside. The man nodded, led Hank to the tent, said bin Laden would welcome them, and opened the flap.

Inside, about two dozen Arabs sat cross legged on Persian rugs thrown on the sand. Among them, black, white-clad servants poured tea from pots with long curved spouts. From the tent door running through the center of the group, a seven-foot-wide, red carpet led to a *dais* holding a throne, on which sat a slim, rather tall Arab with piercing eyes, short black hair, and no beard. He was not a Saudi royal, because the royals all wore beards. Had to be Muhammad bin Laden who came from north Yemen. In contrast to the Saudis, most Yemenis were clean shaven. Behind bin Laden stood a small cluster of attendants, including a few officers carrying pistols, hands near their holsters. They and everybody else were staring at Hank.

He kept his cool, and simply gazed back, aware that he wanted friendship, not challenges. Except for the men in uniform, everybody wore the ubiquitous Arab long white shirts and sandals. But in football, love and war, initiative works best, so he ignored the crowd, strode to the *dais,* offered bin Laden the traditional *Asalamma Alaycum* (peace be with you), and waited somewhat anxiously for a response.

To his relief, bin Laden smiled, answered, "*Wa alaycum essalaam* (and with you, peace)," and reached down to assist Hank onto the *dais*, where another throne now waited. The tension in the tent eased a bit. When Hank was seated, a servant poured him a small glass of the hot, sweet tea the Arabs love in the winter. He raised his glass to his host.

Then, without preamble, bin Laden asked about the war tank, a glass of the hot, sweet tea the Arabs loved in the winter. Hank in the Yemen. Hank was ready for the question. Bin Laden family home was under attack. He had to be worried because the Egyptians had sent 65,000 soldiers across the Red Sea and headed toward his family and friends.

"Don't be concerned," Hank said. "America just sent the Saudis an American fighter-bomber squadron that will quickly end that war and any threat to your family."

Bin Laden sat for a moment with an approving grin, then asked how he could help Hank.

"I'm part of the mission that sent you those American planes. I wanted you to know about them and what they will do for you. I want to be of service any way I can."

"Is your family here?" bin Laden asked.

"My family is back in America," Hank said, "but I have pictures." Hank dug into his wallet and pulled out snapshots of Helen and Faith.

Bin Laden took them and beamed. Rising, he held the pictures high for everyone to see, and called out, "*Jamila bintain* (two beautiful ladies)." The assembled Arabs stirred, laughed, and chattered a little, but mostly, they continued to stare at this strange American and his bodyguard. Most of them had never seen a foreigner, much less a large one in uniform, but the pictures changed them, made Hank human. Progress in what looked to be a long journey.

Bin Laden sat back down, turned to Hank, and asked if he had a specific request.

"I would like to meet with you again," Hank said, "to discuss matters of mutual concern."

Bin Laden stared at Hank for a moment, his brows questioning, head turned at an angle, as if thinking. Finally he said, "I will arrange it."

That was big, just what Hank wanted. Should he push for more?

Bashir whispered, "That enough. Say *salaam*. Let the *medjlis* go on without us."

So Hank stood and offered the usual farewell, "*Maa'a salamma* (with peace)."

To his surprise, bin Laden also rose, took Hank's hand; a gesture of respect, and led the way through the quiet Arabs, past the *ikhwan* warriors to the land rover.

On a nearby hill, among the small black tents, a crowd of women and children stared at him. The women wore the black *burca* and the little children wore clean, white, long shirts for the Muslim holy day.

Bin Laden pointed at the crowd, said, "*Zowdji* (my wives)." "*Kem* (how many)?" Hank asked.

"*Sebaa wa khemseen*, (fifty-seven)," he answered.

Hank started to protest that the Koran says a man could have only four wives, but bin Laden laughed, playfully punched him on the arm, and said, "Four at one time."

Then he motioned for his bodyguards to step back. When he, Hank, and Bashir were alone, he said, "We will meet again and discuss your concerns. I will make the arrangements."

Then he kissed Hank on both cheeks and watched them drive away.

"What the hell just happened?" Hank asked.

"*Hemdu Allah*, I think you did it," Bashir said. "He wants meeting. *Mumtaz* (Great). You hit it just right. Might have been the family pictures. He loves them."

"But why did he agree to meet? Why would he trust me?"

"You come to his *medjlis,* and give him welcome news about the war in the Yemen, especially good stuff, because he thinks his family in danger. He, like you, come to his camp to tell him. And you raise his power among the nomads by bringing America to his camp, pay him respect. You did it. Meet again, win his trust."

"So, what do I do now?" "Wait. See he call you."

"Do I report this to headquarters in Riyadh?"

"Tell them the *medjlis* good. Don't tell his offer to meet. That might leak, upset him, make him change his mind. You want meet. Gain his trust. Tell headquarters you start."

"I learned something about bin Laden back there," Hank said with a grin. "I now know why he likes America so much, we made him rich enough to have fifty-seven wives."

"*Hemdu Allah*," Bashir laughed. "That good, right. Now make him trust you. Find out about King Faisal and the big coup."

Big was right. What happened was big indeed. Bashir was correct, now he had to find out what King Faisal was going to do to consolidate his coup. Who was he going to purge? What did the coup mean for America?

He heard his mother reading a poem, "And I was huntsman and herdsman, the foxes on the hills barked clear and cold."

But there were only goats and camels in the barren Arabian hills. And the future here was not clear. He saw clouds ahead.

Chapter Two

Hank had been an outstanding defensive back on the Fayetteville Bulldog high school state football championship team in 1957. Known for his aggressive play, he had been confident of a scholarship to Duke, State, or Carolina, but all three had told him they were full. If he had been a student, he could have walked on, but his family had no money for tuition. Dad was a mechanic and mom a substitute teacher, and they barely made ends meet. He loved them. They were good people. Dad was a war veteran and mom read to Hank daily from that poet she loved. He never understood the funny words like "dingle," but he grew to like the rhythm and cadence. He desperately wanted to marry his high school love, Helen, but her father would not approve until Hank had a degree or a job. So he went to the army recruiter at Fort Bragg, said he wanted to be a paratrooper. The sergeant gave him some tests and told him to come back in a week.

"You're too smart to be a grunt," the recruiter then said. "You scored really high, especially on language aptitude. You should be an officer. We'll make you a deal. We'll pay all costs for a full-time scholarship at State. When you graduate, we'll make you a lieutenant and you can be a paratrooper. In return, you'll owe us eight years of service."

It sounded like a bargain, so Hank signed the contract. State was only an hour away from Helen, and his father gave him an old jalopy than ran most of the time. He came home a lot to see Helen, and the years flew by until Lieutenant Kean married Helen. It was sheer bliss, the union of two souls in earthly heaven. After he learned how to jump out of perfectly good airplanes, he received orders to defense intelligence at the Pentagon for temporary duty.

"What's this?" he asked his captain.

"Beats me," he said. "I've never seen a junior officer ordered to report to such an important agency. They must have something special in mind for you."

The captain was correct. A full-bird colonel said Hank was to go for an advanced degree at Duke and study Arabic, Saudi Arabia, and nuclear weapons. Then he would go to Arabia, find a man named Mohammad bin Laden, and cultivate his friendship.

"I can't do that," Hank said. "My wife is pregnant, and I don't want to leave her."

"You signed a contract," the colonel said. "We can send you anywhere we want. How would you like to go to Vietnam? If you do what we want, however, we'll put your wife in quarters at Fort Bragg, assign a senior officer to care for her, and send a chopper for you at Duke if she goes into labor. So which is it, Vietnam or Duke?"

The colonel sure knew how to bargain. Hank studied Arabic, Saudi Arabia, and strangely enough, nuclear weapons. When Helen went into labor, a chopper got Hank to the hospital before the little girl, Faith, arrived. The grandparents were overjoyed, but Hank went back to see the colonel at the Pentagon to ask if he really had to go to Saudi Arabia. The colonel sent him to see an official in named Onorato in defense intelligence.

"I'll be your handler," Onorato said. "You locate bin Laden, earn his trust, and learn what the Saudis are doing about nuclear weapons. We'll take good care of your wife and daughter at Fort Bragg. We'll bring you home frequently for updates. Every time we do, we'll give you vacation time with your family. Nuclear weapons are going to be important in the Middle East. You will be on a mission of national importance. Bin Laden will be a special source. He likes Americans and is not a member of the royal family. They trust him, but they won't talk to any American about classified matters. If you do this right, bin Laden will confide in you."

Hank first met bin Laden in that nomad camp in January of 1964, but he did not hear from the contractor until two months later. He worried as he waited, receiving only bits and pieces of information. Bin Laden and other Saudis asked Hank with various

Americans at the embassy and headquarters. Just casual contacts. Had bin Laden rejected him?

The man was an enigma. Hank learned much about him while studying the Middle East at Duke. He was from Asir Province, near the Yemen, not far from where the Egyptians had recently crossed the Red Sea and were fighting. In 1930, bin Laden had been a penniless, uneducated laborer when he made his way north to Jeddah in search of work. In an odd contrast, that was the same year that millionaire Charles Crane had come to Jeddah to meet the newly crowned first king of Saudi Arabia, Abdul Aziz. Bin Laden was a poor carpenter and Crane was a manufacturer of bathroom products who earned the trust of Abdul Aziz just after World War I.

Crane had argued before the League of Nations that the creation of a Jewish homeland in Palestine had violated a major charter of the League; self-determination, because ninety percent of people living in Palestine were Arabs who did not want a Jewish homeland there. Crane lost the case but won Arab trust. That was why Crane came to Jeddah and got the concession from Abdul Aziz to drill for oil in Saudi Arabia. Bin Laden started a small business as a carpenter while Crane brought oil and riches to Arabia. Bin Laden's work in Mecca won the admiration of Abdul Aziz and later, King Saud. He renovated a mosque faster, cheaper, and better than his contract called for. That was why he had gone from poverty to become a billionaire when Hank met him at that *medjlis;* he was honest, skilled, and a hard worker, qualities that mystified the Saudis. Finally, to Hank's relief, an Arab appeared at Hank's quarters with a written invitation to meet bin Laden for supper after evening prayers at a restaurant west of Taif.

"What and where is this restaurant?" Hank asked Bashir.

"West of city," Bashir said. "His excellence, Mohammad Bin Laden, build it top of road that goes down to Mecca and Jeddah. Hangs out over cliff. Where you look down, way far down. It as close to the heaven and the holy city as an infidel is allowed."

If bin Laden found out he was an agent of American intelligence, he would be done for.

"With all the other diners watching, would he dare kill me?"

Bashir grimaced and shook his head, "You out of luck. Bin Laden always eat alone. The restaurant is shut when he go there. It be just you, him, and the guards."

Hank didn't like the sound of that, "Won't you be there?" Bashir shook his head, "The invite is for you. You soar solo."

Maybe soar off the cliff, but he had no choice. He would do this.

Thank God he had provided for Helen and Faith.

He drove the rover west to the restaurant. In the empty parking lot, guards stopped him until he produced his invitation. Bashir was right; there were no other diners, just bin Laden and enough bodyguards to easily toss Hank over the edge. But the restaurant was fantastic, cantilevered well out over the semi-darkness. He looked down. The view was the same as jumping out of a plane, but without a parachute. If they tried to toss him over, he would take several of the bodyguards with him.

Bin Laden rose all smiles to grab him by the shoulders and kiss him on both cheeks, like a mob boss. A kiss of death? Hank took a seat, too damn close to the edge. One of the guards spoke enough English for them to converse.

"Show me the little pictures again," bin Laden said, "of your beautiful wife and daughter. You are truly blessed. Here in Saudi Arabia, we truly love our children."

A waiter brought hot, sweet tea, and Hank started to ask a question.

"First we eat," bin Laden said. "Then we talk about your concerns." The waiter brought a large, round silver platter to the small table. Centered on the latter was the exquisitely prepared carcass of a goat. Around it were rice and fruit. This was the "goat grab" he had been told about. The idea was to reach out with your right hand and rip off some meat to stuff in your mouth, following it with rice and grapes or dates. Hank had asked Onorato why they use just the right hand, and the guy had scoffed, "Because the Bedouins have no toilet paper." In spite of that, this goat tasted delicious. The skin was crisp and flavored and the meat came off easily. Sweet grapes, moist rice, and soft dates finished the meal.

Bin laden sat back, beamed, and said, "Good." Hank nodded in agreement.

"Now, my American friend," bin Laden asked, "what can I do for you?"

This was it, he'd never have a better chance.

"Saudi Arabia is changing. Faisal is now king and Saud is talking to Nasser in Cairo. This has grave implications for both our countries."

Bin Laden nodded and muttered something about truth, fate, and destiny.

"America needs to understand what is happening," Hank said. "But the royal family does not trust us. They have cut us off. If we are to help you, we must find ways to communicate."

Bin Laden raised his hand. In silence, he leaned close and peered directly into Hank's eyes, holding the contact for a full minute.

Hank steadied, and met the stare. It's crunch time. Over the edge?

Then, thank God, bin Laden waved the guards back, out of hearing.

"Your words are true," bin Laden then said slowly, making sure Hank understood. "King Faisal is moving Saudi Arabia in a new direction, a dangerous path that will change everything. Difficult decisions need to be made before catastrophe comes to us."

Then he sat back quietly, with his head lowered and eyes closed.

He seemed to be praying.

Now was the time to step in.

"For America to help you," Hank said, "we need information, facts. You can provide these through me without the censorship of state departments or evil men with hate in their hearts."

Bin Laden sat up, smiling.

"You speak the truth," he said. "We will meet again."

Hank tried not to let his triumph show as they shook hands. The following day, he drove down to the embassy annex at Taif to send an encrypted message to Onorato and summarize the success of this second contact.

CHAPTER THREE

Agent Onorato, Hank's handler, lived in McLean with his wife and two boys. Raised in Abingdon, Virginia, Onorato was a Virginian born and bred. At Emory and Henry College, he studied under an outstanding professor of Lebanese heritage. The man was so impressive that Onorato decided to specialize in the Middle East and learn Arabic. Answering an advertisement for government employment in the Middle East, he maxed some tests, and soon was working on the Middle East desk of the defense intelligence agency.

A dedicated patriot, Onorato was of average size, strength, and looks, which made him perfect as an agent. A hard worker with outstanding intelligence, he won many commendations and rose rapidly through the ranks of various intelligence agencies. He served in Cairo, Riyadh, Beirut, Amman, and Jerusalem, rising from agent to handler, and eventually to senior official. What he lacked in physical statue, he made up by tenacity and endurance. With large eyes and big ears, he reminded Hank of an owl. That first impression lasted, and when Hank met Onorato's two sons, he saw only two little owls.

Onorato circulated a classified summary of Hank's two contacts with bin Laden. The summary went to those with a need to know, and shortly afterwards, a C.I.A. agent named Steve Blevins showed up at Onorato's desk with a copy of that summary.

"I have a demonstrated agency interest in Saudi Arabia," Blevins said. "Bin Laden is high on my list, and I want to be copied on every contact Kean has with him. Here are my agency credentials."

Blevins looked like an agent, but he had hard eyes that worried Onorato. After verifying Blevins's identity and need to know, however, Onorato put him on the list. Then he summoned his researcher with the best C.I.A. contacts.

"Dig up everything you can about C.I.A. agent Steve Blevins," Onorato said. "He worries me. I want the entire scoop, everything."

In Taif, a week later, another invitation arrived. Hank was to come to bin Laden's permanent winter camp. A guide would escort him, and again, Bashir was not invited. Whenever Hank did not have time to go to the American embassy annex in Taif, he used an encrypted short-wave radio. He didn't like doing that. Short-wave was dangerous. It could be heard and its code broken. He needed to report this second invitation quickly, however, and ask why Bashir was again being left out, so he risked sending the message.

"Bin Laden thinks he is in danger," Onorato replied. "He was a favorite of King Saud, a trusted member of Saud's council. But Faisal is still consolidating the coup in which he ousted Saud, and he cannot trust anybody who had been Saud's friend. Bin Laden feels the danger, and he, too, can trust only people he knows. Bashir is not one of those. You have an opportunity to make yourself someone he will talk to. Go to his camp and grab that opportunity. You do not need Bashir. You can do it on your own."

When Hank reported the new meeting to Bashir, the interpreter warned again.

"Bin Laden's camp is in the remote forests of Asir Province," he said. "Two times the height of Taif. Cold and rain. People there hate foreigners, especially Americans. They think Queen of Sheba lived there and her gold is still somewhere in the hills. Not want gold rush to ruin the forests. You be alone among them and in great danger. This be very bad for you."

Hank was warned, but not deterred. The meeting was on a Friday, and when Hank rose that day, a clean-shaven, young, trim Arab waited outside.

"I Mustafa," he said in barely passable English. "I your servant and guide when his most eminence bin Laden summon you to him."

That sounded like a more permanent arrangement. Good. "Where are we going?" Hank asked.

"To permanent winter staying place," Mustafa said. "You be there many days. It would good to pack many things. The women wash for you. But they not know about western clothes. So you bring extra uniform."

Several days didn't sound like a one-night stand. "Where'd you learn English?" Hank asked.

"Bin Laden insist," Mustafa said. "He make many of us learn English. It is good for him to do this. I learn about America. I like to know more. You teach me. Good."

Bin Laden was no dummy. Working with Americans, he needed men who talked the talk.

"Is this Asir Province where the Queen of Sheba lived with her gold?" Hank asked.

"*Na'am* (yes)," Mustafa said. "Gold still there. Before Queen Sheba, Asir be Garden of Eden. Snake come, ruin Eden. Asir people think foreigners be snakes. Ruin Asir."

Following Mustafa's guidance, Hank drove south from Taif on a fairly good, twisting, new, paved road into gradually higher hills. The road was well built; Bin Laden must have had the contract. After several hours, they had climbed into a region not so barren, with taller trees and lush vegetation, almost like the hills Hank liked so much back home. Then they came to a road blocked by a squad of armed men that did not look friendly.

"They *harb* (soldiers)," Mustafa said. "Not want snakes in Asir. If you snake, they kill. No worry, I have papers for you. Stay in car. I show them."

The soldiers did not look impressed by the papers, and Hank bemoaned again his lack of a weapon. The men called several times for him to dismount, but each time Mustafa protested and he remained in the rover. They raised their rifles and started toward him, but Mustafa called out bin Laden's name, and they stopped. Finally, they backed off and allowed the rover to proceed.

"That was bad," Hank said.

"They stupid," Mustafa said. "Not can read paper. I told them you friend of Bin Laden. Said he punish them if they hurt you."

First the *ikhwan* and now the *harb* wanted to kill him. Not a friendly place. As he drove on, however, the serenity of the forest, growing ever taller, calmed him. Instead of sand and barren rocks, verdant greenery was everywhere. "It's really beautiful here," he said. "I can see why they don't want foreigners to come."

"Praise be to Allah, the mountains are Arab glory," Mustafa said. "In the province of Asir, the average hill is very high. Asir has great forests thick and tall. Much rain make small rivers with fast water and many fish. Be beautiful white beaches on Red Sea. Truly, this be where the Garden of Eden was before the snake."

Tall trees indeed surrounded the winter camp, which held large tents with wooden sides. Bin Laden must come here often, because this was a permanent place. Hank needed to tell Onorato about this winter home and the new highway that tanks could traverse. Cooler and clearer than Taif, Asir was a paradise away from the sweltering desert heat on the gulf. It had taken them almost seven hours of driving on that road, and the Pentagon needed to know that Egyptian soldiers would have a tough time fighting north from the Yemen through these wooded hills on that twisting road, especially if the Saudis had American airpower.

Mustafa led him to a large, separate tent. "This your place. Next to bin Laden," he said. "After evening prayers, I come take you to him for dinner. You have water here. Bathe and drink. Wear a clean uniform. Leave dirty one on the bed. The women clean it."

Fearful of listening devices, Hank had to store everything in his head. And he couldn't take notes that might be found and show he was a spy. If anything happened to him in these hills, only the animals would find his body.

Bin Laden greeted him ceremoniously and introduced him to ten other men who appeared to be staff and contractors. They dined together around a large table that held four goat-grab platters. They ate leisurely and talked casually of work and war. Hank listened carefully, trying to understand the dialects and remembering anything to report to Onorato. After the pastries, the others left. Hank was alone with bin Laden and a contractor who acted as an interpreter. Bin Laden stopped smiling. It was time for serious talk.

"Let me tell you about the coup and the removal of Saud by Faisal," bin Laden said softly as if he feared listeners. "We must be careful, for Faisal is known to act swiftly and cruelly. If he hears what we are talking about, I will die, and you will be in great danger."

Hank leaned forward and asked, "Why are you in danger? You do very good construction work that Saudi Arabia needs. The royals value you."

"Faisal hated Saud," bin Laden said. "Thought he was weak. Saud went to Egypt to scheme with Nasser against him. Faisal now says he should have not let Saud go free. Says he should have killed him when he had the chance."

This was important. Hank pressed on, "The royal family has many sons of Abdul Aziz. They have great power. Would they have allowed Faisal to kill their brother, Saud?"

"Yes. They are frightened of Faisal and what he plans to do. He is vindictive."

Onorato needed to know this, "What plans?"

"Faisal is going to seize the American assets of Aramco without any compensation. Then he will raise the price of oil from five to over thirty dollars a barrel."

Wow. Lord let him live to report it, "What is Saud planning with Nasser in Egypt?"

"Saud seeks to persuade Nasser to attack Saudi Arabia and put Saud back on the throne."

To have a communist like Nasser, controlling Middle East oil would be catastrophic. To prevent that, America would have to come to Faisal's aid, no matter what he did to the price of oil or to Aramco.

"America will stop Nasser," Hank said.

"I hope you will help make that happen. That is why I agreed to speak to you. Muslims cannot allow an atheist like Nasser to seize Mecca and Medina. Do not worry about what Faisal might do to me. I can handle him. Tell your people what I said."

Hank went to his darkened tent. In his boxer shorts, he lay on the bed until he heard stealthy movement in the tent. A *harb* assassin? He tensed to spring up and fight. Then he heard a woman softly humming. He smelled perfume and felt a small, soft hand moving lightly across his back, expertly caressing him. Thank God, he was lying on his stomach. If she had touched his erection, he would have exploded. Turning quickly, he caught a soft hand. Lifted her. Delicate and light. He carried her to the tent flap and set her gently outside. Truly beautiful.

"*La,* (no)," he said.

"*Na'am* (yes)," she pleaded.

"*La,*" he repeated in a stronger voice as he lightly slapped her behind, sent her on her way, and closed the tent flap.

He did not sleep well, his thoughts alternating between Helen, what bin Laden had said, and the beautiful humming girl. He was groggy and still barely awake when Mustafa came to the tent after breakfast.

"I show you the forest, many cold streams, and white beach by the Red Sea," he said. "Bin Laden order us to be back by evening prayers."

The forest was grand, the streams flowed swiftly, and the white beaches were wide, empty, and unsoiled. A true paradise, with a hint of defiant dervishes in the darker, deeper woods. He didn't want to end the tour, but Mustafa insisted they return to camp, and after prayers, Hank put on the fresh khakis the women had left on the bed.

Bin Laden waited for him alone, serene, and smiling.

"A man must be with a woman to keep his manhood," bin Laden said.

"My woman waits for me in America. My manhood is for her."

"The girl's name is Jamila, the beautiful one," bin Laden said. "She wants your child. She thinks he would be a boy, and would become strong, a great warrior."

"Can you make her understand that I already have a woman?"

Bin Laden shook his head. Then, over a light meal, they avoided dangerous talk. That night, Jamila did not return to his tent. In the morning, bin Laden kissed him on both cheeks and waved goodbye as Hank and Mustafa returned to Taif.

CHAPTER FOUR

Two days later, Hank went to Jeddah and the embassy annex to send an urgent, classified, encrypted message to Onorato.

"Bin Laden believes that deposed King Saud is working with Nasser in Cairo on plans to attack Saudi Arabia, put Saud back on throne, and give control of Mecca and Medina to Nasser. If that is done, the Muslim world would explode. In order to restore Saudi Arabia's depleted finances that Saud plundered, Bin Laden says King Faisal plans to soon seize American assets in Aramco, without compensation. Faisal will take complete control, installing a new oil minister instructed to raise the price of oil from five to over thirty dollars a barrel."

In a week, he had his reply.

"A plane will pick you up at the Jeddah International Airport in two days and bring you here. The military mission in Taif will take care of your personnel goods while you are gone, including your land rover. I am setting up a briefing in our conference room for several intelligence agencies and a representative of the state department. Be prepared to brief them on the contents of your recent message to me. Do not inform Muhammad bin Laden about this briefing. Your information will be evaluated. While we wait for the results of the evaluation, you will be given thirty days leave and transport to Fort Bragg and your family."

Hallelujah! He would see Helen and Faith, a daughter he hardly knew. He jumped up and almost ran around the embassy annex headquarters. In Taif, as he packed, he sang his and Helen's favorite song, Fats Waller's "Two Sleepy People." It always reminded him of their younger days.

"Two sleepy people by dawn's early light, too much in love to say good night."

His boring travel arrangements were a pleasure. He would see his ladies, mom, and dad. He contacted Mustafa and Bashir to let them he would gone for about a month. Told Mustafa to tell bin Laden that when he came back, he would bring more pictures of Helen and little Faith.

Two days later, Bashir took him to the airport. "Where you going?" Bashir asked.

"To America. Tell bin Laden I go to report his words to important people in Washington. I will be working there for him and Saudi Arabia."

"You return?"

"I think so, but that's up to the army. When I signed that agreement, I told you about, it gave the government complete control over me. They pay for everything, even a house and medical care for my wife and family. At the time it seemed like a good deal, but now, I'm not so sure. They order me around a lot and tell me what to study, even strange things like nuclear weapons. I've got bad vibes about that, but at least I'll get to see my wife and baby."

At the Pentagon, Onorato said Hank's message had stirred things up.

"Three intelligence guys and a state department hack will be coming to our conference room tomorrow. They want to know if you make sense or are a complete nut."

"What do you think?" Hank asked.

"You're a nut that just possibly might make some sense."

Three army colonels and a state department suit sat on one side of the conference table while Onorato introduced Hank from the opposite side.

"Lieutenant Kean is a fully trained and qualified agent," Onorato said. "We sent him to Saudi Arabia to search out Mohammad bin Laden and gain his trust. Kean's mission was to find out what was really going on with the Faisal coup, what new direction the kingdom might take, and what new problems Faisal might create for us. Kean has just returned. He met with Muhammad bin Laden three times, and you have seen his report. He's here to expand on that report and to answer your questions."

"When did you meet Mohammad bin Laden?" asked a large colonel wearing good medals from the Korean War.

Hank disliked the situation. The three colonels looked like they were a court and he was under a court-martial, and they all looked as if he had already been found guilty. The state department suit was frowning at him over black, horn-rimmed glasses.

"We last met three weeks ago," Hank said. "At his winter home in the mountains of Asir. A previous meeting was three weeks before that at Taif, and the first, two months before that, was in a nomad camp above Mecca."

The colonels briefly huddled and took notes on yellow pads.

The guy from state wore an expensive dark suit. His glasses and regimental tie gave him the look of a scholar, certainly not a fighter. He was a thinker, too lightweight to fight.

"Where again did you first meet?" the big colonel asked. "In a nomad tent north of Taif. I went to his *medjlis*."

"At a what?" asked a second colonel, a smaller man, wearing no medals. "What kind of a camp was it?"

Hank straightened in his chair and started to answer with sarcasm. That asshole didn't know shit, but he was going to decide American policy in Saudi Arabia.

Before Hank could ruin himself, the state suit stepped in.

"Let's let this agent talk and not waste time showing our ignorance."

At least the state department guy knew his stuff and had balls.

"A *medjlis* is a meeting where people ask favors from someone important," said the third colonel, a warrior. "And Taif is the summer capital of Saudi Arabia."

This warrior also knew his stuff. Had to watch him. The state suit was still an unknown.

"That's right, sir," Hank said. "I asked him to meet later, and he agreed."

The smaller colonel scoffed and started to interrupt.

The big colonel put his hand on the guy's arm and held him back. "Why don't we hold our questions until after the brief?" he said while holding the guy down.

The state suit smiled and the fighter laughed.

Hank then related how he met bin Laden and gained his trust. How Bin Laden wanted Hank to relay messages to people in America who could help Saudi Arabia. He ended with bin Laden's fear of Faisal's wrath and Saud's conspiracy with Nasser.

The state suit then stepped in, "Do you believe King Faisal will seize Aramco?"

"I do," Hank said. "Bin Laden has worked with the royals for over thirty years and knows how they think. He would not say such a thing carelessly. I also believed him when he said that Faisal was determined to raise the price of oil and have money to make major changes in Saudi Arabia, changes that would affect America."

The smaller colonel scoffed again and said, "America will go to war if he does."

Hank started to answer, but state again spoke, "Do not send our soldiers to war so lightly."

An internecine battle. He sat back to watch.

"Let's argue that another time," the big colonel said, still holding the smaller man down. "I want to find out what this agent knows, so I'll have a basis to decide if he's for real. I don't think we would go to war over oil, but we might fight if Nasser invaded Saudi."

Hank then spelled out bin Laden's concerns about Faisal. When he was done, he asked for questions and the fighter asked if either Hank or bin Laden might be in danger.

"Bin Laden thinks we would be," Hank answered, "if word gets to King Faisal about what I just said. If my report leaks to Faisal, bin Laden thinks he will be in deep trouble, maybe terminal, and Faisal will come down hard on me."

The state suit raised his hand for attention and said, "What I am about to tell you is for high-level use only. Our relations with Saudi Arabia would be harmed if this were leaked to the media before the royal kingdom makes it public."

He had their attention, especially that of Onorato and Hank.

"As you know," the state rep continued, "King Saud exhausted the riches of his kingdom by his profligate and wasteful spending. That was why Faisal got rid of Saud and also why none of the other sons of Abdul Aziz objected. Faisal took over a country that could not pay its immediate bills. He was in desperate straits until Mohammad bin Laden intervened by giving Faisal a billion dollars. That's right, a billion dollars, all of bin Laden's liquid assets. The infusion of that cash solved the kingdom's immediate crisis and gave Faisal time to meet his kingdom's urgent need for cash. We were not sure how Faisal would provide for his long-term need for cash until I heard Lieutenant Kean confirm what we believed Faisal might do; seize Aramco and raise the price of oil. At any rate, Muhammad bin Laden has insured his own survival and become a trusted asset for King Faisal."

Hank was dumbfounded. Bin Laden had not hinted what he might do. He had only said that he could take care of himself. Hank wanted to return to Saudi Arabia and ask him what this news meant for America and Hank's future there.

"What this implies for the safety of Lieutenant Kean," state continued, "is not clear. That is contingent on what bin Laden told Faisal about Kean's role. I suppose if bin Laden told Faisal that Kean is a spy, we probably should not send the lieutenant back there."

The three colonels hastily scribbled notes about Faisal's solution to his immediate and future need for money. The meeting then broke up so they could report to their agencies.

"How did I do?" Hank asked Onorato when the others had gone. "Not for me to say," Onorato answered. "We'll know in a month and you'll either be a hero or a nut case. In any case, there is a risk, a concern about whether King Faisal might punish you. I need to think if I want you to take that risk."

"I have to go back," Hank said. "I want to confront bin Laden. Did he expose my role to King Faisal? If he did, I failed and he was faking all the time with me. But maybe he wasn't faking. Maybe he was and still is my friend. I need to know. I have to look him in the eye. I know that sounds crazy. What does that make me?"

"A nut case with balls."

CHAPTER FIVE

Onorato's executive jet waited for Hank at Andrews's airfield in Maryland. It would a two-hour flight to the Pope Air Force base near Fort Bragg. Time to ponder his fate if he returned to Saudi Arabia and to anticipate seeing Helen. God, how he missed her. She had been a part of his life since they met at Fayetteville High School almost ten years ago. He would never forget first sitting behind her in their history class. Her long, blond hair tumbled before him and he had an overwhelming desire to touch the abundant strands. He called it an historic moment. They walked out together and had never been far apart until the army sent him away. She was 5' 9" and with heels, she almost looked directly into his eyes at 6' 2". After football practice, his custom was to watch her at band practice. She was a baton twirler and he loved how she strutted out with head held high and laughing as she preceded the band. From the start he thought she was gorgeous in bobby socks, sweater, and skirt. He saw the real woman when he went to where she worked at the Dos Hermanos restaurant. It was not a fast-food joint out on the strip where most of the soldiers went, but a fine place in an upscale neighborhood. It had been there for years and was delicious dining with white tablecloths and fine china. She was a greeter, because she was beautiful and outgoing. When Hank walked in and saw her in heels, black dress, and hair swept back, she wasn't just gorgeous, she was breathtakingly beautiful. No wonder Dos Hermanos made her a greeter. No wonder he was in love.

When the jet landed, he saw her on the tarmac standing by a military sedan, just as he had always remembered her; tall, beautiful, and smiling, with that full blond hair swept back. He scrambled from the plane, ran to her, and swung her around in a bear hug.

"Careful." she laughed. "Don't damage the goods."

"I can't help myself," he almost shouted. "It's been too long."

He put her down and belatedly saluted the smiling major holding a sedan door open for them. The major turned out to be the Bragg officer assigned by the Pentagon to take good care of Helen while Hank was in Saudi Arabia.

With the officer sitting in front, the driver took them to Helen's quarters at Fort Bragg; a modern, good-sized, two-room bungalow.

"Are they treating you right?" Hank asked.

"Right, and more," she said. "They spoil me. This major makes hospital appointments, sends people to clean the house, and if I have to go to military personnel with a problem, he escorts me there. If I dared ask him to shop for me, I think he would do it. He's great, always available. He's been a Godsend. And if you add in the fact that both of our parents are nearby, I've been as blessed as possible without you."

Onorato was more than living up to his part of the bargain.

As Hank was getting out of the car, little Faith ran squealing in joy toward him and jumped into his arms. She was a giggling, beautiful child.

"She's happy," Helen said, "because you're here for her second birthday."

"That's not for months," Hank protested.

"We're holding it early, so you can be here for it."

That was the way everything went. Everybody was prepared, happy he was home, and making his stay memorable. His father took time off from his job at the Ford dealership to visit like old times and complain about politics as he always had. His mother took a vacation from her teaching. He went to visit them at the home where he had been raised in Fayetteville, and he sat for hours on their back porch while, as always, she read to him the poems of the poet she loved as they watched Dad work on an old jalopy.

"When I was at a nomad camp in the Saudi high desert hills," Hank said, "I heard your voice, just as you are doing now, reading from your poet. I don't understand him, never could, but I remember a few words now and then."

"What words?" she asked.

"Words like 'dingle' night. I'll never forget my first dingle night with Helen."

She laughed, "Poets use words beautifully."

Hank agreed and then turned serious, "You really helped me learn Arabic. I didn't understand many Arabic words, just like I didn't understand many of your poet's words, but the entire Koran is a beautiful poem, with meter and rhyme. So as I studied Arabic, I listened to the sounds, heard the rhyme, and felt the meter, just as I did when you read those poems. You helped me become almost fluent."

Helen's parents closed their physical-therapy shop for several days. They talked as they always had about retiring and moving to Florida. As usual, it was just talk. They wanted to stay near Helen and Faith, and near their patients. It made them feel needed. They wanted to know what Hank was doing in Saudi Arabia and the army.

He had only a month to make up for the year he had missed, especially a year when he could have been teaching Faith to walk and talk. Now, he wanted to help. Maybe buy Helen a new car, but his dad said he could keep her old wreck running. "Save the money," he said, "you'll need it." Hank saw the start of a problem with his mother; she worried because she kept forgetting things. Could Dad take care of her? Helen's parents said they still wanted to keep their therapy clinic open. Hank's old football coach came by to talk about the Bulldog's championship year when Hank was an all-state linebacker. He said Fayetteville had never again fielded a team like Hank's. Hank tried to teach Faith to ride a small cycle, and exhausted them both in the effort. He had lost a critical year. But he and Helen made sure he had his manhood, and that she still appreciated it. There were so many people to see and so much to do that almost a month had gone when Onorato sent for him. He had to leave again and it was harder than before.

The plane waited at Pope Field, and he could not avoid leaving. Going was so much more difficult after spending time with Helen and Faith that he went to the military personnel office at Fort Bragg to see if he had a choice. They said he had to obey lawful orders. He talked to a military attorney and was told the same thing. If he refused, he could be court-martialed. He had to go. So after tears and hugs, he went back to the Pentagon. Onorato told him that he was now a captain, had a commendation medal, and would be receiving generous incentive pay, but he had to go back to Taif and learn his fate.

"The colonels must have believed me," Hank said. "But if they really think King Faisal might be a real danger to me, why send me back so I can be tossed over a cliff?"

"That's why you get incentive pay," Onorato said. "And now we have a new challenge for you; bin Laden's son, Bakr. We think he will be the one that takes over if bin Laden ever disappears. Bakr's at Miami University now, but he'll soon be coming home for summer break. Meet him, make friends, and gain his trust."

"Why me? Send somebody else."

"We trained you for this. We knew right away you could do it. You were a top-notch football player and a paratrooper who could handle himself physically. The I.Q. tests made us think you had some smarts, so we sent you to college and you excelled. Then we set up a special program on Arabic and the Middle East and again, you proved you had the smarts. You had maxed the language aptitude test, so we knew you could learn Arabic. We were right about you because you found bin Laden and earned his trust. You're the one we need. Your mission now is to gain the trust of the son, Bakr, in case the father disappears. One final thing; we are hearing elusive rumors about nuclear weapons in Arabia. If you hear the smallest hint of anything about that, I want to know it immediately."

What would Onorato do, if he disappeared, too? But there was no alternative. He had to go back to Asir and confront bin Laden. So, reluctantly, he did some research on the son, Bakr, before he boarded the waiting jet and headed back to for Saudi Arabia. He wanted to reassure himself about bin Laden's friendship. He wanted to tell the contractor that Washington had heard his concerns about Faisal and Aramco. King Faisal was a cloud over everything. Would he seize Aramco? Would he raise the price of oil to unheard of heights? Would he link Hank with Saud as an enemy? Would he make Hank disappear? Hank was a nut case with balls who might never return from those barren hills with their vengeful king.

CHAPTER SIX

Onorato's researcher finally got back to him with a full report on Steve Blevins.

"It was like pulling teeth," he said. "I had to call in all my favors, but here it is."

The report was quite large and in great detail. Steve was an army brat, just five years old with his parents in Schofield Barracks on Oahu when the Japanese attacked. His father went west with General Krueger's Sixth Army to the South Pacific. Steve and his mother went east to Alexandria, Virginia to live with her parents. Steve became an ardent patriot as he followed the progress of the Sixth Army from Port Moresby to Reboul, Leyte, and Luzon. Just one month before the war ended, however, Steve's father was killed by a sniper in Zambales Province in the Philippines.

General Krueger headed a campaign to raise funds for Onorato's family, his mother was able to send Steve to Episcopal High School, an expensive, five-year, private, college-preparatory, boarding school. E.H.S. was a small boys' school that emphasized discipline, academic excellence, small classes, daily recitation, and mandatory study halls. It required five years of Latin study, and that made it easy for Steve to learn languages. He must have been an outstanding student, for he easily won admittance to Georgetown University's law school on the campus overlooking the Potomac River. He easily passed the bar and entered a large law firm, but must have found the firm too dull, because he sent his resume to the C.I.A. The agency hired him quickly. He was brilliant and adept at languages. He volunteered for duty in the Philippines, where he went to the site of his father's death and swore vengeance on America's enemies. He spent the Vietnam War first in Manila, gathering intelligence and then in Clark Field, where he worked on Vietnamese matters and boat people escaping the communist takeover.

In 1968, a senior C.I.A. official came to the Philippines and summoned Steve to a very private meeting.

"The agency has a special top secret, eyes-only mission for you," he said. "A Phoenix team member, Jack Elliott, has just deserted in Hau Nghia Province. He is a traitor now working with the Viet Cong. He knows too much about the agency. Find and eliminate him. Here is a dossier, containing everywhere he went in Vietnam while with Phoenix and everybody we knew he came in contact with. Assemble a team you can trust to keep their mouths shut and go into War Zone C. Work with the 25th Division at Cu Chi. You have an unlimited expense account."

Steve recruited David as second-in-command, Jim for listening devices, Ron as a weapons expert, Tom for data maintenance, and Sharon as a computer expert. All agreed to help him kill Jack Elliott. With agency assistance, they went to Cu Chi and began the search. In less than a month, they found Elliott hiding in a remote Montagnard village and completed the mission.

The agency was pleased and thereafter, kept Steve's team together for special missions. Over the next eighteen years, they killed enemy agents in Manila, foiled protestors in Okinawa, found Muslim terrorists on Mindanao, and located traitors in South Korea. They became a permanent team under a special senior handler.

Onorato told the researcher to watch Blevins and report his movements.

Chapter Seven

At Taif, the land rover was waiting, and Mustafa guided Hank back up the same twisting road to bin Laden's camp in the mysterious high hills of Asir. They chatted as they drove, and Mustafa said the camp had become more like a permanent home. Bin Laden used it to live and work as far from King Faisal and Riyadh as possible. Hank's tent was ready and Mustafa said bin Laden had a small welcoming meal for him that evening.

At the table, bin Laden reported that Nasser had sent Saud away because he was too weak and could not deliver Saudi Arabia to the Egyptians. Said there was less danger now, for either of them.

"But you need to stay here at camp," bin Laden said, "because my son Bakr is coming home in just a few weeks, and it is important that you meet him."

"Bakr?" Hank asked, feigned ignorance.

Bin Laden went on to tell Hank about Bakr's attendance and studies at the University of Miami. When Hank was next in the Jeddah embassy annex, he reported no imminent danger to him from Faisal, no hint of war with Egypt, no sign that Aramco was about to be seized, and that Bakr would be home soon. Then Hank relaxed and went with a more positive flow.

Bakr turned out to be twenty-one, some three years younger than Hank. He was halfway toward earning a bachelor's degree at Miami, combining business and political science. He was about six feet tall, slender with a sharp, clean-shaven face, and a long nose. He seldom smiled and his piercing eyes never seemed to relax. Whenever Hank glanced his way, Bakr was staring, studying, and appraising him. Definitely one to watch. Hank reported to Onorato that Bakr was home, watching, and like Faisal, dangerous.

Then, just as bin Laden had warned them, Faisal seized Aramco without offering any compensation. The king announced a new oil minister, Ahmed Yamani. Bin Laden told Hank to remember that name because Yamani was going to have great impact worldwide on the price of oil. Sure enough, shortly afterwards, Yamani raised the price of Saudi oil from five to thirty dollars a barrel.

Suddenly, the Saudis had more money than they could spend. Bin Laden was flooded with lucrative government contracts, and Faisal decreed that anyone seeking a government contract had to go through him. The billion dollars the contractor had given Faisal was coming back rapidly. Bakr was reluctant to go back to America with all the new work going on, but bin Laden sent him away. Hank suspected bin Laden was delighted with the new contracts and wanted to prove to King Faisal that he could handle everything by himself. Onorato wanted to know if any of the new contracts had military implications.

"Many new roads," Hank reported. "A new secret base in northwest Saudi Arabia near the border of Israel, and a new airfield at Khamis Mushayt near bin Laden's camp in Asir."

"Concentrate on that military base near Israel," Onorato said.

All Hank could learn about the camp without arousing suspicion was that the base housed infantry, artillery, and a strange new factory complex. Bin Laden was reluctant to say more, because everything about the place was, for some reason, very highly classified. Hank had no doubt; however, it could be a launching pad for an attack on Israel.

"Keep looking," Onorato said. "Listen for nuclear hints."

Then came the news from Fort Bragg, Hank's reunion had been a little too joyful and Helen was pregnant.

"Let me go home," he pleaded with Onorato.

"Not a chance. Too much is going on in Saudi Arabia, but I'll make you a deal. When things calm down, I'll bring you home, maybe in December in time for the birth near Christmas."

Bin Laden gave Hank a few more details about the secret base near Israel. Its roads were especially wide and the new factory had many large buildings. Bin Laden was making money hand over fist, and he brought Bakr home to help manage the new contracts.

Hank had Mustafa lead him often to the new airfield at Khamis Mushayt near bin Laden's Asir hideaway. The base was not a top-secret project, and over the months, Hank sent many details back to Onorato. The international airfield complex would house several foreign airlines, as well as a separate Saudi military airfield that could be used against the Yemen.

True to his promise, a happy Onorato sent Hank home to Fort Bragg in December in plenty of time for the birth of a little girl near Christmas. The base hospital treated Helen like a queen, and of course, the grandparents were overjoyed. They named the little girl Hope. Hank was allowed to hold her carefully, and both sets of grandparents pitched in joyfully. After a few weeks, Hank realized he was completely superfluous, and he went back to Saudi Arabia, taking with him a full heart and new pictures to show bin Laden.

CHAPTER EIGHT

Bakr came home from Miami for spring break and stayed. Hank did his best to cultivate and improve their relationship. Bakr did unbend a bit after Miami beat Virginia Tech in a bowl game, he said, "The Virginia Tech team were Hokies. What's a Hokie?"

"Nobody knows," Hank said and laughed. Bakr smiled for once. It seemed to break the ice, and Bakr let drop the fact, then he was taking a course in the history of nuclear weapons. That intrigued Hank and he made an excuse to go to Taif and report it.

Onorato answered immediately.

"Talk to Bakr about that nuke course," he said. "Why? Is it related to the construction of that factory on the new base near Israel? Stay alive."

A major break came when bin Laden and Bakr had to go to Jerusalem to repair the dome of the Noble Sanctuary. They asked Hank to go with them.

Hank quickly reported this to Onorato, who was elated and ordered, "Find out everything you can about Jordanian military defenses around the Old City and Bethlehem. Who mans the lines and with what equipment?"

At the Dome of the Rock, bin Laden explained that the holy sanctuary was a shrine, not a mosque, the most sacred Muslim shrine in the world. Everything included, the shrine occupied some thirty-five acres of gardens, mosques, and the sanctuary itself. The entire shrine was magnificent, but the Dome of the Rock was the crown jewel. Bin Laden proudly showed Hank where he had previously replaced the gold leaf, now in need of repair, with its ornate Arabic inscriptions on the exterior of the dome. The interior was quiet and serene, with many Koranic sayings written in a circle around the inside of the dome and the sacred rock displayed below in a recessed center. Hank was not permitted to touch the rock, from which Muhammad and his steed had sprung up to heaven to receive the Koran from Allah.

When Hank asked to see the Via Dolorosa and the Church of the Holy Sepulture, Bakr escorted him up the Dolorosa, pointing out each of the Stations of the Cross along the way. The inside of the church was under repair, however, and Hank thought it could not match the splendor of the Holy Sanctuary.

Hank then asked if he could visit Bethlehem, and Bakr commandeered a military vehicle and a Jordanian major to guide them because it was a war zone. Driving south from Jerusalem, Hank saw what Onorato wanted; the Jordanian defenses. The front was just a few hundred yards to the west of the highway; they were on and on those redoubts Hank saw only a thin line of trenches, behind which were neither tank nor artillery positions. It was an extremely poorly prepared defense. An Israeli attack would quickly and easily break through there. At Bethlehem, Hank broached the subject of the Jordanian defenses with their guide.

"Do not concern yourself," the major said. "If the king gives the order to attack, we will overwhelm the Jewish dogs, drive them into the sea, and kill every man, woman, and child."

"I can understand why you would kill the men," Hank said, "but why kill the children?"

"Because they killed ours," the major said and pivoted away.

As soon as he returned to Asir, Hack wanted to tell Onorato about the Jordanian defenses, but he could not go to the embassy annex at Taif. He had to risk another short-wave message. Sent over the air, they were risky, even if encrypted. But he had to do it, and quickly. He kept it short and hoped for the best.

Not long after the Jerusalem trip, perhaps inspired because Hank had seen the holy sanctuary, Bakr began to broach a new idea to Hank.

"You should become a Muslim," he said. "It would be easy. Just vow that that there is no God but Allah and that Mohammad is His prophet. You would be one of us."

"It is not as easy as Bakr says," bin Laden cautioned. "You would have pray five time a day, fast during Ramadhan, give alms to the poor, and avoid alcohol and pork. It would be a major commitment, and your life would have to change completely."

"I would not be a very good Muslim," Hank protested. "I like my beer now and then. Bacon and eggs are among my favorites. I could not change."

"But we could take you to Mecca to see the mosque we renovated," Bakr said.

"I couldn't go to a football game with you," Hank said, "and enjoy a beer and a hot dog."

"We could make occasional exceptions," Bakr said.

Hank always found ways to change the subject and avoid any commitment, and the two never really pressed him. Eventually, they gave up.

"Bakr is an intelligent man," Hank told Onorato. "I can understand why you think he might be the future of the bin Laden operation. But he is volatile and dangerous."

When the six-day war of June 1967 was fought between Israel, Jordan, Syria, and Egypt, everything changed. As Hank had forecast, the Israelis easily broke through the thin Arab lines, seized the Old City of Jerusalem, and captured the Noble Sanctuary.

Bakr was irate.

"America helped the Israelis," he said.

"The Arabs did not fight well," Hank countered.

"King Faisal will not let the dome remain in Israeli hands," bin Laden said.

"The Arabs will have to fight better," Hank replied.

"They need weapons," Bakr said. "Tell me about American suitcase nuclear weapons."

Wow. Unexpected. Hank sat back with wide eyes. He couldn't give Bakr classified details, but Bakr would suspect if Hank didn't tell him something. So he spelled out some unclassified stuff Bakr could have read in the library at Miami. "I don't know a lot," Hank said, "but they weigh 162 pounds and can be easily broken into two parts so that paratroopers can jump with them. They have two yields, three and ten kt. They are more powerful than the bombs we used on Japan, because they are fusion devices that can be remotely set off by a timer or a radio signal. Why do you want to know about them?"

"I want to use them against the Israelis," he said.

Bin laden had been sitting back quietly, eyes shut and elbows on his knees. Now he looked up, sat forward, and raised a hand to stop Bakr. Turning to Hank and said, "If King Faisal believes that America helped the Israelis capture the holy sanctuary, he will take drastic measures, regardless of the consequence. If he had these weapons you talk about and thought America had helped the Israelis capture the noble sanctuary, he would use the weapons against New York or Washington."

Bin Laden paused to let his words sink in. Then he continued, "Make sure you tell your contacts at the Pentagon exactly what I just said."

Shaken by the idea of nuclear weapons in Arab hands, Hank didn't know what to say. He agreed to report bin Laden's words to the Pentagon. Then he sat back and wondered. Did bin Laden or King Faisal know about the messages he was sending Onorato? The possibility that he had been compromised worried him.

Sleepless nights ensued.

CHAPTER NINE

Hank's short-wave messages might have been compromised. He had to find a way to get out of Saudi Arabia before Faisal's police came after him. Several weeks later, he went to the construction site of the new airfield at Khamis Mushayt in order to meet bin Laden when the builder returned from visiting the new mystery military base near Israel. As he waited, he questioned a few contractors about their current projects, hoping to garner a few tidbits of data to report. Bin Laden was late, not arriving on time in his private plane, but hopefully, with new details about the base that Hank could report.

Searching the sky for sight of an arriving airplane, Hank saw instead an unusual helicopter and heard the unfamiliar whopping sounds of chopper blades. A black, unmarked helicopter landed on the tarmac close to his group. Before the craft had fully settled, four masked men in black uniforms with no identification insignia jumped from the craft and ran toward Hank and the contractors. Three of them carried submachine guns. The fourth pointed a pistol at Hank.

This was the end. Faisal had intercepted his messages. These men would seize him. He rose to defend himself, but one of the attackers jammed a gun barrel in his back. The leader grabbed Hank's arm and pulled him to the chopper, already rising. The other attackers pointed their weapons at the cowering contractors and followed aboard.

He was going to prison, torture, and death. But the chopper did not turn east toward Riyadh. Instead, it turned west, where he could be dropped from a thousand feet into the Red Sea.

Once airborne, however, the men took off their masks and grinned at him. Shocked, Hank expelled a breath; he didn't know he had been holding, they were American special forces soldiers, a captain and three sergeants. What the hell?

"Relax," the captain said, offering a hand. "You're safe now."

Hank tried to throw himself at the guy. Restrained only by the seat belt, he exploded, "Relax, hell! Those were my friends back there. You scared the shit out of them. Why attack them?"

"I had to," the captain said. "We needed to get you out of there, and fast. But if we can get you out of Saudi airspace, you'll be safe. You're going to the American embassy in Cairo."

Alarmed and aware that bin Laden might also be in danger, he asked, "What am I safe from? Why am I going to Egypt? My gear is back at bin Laden's camp. What's going on?"

"We were ordered to get you out of there," the captain said. "Your contact, bin Laden is dead. And the Saudis think you were somehow involved. If they had caught you, you would have either quickly lost your head or spent the rest of your life in a Saudi stink hole. The police are at bin Laden's camp right now, looking for you. My orders are to get you out of Saudi Arabia to the defense *attaché* in Egypt. A plane is waiting to take you to Washington."

At the Pentagon, Onorato explained, "Bin Laden died in a plane crash. There was something odd about the circumstances of the crash, however, and the Saudis think you were somehow involved. They were coming for you, and we think they will continue to look for you. We're going to hide you first in the 101st Airborne Division at Fort Campbell and then, in a few months, you'll be in Vietnam."

He had already spent too much time away from his girls in Saudi Arabia. He hardly knew Faith and Hope, and now he was going away again. It wasn't fair. Helen would once more have to run their family without much help from him. He couldn't take it. It was just too much. It hurt down deep. Finally, he gathered his thoughts and objected, "My going to Vietnam will be really hard on Helen and our daughters."

"We will do everything we can to help and protect them," Onorato said. "We'll promote you to major and move your family into better quarters at Fort Bragg. You'll have a month with them.

I'll assign a team to give them assistance while you are in Vietnam. Headquarters at Bragg will watch after them."

"Why do I need to go to Vietnam?"

"The Saudis won't find you there. Vietnam will give you some combat cover."

He'd made a bad bargain with the devil, but it was a joy to spend time with Faith and Hope, and to be with Helen again. He packed as much as he could into the month he was given, and then he went to Fort Campbell.

The 101st Airborne Division, the Screaming Eagles, was preparing to go to Southeast Asia. Hank joined the First Brigade, and after a month of intensive training and a few parachute jumps, he and the brigade went to Vietnam. They set up a headquarters at Cu Chi, in War Zone C, just a few miles west of Saigon, and began operations.

Hank went on patrols in hot, wet jungles infested with biting red ants. Slept on the ground. Went days without a shower. Flew helicopter missions to cover his units. By the end of 1967, his brigade had been fighting in the jungles of War Zone C continuously for three months. The pace was faster than he thought possible. By Christmas, he was dog tired. Then the Tet Offensive began as North Vietnamese units poured down the Ho Chi Minh Trail and the Viet Cong emerged in force from their tunnels.

He barely had time to write Helen.

"We have been fighting almost continuously since I got here. Even at night we're kept awake by the thump of incoming enemy mortars and crack of our responding howitzers. In base camp at Cu Chi, we keep our flak jackets very close. When I fall asleep, I dream of holding you in a nomad's tent near Mecca, and it gives me little rest. The only time I can relax is when I'm riding high up in a chopper because the fog of war is far beneath me. But the quiet doesn't last long because when daylight comes, I have to hover above my battalions, looking for an ambush, and the fighting always starts all over again. America has been here far too long. And now, we're pulling out of the wet triple canopy jungle and heading back to defend the capital. That looks to me like a retreat. The war isn't getting any better. It's a crazy business I don't like and it's time we all went home."

She sent him beautiful pictures of Faith and Hope and told him they were well, loved him, and were waiting for him to return. She said she prayed every night for him. She hoped that the Vietnam War would soon be over. She wanted him home safely.

Her letters were a bursting ray of sunshine in a dark period of his life.

CHAPTER TEN

Two months later, Hank was in a helicopter, flying over Route One from Tay Ninh east toward Saigon, a thousand feet above jungles filled with enemy soldiers, red ants, and poisonous snakes. He had risen before dawn to fly cover for a battalion headed to Saigon. At cruising altitude, he was in sunlight above the clouds, and the darkness of war was far below. Felt good. The roar of the craft's engines hypnotized him and he almost fell asleep. He didn't need to hurry. He had a personal question to ponder.

In several briefings in Cu Chi, intelligence had repeatedly spoken about the possibility of an attack on an orphanage north of Khiem Cuong. The orphanage was not far from Hank's current location. During these briefings, the name of the director, Waters, had been mentioned. That name brought back bad childhood memories.

He and his family had been at Schofield Barracks in Hawaii just before the Korean War. Hank and a buddy, Charley McMillian, both just nine years old, had been accosted by an army deserter named Waters. Hank had seldom run across that name, but when he did, it always brought back those bad memories. Now, these were refreshed again by that name. Maybe he could visit the orphanage and satisfy his curiosity. Weeks had passed without an opportunity, however, and the idle curiosity had slipped his mind.

Then a radio call came over the intercom in his helmet, "This is a call to any helicopter near an orphanage north of Khiem Cuong. An official there has been wounded. A medic on the scene says the hospital at Cu Chi might be able to save him. Any chopper in the area please respond. An American team is at the orphanage and they say there's a lull in the fighting."

An opportunity! He could go to the orphanage, pick up the wounded man, and meet this guy Waters. Then he could return and fly over his men coming east from Tay Ninh. He answered the call, "I'm close to the orphanage and will respond."

He gave an affirmative nod to his pilot, and the chopper turned south. Why would the Viet Cong bother to attack an orphanage? Why attack kids? There was an American national guard unit on site. He hoped it had been able to protect them.

To pick up the wounded guy that would be risky, and he had been repeatedly warned by his football coach, his superiors, and Helen that aggression was his flaw. But this rescue might save a life, and he didn't believe the smart asses who said no good deed ever went unpunished. He checked his gear and made sure his door gunner was ready. Why was America fighting in this God-forsaken land? Maybe someone thought evil would win if the good guys stood aside. Maybe, but Vietnam was looking more and more like a mistake. Too many of our guys had died, and soon, he might find dead kids. It was starting to be another bad day.

So many twists and turns that had brought him here. To receive an education, he signed a contract to serve eight years on active duty. At first, it looked like a good deal, but that contract had resulted in his being put into top-secret intelligence operation and given him a valuable education. But it had also made him an agent, a spy with an unlimited obligation. Unlimited? How had that happened? Where he went, what he studied, the government had complete control. Why did he need to become a paratrooper? Why had they made him study nuclear weapons? He failed to see the connection. His work in the Middle East with bin Laden and Bakr had resulted in early promotions and extra pay, but bin Laden's sudden death had put him under suspicion by the Saudi authorities. And the army had made it worse by sending him to hide in Vietnam. His good deal had gone bad.

A few miles from the orphanage, the pilot called for an update, "We're five minutes out. Will we take fire coming in?"

"The jungle to the west is not secure," a voice answered. "Come in from the east. I'm on the road there with several men. When I hear or see you, I'll drop red smoke. There'll be room for you to land near the smoke. Any activity west of the orphanage is hostile. If you see any movement out there, take it under fire."

Hank's Huey landed on the road without incident, and after the dust settled, he stepped out and met an armed group; two American officers and a Vietnamese major.

One of the Americans, a captain, reported, "I'm Gus Bean, Advisory Team Forty-Three. National Guard from Massachusetts. This is Major Manh who commands the Viets, and this is Captain West who built the orphanage."

Bean's handshake was firm and he looked Hank straight in the eye. He was trim and cool. Hank liked him.

"What happened here?" Hank asked.

"Mortar rounds hit a few hours ago and a Viet Cong squad broke through our fence on the west. The attack wasn't too bad, because a Phoenix team had showed up earlier and alerted us. We handled the fight well until an incendiary mortar round hit the community building and started a fire. It got out of hand for a time with lots of smoke and confusion, but the V.C. broke off and the fight looks like it's over. We found several Cong bodies inside the fence, and we have minor injuries to seven South Vietnamese soldiers. None of my team or any children from the orphanage was hurt, but the director took a bad hit. He was really unlucky, because he had on a flak jacket and the bullet hit him in the stomach, just below protection. If it had hit six inches higher, he would have been sore, but okay. As it is, he's in bad shape. My medic put on a compress and gave him morphine. Once we get his stretcher on your chopper, my medic will go with you to Cu Chi to take care of the director until you get him to the hospital. I'll stay here for a while, but I need to have my medic back soonest, in case the Cong hits again."

"Where is the Phoenix team?" Hank asked. "They left after the attack broke off."

"Okay," Hank said. "I should be able to have your medic back in about an hour. But why would the Viet Cong attack kids and an orphanage?"

Major Manh spoke up. He was small, all muscle, and showed little stress from the recent attack. "That's how they work," he said. "They destroy anything that helps the people. They set off bombs in the marketplaces, schools, and hospitals. This orphanage is helping our kids and making a better future, so the V.C. wanted to blow it up, even if they killed our children."

"We held them off," the engineer captain said. "And I can rebuild the building that burned. I'll also reinforce the fence and spread Agent Orange to the west, where the V.C. used the jungle for cover."

"Thank God, no children were hurt," Major Manh said. The pilot waved that he was ready to take off.

"If you see anybody in the jungle to the west," Bean said, "the bad guys may be getting ready to attack again. Take them under fire. Let us know what you see out there. Thanks again for your help. Try to get to Cu Chi A.S.A.P. and save Director Waters. Send my medic back as soon as possible. Take care."

"Will do," Hank said, "but keep your heads down. If we start shooting, we don't want any of your guys hurt."

As the chopper rose, Hank saw the nametag of the wounded director "Waters." Any relation to the deserter in Hawaii? Maybe Hank could talk to him in recovery. He saw no movement in the dense foliage west of the fence, no dark shapes that might be a new attack. So he ordered his pilot to head at top speed for the army hospital at Cu Chi. Bean's medic worked on Waters. Could he possibly be the guy from Hawaii? It seemed impossible. He looked to be about the right age. He also looked really bad; very pale, no breathing, and completely inert. Hank told the pilot, "Call in and make sure there's an ambulance waiting when we land. This guy looks like he's really in bad shape."

"He's worse than bad, major," the medic said, "he's gone."

Another poor day had just gotten worse. Hank had wasted time in a risky effort to get the director to the hospital, only to have the man die. Now he'd never get to talk to him and satisfy that curiosity. And he might be late in flying cover for his men in the convoy coming east. America had been fighting this poor war for too long, and violent memories were starting to build up. If he survived, he would never come back to this God-forsaken hell hole.

Two months later, when Hank landed his chopper to pick up some wounded soldiers, a mortar round hit nearby and killed his pilot and door gunner. The blast also smashed Hank's right arm, broke an ear drum, and gave him a concussion.

He went home with a Purple Heart and a Silver Star.

CHAPTER ELEVEN

From his hospital room at Fort Bragg, Hank called Onorato. "I want out," he said.

"No way," his handler said, "your knowledge of Saudi Arabia is getting more important every day. You quit, you go to jail in debt, and we kick your ladies out of Fort Bragg. Just lie low. Wait until we contact you."

Hank showed his government contract to the adjutant general at Fort Bragg. After study, the colonel said Hank had to serve at the pleasure of the government, whether in the army or as a civilian. It was binding. His maze had no exit. But when he went home to his three lovely ladies, the army tried to make it right by giving him additional time to recover. They sent him back to Duke to earn an advanced degree. He wanted to study economics, but Onorato made him also take refresher courses in the Arabic language, the Middle East, Saudi Arabia, and nuclear weapons. During his two years of study and recovery, he stayed at Bragg with Helen and the girls, and by 1972, he was well. Promoted to lieutenant colonel, he was given command of an airborne infantry battalion in the 82nd airborne division.

Helen was not pleased, "I worry about the parachuting. You have just mended from Vietnam. You could be hurt again."

"These new parachutes make jumping easier," he said. "I won't overdue it, but the men expect me to be with them. I like them, especially the Hispanics. They are hard-working and loyal. I think they would do anything for me. I have so many Hispanics in my battalion that we are not called A.A., All-American, like the rest of the division. No, my battalion is M.M., mostly Mexican. I love it."

"You're nuts," she said. "Always have been." "That's why you married me."

Hank took care as he jumped. In his three years of command, he suffered only minor cuts and bruises from a few bad landings in trees and ditches. The army commended him and sent him to the prestigious Army War College. He guessed Onorato was behind the selection.

"You're wrong," Onorato said. "The Arab-Israeli War of 1973 resulted in an oil embargo, and the Middle East is heating up. The army needs your Saudi experience more than ever. That's why you were picked for the War College. You're a shoe-in for full colonel, maybe even general officer. Write your thesis on Saudi Arabia."

When Hank told Helen about the college, she pointed out that their girls were at a particularly vulnerable age, "We can't go with you. Faith is in Fayetteville High School, and Hope is almost there. It's a critical time for them. I can't ask them to leave their friends."

"The war college is just a year," he told her. "I'll set it up for you to stay right here at Fort Bragg. I'll have use of a helicopter to come home now and then. And after the college, I'll ask to be returned to Fort Bragg."

The war college was at Carlisle, Pennsylvania, a quick helicopter flight, and Hank came home often, more than just at Christmas and Easter. As Onorato suggested, he wrote his thesis on the Saudi's increasing need for water, explaining how they could solve that problem through desalination. The college liked the idea, the state department talked to Saudi Arabia about it, and the Pentagon promoted him early to colonel. Washington was interested in his thesis, and Senator Tompkins of South Carolina called Hank down to his office for a special briefing on Saudi Arabia. After graduation and per his request, he was assigned to the special warfare center at Fort Bragg. He moved his family to larger colonel's quarters there on Smoke Bomb Hill. His daughters stayed in school at Fayetteville High School. Life was good.

Helen was happy, except for the fact that he had to make frequent trips to Bad Toelz, West Germany to visit the Tenth Special Forces Group. That group had responsibility for the Middle East and

Hank trained with them to parachute carrying suitcase-sized nuclear weapons. Those were the ones he had told Bakr about. Life was coming full circle. It worried him.

Helen didn't like it either. "Nuclear weapons frighten me," she said. "Don't be concerned," he said, thinking about Bakr. "I just need to know about them."

Saudi Arabia was making waves about America's supporting Israel, and a revolution started in Iran. Hank was in demand as an expert on the region, and his future looked promising, his promotion to brigadier general seemed sure. On a night parachute jump in damp windy weather, however, he landed in a ditch and hurt his back badly. Good surgeons worked on him, but the damage was too great. He retired with a medical disability.

"Stay in touch," Onorato said. "In Iran, the shah is out and *Shiite* hardliners have taken over. Saudi Arabia is funneling money to terrorists. Your knowledge of the Middle East is getting more valuable every day. We could recall you at any time. Save your uniforms. Be ready."

Chapter Twelve

Happy to finally be together and looking forward to a more peaceful life, they moved to Hilton Head Island on the South Carolina coast and bought a home in Port Royal Plantation. Faith went to Clemson University and Hope attended nearby Sea Pine Academy. Hank worked to strengthen his back with physical therapy, exercise, and karate, and he used his economics degree to join an investment firm. Hilton Head had wide beaches, mild weather, and good fishing in the ocean. For three years, the Kean family was happy.

Then Helen began to experience strange symptoms. She vomited without any signs of flu. She had dizzy spells and fell asleep at odd times during the day.

Hank took her to the Hilton Head Hospital and the doctor administered all sorts of tests, from CAT scans to M.R.Is. While they waited for results, Helen took pills that lessened her symptoms. When they went back to the hospital, the doctor met Hank separately.

"She has a brain tumor," he said. "Are you sure?" Hank asked.

"Absolutely, but you should get a second opinion."

Hank took Helen to the Mayo Clinic. The results were identical.

Back on Hilton Head, he asked the doctor, "How are these things handled? What's going to happen to her? What choices do we have?"

"Each tumor is different," the doctor said. "The type, location, and speed of the growth determines whether we can operate. But because of the type and location of Helen's tumor, I'm afraid we can do nothing except make her comfortable until she goes."

"How long does she have?"

"My guess, and it is only a guess, is about six months."

Hank almost collapsed.

Everything changed. Faith and Hope stayed home from Clemson. Hank hired a caregiver. He had to work, but he could only bring himself to spend part of each morning at the office, while the girls, or the caregiver, were around. During the rest of the time, he worked from home using a computer his firm provided. He used his phone for conferences and client outreach. His firm supported his decisions. Helen's doctor prescribed steroids and a narcotic for pain. Gloom settled in at the Kean home as a vibrant and lovely woman slowly deteriorated into a vegetable. The girls cried a lot, and Hank struggled to keep going.

The end came that fall. The military chaplain and cemetery at nearby Beaufort took care of the details. The fall weather was cool with a brisk breeze that sent dead, brown leaves tumbling around to mingle with the haunting echoes of bugles sounding taps.

Helen had fallen in love with Frost's poetry and toward the end, when she could not see well, Hank had read to her. She smiled as she listened, often falling asleep. At her graveside, he read "Stopping by Woods on a Snowy Evening," although he choked up several times. Then she was gone.

Chapter Thirteen

When Faith and Hope went back to Clemson in January, Hank was alone, and he could not bear being in the house he had shared with Helen. So he sold it and bought a two-bedroom apartment near work. He was not comfortable being around people who had known Helen. He could see the pity in their eyes, just as he knew they could see the despair in his. The only person he could talk to was Paul Ruth, who had handled the probate questions.

Paul seemed to understand, and they became good friends, Hank's only one. They played a little golf, shared an occasional lunch, and had a few drinks after work. Except for the times when Faith and Hope came home from Clemson, Hank was isolated. His daughters urged him to get out more, but he refused. The only times he went out were to the office, give seminars on investments, or to see Paul.

Then in 1986, he received a letter from a woman identifying herself as Mrs. Ahn Manh. Postmarked El Paso, Texas, it said, "The kind people at the Fort Bliss hospital gave me your address. My husband is Colonel Nung Manh, formerly of the South Vietnamese army. He is a patient at the hospital. With our son, Le, we escaped from South Vietnam in 1975 and went to the Philippines. Three years later, we were given asylum in the United States. We are living in El Paso, and like it very much. Our son graduated from the University of Texas here and married a wonderful American girl. They have two lovely daughters and a computer business. I work at the public library, and the United States pays Nung a small pension. He gets medical treatment at the Fort Bliss army hospital. He had a stroke, and now has diabetes and high blood pressure. He met you during an attack on an orphanage in Hau Nghia Province during the Tet Offensive, and he has important information to give you. I hope you will come and speak to him. You will not be disappointed. Thank you."

It was signed Ahn.

Hank read the letter several times and then went to see Paul.

"I'm skeptical," he said. "I read in the *Army Times* and in letters from several associates about extortion scams or drug schemes run by Vietnamese who had fled their country for the United States. I know that most refugees are honest, hardworking people, but a few have gone bad. On the other hand, it's possible that I might have known her husband during the Tet Offensive. I was in Hau Nghia Province, and I may have met this Nung Manh then, but I really can't place him. I'd like to hear what he has to say."

"I don't think a phone call would do it," Paul said. "That's for sure. I may fly down there."

"Why? That would be costly. Besides, you said this could be a scam."

"I want to know what he thinks is so important."

"I think you're just bored and lonely. Let Fort Bliss handle this." Hank decided to ignore Paul's advice and go to El Paso. Quickly, his manager agreed to finance the trip. A group of doctors there had a retirement plan with the firm, and they were good customers.

Hank wrote Ahn Manh.

"I will be in El Paso in February and I will call you then. If you and Colonel Manh would like to meet, send me your phone number."

He told himself he wanted to learn what Colonel Manh had to say, and the visit made good investment sense. To discuss current strategy and their portfolio performance, he set up a conference at the El Paso Marriott. Six accepted and four brought their wives. He gave them a complete update. The partnership's retirement account and the doctors' individual portfolios were in good shape. Because Hank's firm had put them in balanced portfolios, gains in their bonds had compensated for their losses in stocks. When he finished, he asked the senior partner for comments.

"Well done, Colonel Kean," the man said. "I have no questions. Frankly, I was worried about our stocks. They seem to have underperformed, but you reassured me. Thanks for coming and for your presentation. Others may have questions."

There were none, so Hank changed the subject.

"While I was in Vietnam, one of the people I dealt with in the jungles was a major in the South Vietnamese army. He would have been badly treated if he had remained in South Vietnam, so he escaped from Saigon just before the North Vietnamese took over. He took his family to the Philippines as Boat People. He's here in El Paso, a little over sixty, and pretty sick. The military hospital at Fort Bliss is treating him. Ten years ago, he had a stroke, and he now has diabetes and high blood pressure. Is he young for all that?"

"That's my field," a tall, slender doctor said. "I am sure you have heard of the disaster of the Love Canal, a catastrophe caused by dioxin in the drinking water around Niagara. During the Vietnam War, the United States sprayed the same dioxin on the jungle to clear the foliage and deny concealment to the enemy. The spray they used, Agent Orange, could be the cause of the colonel's symptoms."

Hank went to the Army hospital at Fort Bliss to meet its commander, Colonel Goodwin. Using the name of a doctor as a reference, a good friend Hank had known for many years, he had written *Goodwin*, the current commander, and asked to discuss Nung Manh. Goodwin had agreed and Hank went to his office. He was a chubby, cheerful man, but he immediately offered a stern caveat.

"I can give you only a general report," he said. "I can't reveal anything of a personal nature. This discussion must be off the record."

"Of course," Hank said. "But you seem cautious."

"I am. Government agencies have shown an unusual interest in Colonel Manh. The extent of their inquiries seemed extreme and raised a flag, so I checked with the doctor who referred you. He spoke highly of you and asked that I help out. If he hadn't given you such good marks, I would have refused to discuss Manh at all. As it is, I need to be off the record."

What government agencies were interested in Ning Manh? And why? But Hank was there to learn about Manh's medical condition, so he pushed ahead.

"I guess I understand," Hank said, "but what can you tell me about him?"

"He has been a patient here since 1976. Ten years ago, he had a stroke. In Vietnam he operated in the jungles, which the Americans had defoliated. We have seen many similar cases, and our conclusion is that he was exposed to Agent Orange. He has only a few months. His son is in business in El Paso. The boy's doing well and can take of Manh's wife if he passes. I think she'll be fine. But she should be prepared. He could go at any time."

That wasn't particularly good news for Manh, but Hank now, at least, had some facts to work with, so he called the family. He knew that talking about Vietnam, a country he hated, would be painful for him, and he almost felt like not doing it. It would be too much like returning to a war that had failed him and America, killing many of his friends, and he didn't want that. He still had bad memories he had hoped to forget, as well as some worse dreams. Seeing Manh might set them off. Not a good idea.

At least he could find out what Colonel Manh thought was so important. And he really wanted to offer some support for the colonel and his wife. The man had been a staunch ally and helped the Americans under difficult circumstances, dangerous for him and his family. He was now ill in a land far from home. He might really need help and to Hank, loyalty went both ways, up and down.

It was still early afternoon, and he was not due at the El Paso airport until noon the following day, so he phoned Ahn Manh and arranged to meet at their place after she came home from work. He would listen to Colonel Manh, although he really wanted to get back to Hilton Head and be left alone with his memories.

In the hours that he waited, Hank recalled how his pilot and door gunner had been killed, how Director Waters had died on Hank's helicopter and how Bean and West had met him after the attack on the orphanage. This Colonel Manh must have been there when Hank flew in to rescue the director. He was not returning to a happy place.

CHAPTER FOURTEEN

The Manh apartment complex, the Cielo Vista, was a modest development of single-story, one-and two-bedroom places. If anything, the run-down appearance of the buildings led Hank to believe the Manhs weren't dealing drugs. If they were, they were hiding their money well. And if the two of them were scam artists, they weren't successful ones. He felt more kindly disposed toward them.

When he knocked on the door, a small, white-haired, Oriental woman opened it and introduced herself as Ahn Manh. In the living room, he saw that Colonel Manh was a frail, elderly man. After a few pleasantries and some iced tea, they settled down and Manh began to speak. He had difficulty in doing so, and at times, his words were barely audible. But he was coherent and quite precise.

"During Tet," Manh said, "I was responsible for security of the orphanage where I met you. As you may remember, when the Cong attacked us, we were ready because a Phoenix team had come to alert us. The Cong launched mortars from the jungle to the west and blew a hole in the fence. When they charged in, my reaction force handled them well, but one of their mortar rounds hit a building and started a fire. My lieutenant had our defense in good shape, so I went inside the burning building to help."

Manh was bringing back memories Hank had tried to erase, but he wanted to hear what the man had to say. Uncomfortable as it was, he let the colonel continue.

"Inside the building, there was fire and smoke, but I saw the orphanage director and one of the Phoenix men yelling at each other. Then the Phoenix man shot the director. When I shouted, he turned toward me, so I ran outside, hoping he had not seen me well enough to identify me. When I found Captain Bean coming with a team to fight the fire, I told him that the director had been wounded. Bean called for an evacuation to Cu Chi. You landed about an hour later."

"You say a member of the Phoenix team shot Waters?" Hank asked. "Do you remember who the Phoenix team were?"

"Certainly," Manh said, "they were Elliott and McMillian. McMillian shot Waters."

Shaken, Hank stood and paced the room. Was Director Waters the deserter who had assaulted Hank's buddy, Charley McMillian, in Hawaii almost twenty years ago? It seemed impossible. Had McMillian taken revenge, using the cover of a V.C. attack?

"Do you know that Waters died on the way to Cu Chi?" Hank asked.

Manh fell back on the sofa and closed his eyes.

"Nung must rest," Ahn said. "I can continue. We knew we were in danger because the Cong leader, Major Quan, had ordered his men to kill Nung. We had to leave Quan's area, so Nung arranged a transfer to Saigon, and we adopted one of the boys, Le Trang, and took him with us. Because of Nung's experience, he was promoted to colonel and had the rank to protect us. When the South Vietnamese government started to fall apart, he arranged for a boat to take us to the Philippines."

Boat people. What an ordeal. No wonder this Manh was in bad shape.

"It was rough," Ahn said, "but we evaded the patrols and made it to the Philippines. We were questioned often and made to wait to enter the Unites States. Finally, we were sent here. For a while, things were peaceful. Le graduated from high school and the University of Texas at El Paso. He married Nancy and started a family. Then government people came and began to ask where Nung was during Tet. We were afraid. So we asked Fort Bliss for your address, as well as that of Captains West and Bean. I decided to write all of you, but you were the only one that answered. I'm sorry if we bothered you."

It wasn't really a bother. This guy had been an ally and now needed help. And he had handed Hank a bombshell from long ago.

"That's okay," Hank said, "but was the killing the important thing you wanted to tell directly, rather than by letter or on the phone?"

"No." Nung sat up with an obvious effort. "I must tell you. Several years ago, Colonel Orzon, a Filipino officer visited us. He had helped us when we were waiting to go to America. We had become friends and because he interceded for us, we were grateful. He had just retired and come to America to celebrate. So we talked, played chess, and drank many beers. When he was perhaps a little drunk, he told us some stories, the most important of which was that the Philippine Sayyaf terrorists had stolen two small nuclear weapons from an American depot in West Germany."

My God. Here came the nukes again. He couldn't escape them. "That's absurd," Hank said. "Nuclear weapons were never stolen from West Germany. I would have known if anything like that had happened."

"I must respectively disagree," Manh said. "The theft did occur and you did not hear about it because there was a cover up. The stolen bombs ended up in Saudi Arabia."

Hank paced the room in dismay. If this had really happened and it turned out that Bakr was involved, it would be a catastrophe.

"Did Orzon say anything more?"

"Yes, he said that the Saudis intended to use the bombs against the Iranians. If the Saudis were successful, neither Israel nor America would have to attack Iran. When I asked Orzon for proof of this scheme, he smiled, took a swig of beer, belched, rolled over on the couch, and passed out. He never mentioned the subject again. I tell you this because now I hear that Iran is starting to build such a bomb, and if we attack to stop them, a major Middle East war will start. It would be better for us if the Saudis had those weapons and could use them to prevent Iran from getting their own. You should find out if Orzon was right. My son, Le Trang, can help. He wants to talk to you."

Philippine terrorists stealing suitcase nukes and selling them to the Saudis. It could not be true, could not have happened. As a member of the nuke community, Hank would have heard if such a theft had occurred. It would have been a major story that nobody could have covered up, not even the White House. This had to be a stupid fabrication made up by a drunk to impress his drunken friend. Hank decided to ignore the whole absurd idea. But the McMillian and Waters thing was different. Was Phoenix McMillian really Charley McMillian? Was Director Waters really deserter Waters? If so, did McMillian use the cover of a V.C. attack on the orphanage to take revenge on Waters for the deserter's sexual abuse when Charley was nine years old? Hank had to know.

Chapter Fifteen

That evening, at the Marriott, Hank wrote himself a brief memo, "Elderly Philippine drunk retired Colonel Orzon claims Filipino terrorists steal suitcase-bombs from American depot in West Germany. Sells them to the Saudis. Is Bakr involved?"

He looked at what he had written and laughed. He had worked with those bombs through the Tenth Special Forces. Security was unbelievably so tight around them that theft was impossible. And if somehow a theft had occurred, all hell would have broken out. Nobody, no matter how powerful, would have been able to cover it up. And why would anybody do something like that? If Saudi Arabia had such weapons, Iran would react by getting their own, and a nuclear arms race would start in the Middle East. Inevitably, some weapons from Saudi Arabia or Iran would fall into the hands of people willing to use them against Israel or America. The whole thing was alcoholic nonsense. But then he recalled Bakr bin Laden asking about suitcase bombs to use against Israel. Bin Laden said King Faisal would use them against America if we had helped Israel seize the Dome of the Rock. And Hank had facilitated that by reporting the weak Jordanian defenses around Jerusalem. It was just plausible enough for him to question Le Trang about it.

Hank found Le waiting for breakfast in a small corner *café*. Black hair, slight build, clear skin, and attractive, he had a firm handshake and did it with a smile. "I am Le," he said. Hank immediately liked him.

"You are Colonel Manh's son?" Hank asked.

"No," Le said. "I was adopted by them. My father and mother were killed by Major Quan, the local Viet Cong leader, and I escaped to the orphanage with Waters. I met Nung Manh there, and when the Manhs decided to escape, they took me with them. We were among the first boat people to cross the South China Sea to the Philippines and be attacked by pirates on the way. In the Philippines, my only bad moments were when American agents questioned me about the Viet Cong commander, Truc Quan, and his attack on the orphanage. But I didn't know anything, so they left me alone. In El Paso, I learned English, earned a college degree, and married Nancy, a girl I met at Texas, El Paso. We have two beautiful daughters, Kay and Samantha. We are computer programmers, good ones, both of us. We've written programs that will make us rich."

Enough of the background. Hank wanted to know about Waters, "Tell me about the orphanage and Director Waters."

"There is good news and bad. The good news is that the place was clean and protected us. The bad news is that Waters was a pervert and dangerous. He watched us when we showered, and he came into the dorm in the dark and stood beside the beds of young boys. In the year before he died, two boys disappeared. The director said they had gone to the hospital and run away. But I was their leader, and those kids hadn't told me they were sick. They never said they wanted to run away."

Waters was starting to sound really bad, and Le couldn't help with the real identities of Waters and McMillian. Maybe he could help with Orzon and the story about nuclear weapons.

"What can you tell me about this Colonel Orzon?"

Le pulled away, as if he wanted to avoid Orzon, but he quickly recovered. "In the Philippines, he was a captain in the Philippine army. When he came to El Paso, he was a retired colonel. He had money and seemed like a good man."

"Did you hear his story about the Sayyaf?" Hank asked. "And nuclear weapons?"

Le glanced around, as if he didn't want anyone to hear.

"That is a very dangerous subject. Most of Orzon's stories were dumb drunken rambling, but the stuff about the Sayyaf and the nuclear weapons was different. It sounded real, and it frightened me. He said that several bombs had been stolen in Germany and taken to the Philippines. And then the Sayyaf sold them to Saudi Arabia. I think there might be some truth to the story."

Le Trang seemed smart and honest. Hank decided he would at least report the story about stolen nukes to Onorato. He said good-bye to Le and went to turn in his rental. The Texas sky was blue and clear, with no storm in the forecast.

That changed at the airport where he had an early afternoon departure. He drove directly to the rental compound near the airport, paid his bill, and was about to load his bags on a bus when two uniformed policemen approached him. The clear Texas sky darkened.

"Colonel Kean," the larger one said, "please come with us. We want to talk to you."

"I don't have much time," he said. "I need to make a departing flight."

"We'll take you to the terminal faster than the shuttle. Just get in the car."

He sized them up. It was decision time.

CHAPTER SIXTEEN

Someone in the cruiser really needs to talk to him? And the car would be the better than here out on the street where they could be seen? Made no sense. He sized them up. On the one hand, they were both overweight, and he had gotten in shape by frequent karate sessions. He thought he could take them down. On the other hand, they were pretty big and might be tougher than they appeared. And they were uniformed officers. Most courts do not like the idea of their policemen being knocked around by anyone, even honorably discharged veterans. Resistance might serve no purpose, other than make him feel good. Stupidity was always bad.

One of the officers opened the back door. Inside, Hank found a trim, middle-aged man in a well-tailored business suit.

"Special Agent Blevins, sir," the guy said, smiling and holding out his hand.

Hank didn't like what was happening. He was on his way to make a departing flight and had done nothing to cause him to be approached by officers and put in a cruiser. So he didn't shake the hand, but instead asked curtly, "Do you have identification?"

"Certainly, colonel," Blevins said, holding out an I.D.

Hank took it and tried to memorize as much as he could. He saw a date that meant the identification was a little over a year old. He memorized the name on the card, Steve Blevins, and he tried to stamp the man's picture in his mind. There was a United States seal emblazoned on the card. It looked real.

"What's going on?" Hank asked.

"I'd like to ask you a few questions," Blevins said. "I have your name from Delta's manifest, and your flight doesn't take off until 1345."

"You know a lot about me. Do I need a lawyer?"

"You do not. But if you insist on contacting an attorney, the process would take more time than you have available. You'd miss your flight, and that would be inconvenient. Besides, you aren't under suspicion of any crime, so you don't need a lawyer. I just want to talk, but I want to remind you that lying to a federal officer is a crime, even if you haven't been read your rights. We will insure you make your flight."

"And I'll remind you that stopping a citizen without cause is also a crime."

The session didn't go well. Blevins asked about Manh, accusing him of drug trafficking and illegal immigration. Impossible. So Hank called the suggestion absurd. Then Blevins shifted quickly to Vietnam and asked about the wounded director Hank had evacuated and who had died on the way.

"Did he say anything on the flight before he died? Anything at all?" "No," Hank said tersely. "He never regained consciousness."

"Tell me about Colonel Orzon," Blevins said more sharply. "What did he tell Nung?"

The change of tone and shift from drugs to Orzon and nuclear weapons set off alarms. Was Orzon's talk of a weapons theft the real reason Blevins was questioning him? How did Blevins know about Orzon?

"Now I know you're fishing," Hank said. "I don't even think you are an agent. Either let me out or I want a lawyer, and I want him now."

"We're at your departure gate," Blevins said. "You are free to go, but let me suggest that you might want to avoid future contact with the Manhs. They and people they know may be in a dangerous business that could turn out badly. Violence might be involved, and that, in turn, might put you or your family at risk. Classified material and violent people are involved."

"What about this is classified?"

"I can't tell you that, but it may be of national importance to the country and of personal importance to you and yours."

Hank stared at the guy in disbelief. Orzon was a drunk, and Colonel Manh was most certainly not a drug dealer. But this agent had just associated both of them with a theft of American nuclear weapons. That made absolutely no sense. But Blevins must have believed the story enough to threaten Faith and Hope. That gave the theft story to Saudi Arabia more credence. The clear blue Texas sky turned dark, Hank's stomach growled, his neck stiffened, and his fists clenched.

He was headed for a fight.

He decided in Atlanta to change his connecting flight from Hilton Head to Washington. He would tell Onorato the story. He let his checked baggage go on to Hilton Head, where his attorney, Paul Ruth, would pick them up. Hank would take only his briefcase and his notes to see his handler.

This was better. Onorato would have everything, and he could make all the decisions. If Hank was going to start a fight, it was better to have all the details on the table.

CHAPTER SEVENTEEN

Once Hank had settled in his seat and the aircraft reached cruising altitude, he took out his briefcase and wrote a summary of his encounter with Blevins. Because nuclear weapons seemed to be more important, he added more details to what he could remember about Bakr studying them at Miami. He then fleshed out his recollection of bin Laden, warning him that King Faisal, or whoever was on the Saudi throne, would use such weapons against America if the king thought America had helped the Israelis take possession of the holy sanctuary. Agent Blevins had just added to his puzzle by questioning him about Colonel Orzon, the Sayyaf, and the possible theft of nukes from West Germany. He had dismissed the theft idea as absurd, but what if the story about terrorists and stolen nuclear weapons was true? An unthinkable danger. And Blevins had threatened harm to Hank's daughters. There was enough smoke that he had to report the Blevins meeting to Onorato. But he would omit the possible killing of Waters by McMillian. That was a personal matter he would investigate on his own.

In Washington, Hank and Onorato talked for several hours and Onorato took copious notes until he closed the meeting and gave Hank his marching orders.

"I concur. This nuclear thing is important. You may have to go back to Saudi Arabia about this sooner or later, but not now. I will run this up the flagpole and see who salutes. For now, just go back to Hilton Head and wait. Don't worry about it. You're on record as reporting your concern. We've got your back."

That wasn't enough. Hank had to do something. For starters, Mrs. Manh had given him Bill West's and Gus Bean's phone numbers. Hank remembered Bill West well because they had spent months together in headquarters at Cu Chi, but he recalled Bean only faintly. They had met just that once at the orphanage during the attack, but Bean had said he was with the Massachusetts National Guard. It was just possible that he might still have friends with the guard. Hank decided to try to track him down. As for West, after leaving Vietnam, he had worked in personnel at the Pentagon. He was now retired in Northern Virginia, but he still might have helpful contacts. He could help. And Paul might also have some ideas. Once home, Hank went to see Paul and told him about Blevins, nuclear weapons, and the Saudis.

Paul had become an increasingly good friend. A tall, ungainly attorney who always held himself erect and spoke as if he was in front of a jury, he had an incisive mind. Extremely well read on matters that mattered, he was ready with an opinion on any subject of importance. Although he was a dedicated liberal, he was a good balance to Hank. Paul tended to think the question through before he spoke, while Hank was ready without warmup to attack. Paul always wanted to talk rather than act. While Hank tended to act quickly, Paul said too quickly. They made a good team.

"He stopped you and forced you into a police car?" Paul asked. "Actually, two officers stopped me," Hank said. "No real force. Just strong suggestion that I get in the cruiser. Blevins was waiting in the back seat. He looked and dressed like a stereotype of an agent and handed me his card."

"Did you get those officers names and badge numbers?" "No," Hank said. "I was too surprised to think about that."

"Well, that's not like the Hawk Kean I know," Paul said. "But I'm licensed in Texas and I can the El Paso Police about them. I'll find their names and determine if they were on official business when they stopped you."

Then Hank went over his notes on the contact with the Manhs, Le Trang, and Blevins. All had mentioned Orzon, the theft, the Sayyaf, and the Saudis. He told Paul about Bakr studying nukes and bin Laden's reaction. Stressed that the problem before them was not drugs. It was the possibility of nuclear weapons in Arab hands.

"You're right, of course," Paul said, "but could there have actually been a theft?"

"I doubt it," Hank said, "but there actually were some six hundred suitcase-nukes in a special ammunition depot in West Germany. I guess we have to consider the possibility of a theft. Ordnance personnel guarded the interior, but regular army units were on the fences. And almost everybody detested the nukes. Anti-nuke and anti-war people hated them, especially the Germans, because anywhere those things might be set off, the ground would be unusable for a long time and Germany treasures every bit of its land. Pressure to get the things out of Germany increased until the president ordered them home. That was when there would have been a complete inventory, and if two had been missing, all hell would have broken out. The fact that there was no uproar means to me there was no theft. What worries me more than anything else is Bakr may have been trying, ever since I knew him back in 1966 to find a way to get Saudi hands on some kind of nuclear weapons. We need to know more about Bakr."

"I have a contact at the F.B.I.," Paul said. "He's Ted Storm, and he could look into the whole thing. He's a good man and we need someone like that on our side."

Did the death of Waters at the orphanage director have anything to do with nukes? Nung had said McMillian was the Phoenix agent that killed Waters. Phoenix agents were from the C.I.A. Was there a connection? He told Paul to ask Storm if he could find out if there had really ever been Phoenix agents named McMillian and Elliott and a theft of nuclear weapons. Hank would be the one to contact Bean and West to see if they could shed some light. They had a plan.

As they broke up, Paul said, "You're too tight wound. Take a break and relax. For far too long, you've been a hermit. Get out more. Riley's on Friday night has a great crowd. Today is Friday. Join the crowd."

"It's hard," Hank said. "When Helen left, she took the bright days with her."

"If you'd get out of that dark apartment, you'd find there're still bright days left."

Paul had a point. It had been five long, depressing years since the funeral, and he had gone out only to work or give investment seminars. Maybe going to Riley's for a drink wasn't such a bad idea. Young professionals went there after work, especially on Fridays to relax from the week, have a drink, a good meal, and maybe meet someone. He could go and see what happened. Faith and Hope had been after him for some time now. They would approve. It had been far too long.

He found himself looking forward to the evening.

Chapter Eighteen

Riley's it would be. He drove the three blocks from his apartment to Sea Pine Circle. He intent was to unwind, sip a bourbon, and grab a quick meal. Riley's long bar was packed with young men and women socializing loudly. They were too loud for him, so he took a booth away from the noise and ordered a hamburger. Waiting, he nursed a bourbon.

Paul was right. Since Helen's death, he had turned inward. And with Faith and Hope at Clemson, he was alone much of the time. He had to make some changes.

He looked up and found a woman standing by his booth. In a white blouse, black skirt, and low pumps, she looked to be in her thirties. Medium-length black hair, brown eyes, and a trim figure, she was attractive and holding a drink.

"Hi, Colonel Kean," she said. "I was at your seminar at the Hilton to learn how to handle my I.R.A. I'm Bev. I'm a hairdresser. May I join you?"

"Be my guest," he said, "but be warned, I've been out of touch for a while."

"I know," she said. "Welcome back." What did she mean by welcome back? "How do you know about me?"

"My shop is across the street from yours. I've watched you come and go. Five years ago, your wife died. You have two grown daughters. I've been to several of your seminars."

He sat back and took in her big brown eyes and just a little not-too-flashy jewelry. She was interesting. He took a chance.

"Can I buy you a drink?"

He ordered her a scotch, another bourbon for himself, and sat back to relax. They chatted, sipped, and laughed. He was enjoying this. But the loud music annoyed him. Finally, his burger came, but it wouldn't be right to eat alone, so he took another chance. "It's too loud here," he said. "I can barely hear you. And the music is lousy. My place is nearby. I've got some good scotch and better music. Let's take my burger there and split it."

"Great," she said. "I'll follow you in my car."

At his apartment, she went to the sofa in the living room as he fixed the drinks, warmed the burger in the oven, and divided it. Handing her a plate and a scotch, he sat on the opposite ottoman. "Tell me," he said. "With all those young studs at the bar, why hit on me?"

"Maybe I prefer a combat hero who gives great seminars," she said. "Maybe I like guys who have hard bodies, great hair with silver streaks in it, and good music."

"Are you serious?"

"I am. Let's hear some of that better music." "I warn you it is really old stuff."

He put on a song that started "You'll never know" and she immediately said, "Sinatra."

He put on another, "There, I've said it again." She hesitated, then asked, "Monroe?"

He nodded and she said, "Good tunes. What's your favorite?" "Waller's *Two Sleepy People,*" immediately regretting it. That was Helen's song.

"Please put it on," she said. "I'd like to hear it."

When Fats Waller came on with that great, slow beat, she said, "Let's dance."

"Not much room," he said, thinking about Helen. "It's enough if we go slow and close," she said.

He hesitated. This was happening too fast. He was out of touch. But he really loved the song and he liked to dance. Then he remembered that in love, war, and football, initiative counts. So he offered a hand and held her fairly close. She was a good dancer. Hit the beat.

When the disc ended, he turned toward the sofa, but she said, "That was the best. Can we do it again?"

He liked her feel. She fit just right. So he put the disc on again and held her a bit closer. It ended "Too much in love to say good night, good night."

"That was the best," she said and led him by the hand to the sofa.

He sat beside her. Not too close. Didn't want to scare her off. For a time, they ate their almost cold burgers and sipped their drinks. Then she moved closer, put her hand on his arm, and said, "You're sweet. I like you."

He stiffened and resisted. But he didn't want to kill the moment, so he put an arm around her. She cuddled close and looked up at him. He stopped resisting and kissed her very lightly and slowly. Her lips were a softness he had almost forgotten. And sweet beyond compare. He could feel the yearning of both of them.

She drew back and said, "That's what I wanted," she said.

Then remembering how alone he had been, he kissed her again, harder this time and neither could stop. They fumbled at clothing and coupled fast and hard. He was a teenager again. In a moment it was over and they gasped to catch their breath. She rested with her arms around his neck, her head on his shoulder. He picked her up, carried her to the bedroom, took off the rest of her clothes, and lay down beside her, said, "Let's do this right."

Later, they dozed, at first with him spooned onto her, his arms holding on for fear she would disappear. When his arm fell asleep and he turned away, she threw an arm and a leg over him. He slept better than he had in months and in the morning, he could not remember his dreams. When the first dim light roused them they made love again and finally rose, satiated, and showered together. As he liberally soaped her firm trim body, he could not believe what had happened. He heard his mother's voice and half recalled the words, "When they awoke, the farm was all white with the dew, and the sun was shining in their Garden of Eden."

If this was Eden, was there a snake in the bush? "Can I stay?" she asked.

"I have a problem," he said. "My daughters are off at Clemson now, but Hilton Head is their home. They were very close to their mother, and they might be upset if they found you here. They might turn away from me, and I don't want that to happen. I lost a lovely lady."

"I dated two pretty good guys," she said. "One was a golf pro who played in the heritage tournament here. When he lost his card, he never came back. The other was a local attorney. He found a client with money and married her."

"Family?" he asked her.

"My parents went to Florida a while back, to live in a trailer. What about yours?"

"Helen's parents and mine also went to Florida, to assisted living. I lost touch with Helen's parents after she died. I go down there to see Dad and Mom for birthdays. They have a nice suite and I help out with the money part. Dad's doing find but Mom's having trouble with her short term memory. They seem happy."

"I need to say something important," she said. "I have loved you for a long time. I went to your talks just to hear and see you. I cried after your wife died. I wanted to comfort you. When I saw you at Riley's, I summoned the courage and went to you. So, for me, last night was special, not a cheap one-night stand. I want very much to stay with you and meet your daughters, but I'll leave that up to you. Let's take the cars over to my place."

He put his arms around her and held her tightly.

Her apartment across from Palmetto Dunes was a block from a semi-circle body of water, adjacent to the Inland Waterway. She was surrounded by a series of upscale restaurants and shops. She was on an upper floor and could see the waterway between the buildings. While she fixed eggs, toast, and coffee, he relaxed on her small deck.

"Pretty nice," he said when she came out.

"I love it," she said. "I walk around the harbor in the morning and do yoga in a place with a great view of the boats on the water to the west. You'd like it here."

"Maybe, but where I am, I can jog on the beach. I train at a martial arts place in the mall there. I can walk to workouts and shop for food on my way back."

"Do you travel?"

"Not a lot, but I just came back from giving a seminar in El Paso."

"Was it worthwhile?"

"A mixed bag. A good seminar but I also visited a sick Vietnamese officer I had known overseas. That wasn't so good. He's dying. I don't do death well."

As they snuggled, he realized she might make his life better. He was starting to look forward to getting out more. Paul, Faith, and Hope had been right.

Chapter Nineteen

In the middle of the following week, Hank was just closing up his shop when Bev called, a quiver in her voice, almost as if she was crying.

"What's wrong?" he asked.

"Please come over quickly," she sobbed. "I need you."

He broke the speed limits on his way and rushed to her door.

She opened it quickly and threw herself into his arms. "Thank God you're here," she said.

"What happened?" he asked.

She pulled him into the room and down beside her on the couch. "An hour ago, just after I got home, there was a knock on the door. When I opened it, five men and a woman were standing there, looking very business-like, suits. Four of the guys were wearing sunglasses and had bulges under their arms that looked like they were carrying something. The guy without sunglasses pushed his way in and two of the bodyguards and the woman came in with him. The other guards stayed outside. Once they were in, the leader showed me a badge. It had the name Blevins on it."

Hank stiffened and stared at her. "Blevins?" he asked. "You're sure?"

"Absolutely," she said. "It's engraved on my mind. I'll never forget it."

"What the hell did he want?"

"He said he was from the treasury department and needed my help. I couldn't understand what he was talking about. I don't know anything that could help the treasury department. I told him I was a hairdresser and couldn't help him with anything but a haircut. Then he said that because of national security or something, he couldn't give me the details, but the government had an interest in you. I didn't understand what he was taking about. He said you were about to ruin some sort of important operation the government was running. He asked me to help."

Hank stood and paced, trying to understand, "Can you describe this Blevins?"

"Not really," she said. "I was too shocked. I would say he was completely medium in height and build. Wore an expensive suit. Had a good haircut. Blue eyes. Brown hair. Firm jaw. Clear speech. Like a highly paid executive or attorney."

That could be the Blevins from El Paso. "Did he say anything else?"

"Not much," she said. "I couldn't understand him. I was too stunned to think. But he rambled on about you working with people that may be trying to harm a program that was important to America, real harm. A potential disaster or something."

"What kind of disaster?"

"He didn't say exactly," she said, "but I think he mentioned that Iran was going to build a nuclear weapon, and that nobody in America wanted that to happen. Then he ranted on about the danger of war if America had to attack Iran. The Middle East would explode. Israel would be attacked. It was all very confusing, especially when he said the people you are supposedly working against are working on a way to stop Iran without going to war. America would then benefit greatly, but you and your associates were supposedly on the verge of interfering. When I said I didn't believe you would do anything like that, he said that would take me to the treasury department in Washington to talk to the secretary who would confirm what he was saying. He again asked me to help him."

"How are you supposed to help him?" Hank asked.

"Report on what you do, where you go, who you talk to. Keep him informed. He said repeated something about nuclear weapons."

Blevins had also asked about nuclear weapons in El Paso. He paced the room, "Can you remember what he said about nuclear weapons?"

"He said that details about those weapons were classified, but he would try get approval for me to know more. Then he emphasized there would be consequences if I didn't help him."

"Did he hurt you?"

"No. But there was definitely a threat. Then he and the body-guards left as suddenly and quietly as they had come. I locked the door and called you."

He sat down beside her and held her tight for a long time until she stopped shivering.

"I'm sorry, Bev," he said. "Blevins stopped me in El Paso. Now he's trying to hassle me and stop me from investigating him. He just mentioned nuclear weapons to frighten you, make him seem import-ant. Don't worry about them. I'll take care of him, but you need to take precautions. Lock your doors. Set the alarm. Paul and I will talk to the Hilton Head police and your neighborhood security."

"Will he come back?" she asked. "Probably not," he said, hoping.

CHAPTER TWENTY

Back at work after his eventful weekend, Hank decided to contact Gus Bean and Bill West and see if they could tell him anything about the Phoenix team at the orphanage during the attack that killed Waters. Bill West had retired from the army and was working in real estate in Northern Virginia. A secretary put Bill on the line.

"This is Hank Kean," Hank said, "from long ago in Cu Chi."

"Well, I'll be darned," Bill said. "Cu Chi was really a long time ago. When my secretary buzzed me, I couldn't believe it, but I hoped it might be you. What a pleasure. But I remembered you as Hawk. Why the name change?"

"Now that I'm no longer a soldier," Hank said, "people call me Peachy."

"Peachy Kean," Bill said. "Got it. How are you?"

They exchanged family updates and told each other that civilians are a lot better paid than army officers, and on top of that, the Viet Cong wasn't shooting at the civilians. Bill said he was working his butt off and not sure he was enjoying it. Hank replied that he was also hard at his new role of investment advisor.

Then Hank got to the point, "Did you get a letter from Nung Manh's wife?"

"I did," Bill said, "but I barely remembered Nung, and Vietnam was long ago and far away, in another life. Nung was a good guy, and at first I wanted to help him, but I couldn't afford to go to El Paso. I actually looked for ways to help out, trying to see what I could do, but I really couldn't think of a thing. Then the demands of everyday life took over, and I let the matter drop. I suppose I should have written her back and at least offered some advice, but inertia got the better of me. She wrote you, too?"

"She did," Hank said and filled him in on what had happened and the fact that Nung was probably dying of Agent Orange.

"He's not the only one," Bill said. "It's going around for a lot of Vietnam vets. I'm in a study group at Fort Belvoir, and we talk about Agent Orange a lot. Several of my buddies from Nam are gone, mostly because of it. What did Nung want?"

How much to lay on Bill? The killing of Waters was one thing Hank knew Bill might be able to clear up, but Hank wasn't sure whether to mention the theft of nuclear weapons. That was dynamite news, maybe too much. He decided to start with the killing. "At first, Nung talked about Waters's death. You probably remember the Phoenix Team on site that day. Well, Nung said they were bad apples working with the Viet Cong. Said one of them shot Waters."

Then Hank decided to go all in.

"Nung then dropped a real bomb. Said he had heard about some nuclear weapons being stolen. Taken out of a depot in West Germany and shipped to the Philippines by some terrorists. Had you heard anything like that?"

"Of course not," Bill said. "That's absurd. Couldn't have happened.

It would have been a gigantic story. What did he say about it?"

"Not much. He claimed a drunk told him the story, something about some Sayyaf Filipino terrorists being the thieves. At first, I reacted as you just did. It sounded absurd, and I was going to drop it, but on my way to the El Paso airport, a federal agent stopped me and grilled me about the theft. So I decided to follow up and report it to the Pentagon."

"A federal agent? What did he want?"

Hank summarized the contact with Blevins, especially the part when Blevins asked if Nung had said anything about a theft of suitcase bombs. Then he asked Bill if he thought the men on the Phoenix team could also have been involved with the theft of weapons.

"The Phoenix agents belonged to the C.I.A.," Bill said. "I agree with Colonel Manh. Many of them were bad apples. I suppose it's not without the realm of possibility that they or the C.I.A. could have been involved with something like that, if it really happened.

But the Vietnam War was years ago in a country now run by people you fought. You should turn all this over to the government. It's way above your pay grade."

"You're probably right. After I reported it, I was going to drop it, but I thought I could to make a quick check with some of the guys who knew Nung. I called you first because I know there's an intelligence outfit near you at Fort Belvoir. Do you have contacts that could check out the Phoenix team there during that attack and at the same time check out that director?"

"Sure. My study group at Belvoir is working on Vietnam. Phoenix is kind of out of their league, but I could ask around. As for Waters, we have some state department guys in our group. I could ask them."

Hank didn't want to call unwanted attention to the killing of Waters, maybe by one of ours, or to the rumor of a possible theft of nukes, so he suggested that Bill just base his questions around the orphanage he had built. That was really all Hank needed. But as long as he had Bill's attention, he decided to push his luck.

"Before I let you go, could you also check into the status of a Filipino army colonel named Orzon who visited El Paso three or four years ago? He had met Nung in the Philippines and helped the family come to America. When he went to see Nung in El Paso, Orzon got tipsy and claimed the Sayyaf were the ones that had stolen the nukes."

"I guess I could check out Orzon with the state guys."

Hanging up, Hank wondered why he had brought up Orzon, because he still wasn't convinced that any nuclear weapons had been stolen. It was probably a waste of time, but the call hadn't been difficult. So he decided to try Bean in Massachusetts. He got lucky. Gus answered after the third ring.

"This is Hank Kean," he said. "We met at that orphanage in Vietnam during Tet."

"I remember," Bean said. "You evacuated the director." "Right on. How are you?"

"Not well. Age, diabetes, and a stroke. The wife takes care of me." "Good luck. But a short time ago, I went down to El Paso to see Colonel Manh who told me that one of the Phoenix guys killed Waters during that attack, not the VC. That was new, and I want to check it out. Fort Devens is near you, and it has an intelligence unit.

Could you ask somebody there about that Phoenix team at the orphanage when the V.C. hit?"

"You mean Elliott and McMillian? Hard to believe they were killers. But you never know. I guess I could ask around. I don't have much energy most of the time, so I'm not up to much. But for you, I'll look around when I have one of my better days."

That night Hank couldn't sleep. Why had he made those calls? The more he mulled it over, the more he thought he ought to drop the whole thing. But he couldn't turn off his mind. Who were those Phoenix guys? Who was that agent in El Paso? And Bean, too, had just said one of the Phoenix was named McMillian. Hank couldn't drop the absurd idea that the agent might have been the same McMillian he had known in Hawaii, a long time ago. And was Waters the deserter that had attacked Charley McMillian back then? He dozed.

It was Hawaii in the March of 1949 and Schofield Barracks was peacefully quiet for the officers, soldiers, and their families. Congress had cut the defense budget. With less money for training, the military on the islands worked a relaxed schedule. In never ending beautiful weather, the soldiers played baseball or boxed for their units. Officers bet on those contests, worked an eight-to-five schedule, and kept up a bare semblance of training. Their wives had bridge groups and daily cocktail hour at the officers' club. The weather was magnificent, booze was cheap and the slot machines paid well. Life was good.

Especially for kids. Hank was nine years old, and it was a great time to be that age. The Hawaiian school did not demand much, the school day was over at noon, and there was never any homework. He and his buddy, Charley McMillian, spent their afternoons swimming in the club pool, running in the nearby woods, gaping at the neighborhood girls, who, until recently, had been sissies and had suddenly become attractive, or hanging around the slot machines to see if they could make a hit after a drunk left a slot primed to pay. It was a joy to be alive in Hawaii, without care, and beginning to learn about life.

One afternoon, while the boys were playing cowboys and Indians in the woods near their homes, they came upon what looked like a concealed camp site. It was roughly constructed, consisted of a pup tent, a crude picnic table, and a bench. A soldier was sitting on the bench and cooking something in a pot on the fire.

"Let's attack," Hank said.

"No, I don't like it," Charley said. "He may be a deserter."

"If you boys want soup," the soldier called out, "I have cups for you."

Slowly, the two of them got up from their attack position and moved to sit on the bench next to the man who was wearing army fatigues.

"What're you doing here?" Hank asked.

"I'm a scout," the man said as he ladled their soup. "I'm training to work deep behind enemy lines if we ever have to fight again in the South Pacific. I'll be sent on long patrols and have to know how to survive."

The soup was good, but the soldier made the two of them nervous. Soon, they broke away, left the woods, and ran back to the housing area.

"Do you think he was really a scout?" Charley asked.

"I don't know," Hank said. "He could be a deserter. I think we should talk to him again and find out. Let's sneak up on him tomorrow after lunch."

By noon the following day, however, Charley had not appeared and Hank decided to scout the camp alone. He moved carefully and crawled stealthily through the bushes until he heard strange sounds from the camp site, grunting and screams. From under the bushes, he saw Charley bent over the table with his pants down and screaming. The soldier was behind Charley and grunting as he thrust into Charley. In terror, Hank pulled back and ran home to tell his mother. Quickly, his father arrived with several men in jeeps and Hank led them to the area of the little camp. He stayed back with the jeeps and could not see what happened, but soon, a soldier emerged carrying Charley, while two other men dragged the scout from the bushes. There was blood on Charley's legs and on the unconscious scout's face.

"Don't look at that," Hank's father said. "Charley will be okay."

As Hank and his dad walked slowly home, his father said that the scout appeared to be a deserter and that there would be a court martial.

"Did that man touch you?" he asked.

"No," Hank said. "We just found him yesterday. He gave us some soup. He said he was a scout, but we thought he was a deserter. We were going to sneak up on him today and try to figure out what he was doing. When Charley didn't meet me after lunch, I went on to the camp alone and saw that something bad was going on. Charley must have tried to sneak up on the guy by himself."

"What do you remember about the man that attacked Charley?"
"He had a pup tent, a bench, and a cooking fire."

"How did you know he was a soldier?"

"He had on army fatigues. He had a pup tent and his drinking cups were the kind the army uses. He said he was a scout, and he had a military name tag."

"What was his name?" "Waters."

In the morning, Hank rose groggily, and at the office, he couldn't concentrate. Visions of the burning orphanage and its dead director mixed with the memory of a sexual assault back in Hawaii. On top of that, he recalled parachuting with those suitcase nuclear weapons in West Germany. It kept him on edge.

He looked out his window at the adjacent golf course, but his view was not as clear as it usually was. A front had moved in, and its winds had brought clouds that obscured his view and depressed him. He had to move on and forget this non-sense. He decided to call Bev, knowing she would cheer him up.

He needed her.

CHAPTER TWENTY-ONE

A year before stopping Kean in El Paso, Steve Blevins had assembled his team in McLean and told them, "We have a new mission. Rumors have arisen that a few years ago, several small nuclear weapons had been stolen from an American depot in West Germany. We are to look into what actually happened. This is an eyes-only mission; absolutely no word about any theft can leak out. Chaos would result. We want to know if a theft took place, who did it, and who set it up. We have only one fact; a Filipino army colonel named Manual Orzon suddenly retired back in eighty-three and came into significant wealth. We need to find him, the source of his money, and if the money came from that theft. It will be easy to find him. We all have contacts in Manila, his home. Use them and find him, but don't raise any flags that might send him into hiding. Just say that you have Saudi money for him and need to know where he is. Get on this fast. We need this yesterday."

Sharon found records in the state department that Orzon had visited a former Vietnamese colonel, Nung Manh, in 1984 in El Paso. Jim bugged the Manh apartment there, and Tom was listening when a Colonel Kean visited Nung in January of 1987. Tom heard Manh tell Kean about Orzon and a theft of nuclear weapons. He also learned that Kean planned to meet the Manh's son to learn more. Because Blevins couldn't find a way to tape Kean's meeting with the son, he decided to intercept Kean on the way to the airport, try to learn what the son had told Kean, and evaluate the colonel.

At the same time, one of Sharon's contacts in Manila told her that Orzon had an expensive home in Zambales Province some fifty miles northwest of Manila. Steve decided to take his team to Zambales, grab Orzon, and interrogate him about the theft rumor.

"Here is a layout of the Orzon place," Sharon said. "The fence is not an obstacle. He has seven caretakers and butlers. Four are outside men, mowing the lawn and patrolling. The three guys inside look like a doorman, a cook, and a personal bodyguard. The doorman sleeps in an anteroom adjacent to the front door, which looks like we will be able to break open with a ram. The cook sleeps by the kitchen, and the personal guard seems always to be with Orzon. All of them appear to be former Sayyaf terrorists that Orzon hired for protection."

Steve set the operation in motion. Ron provided assault rifles, silenced pistols, a door ram, and flash bombs. Tom got night-vision goggles and radios. Sharon provided a layout of the house and grounds. David organized the attack. "We'll hit them two hours after midnight," he said. "Kill the guards, but keep Orzon alive. At night, the four outside guards operate in two shifts of two men each, one before and one after midnight. On patrol, they separate, one going clockwise, the other in the opposite direction. Here is the point where they are farthest apart, and here are bushes for Tom and Jim to wait. When the guards reach the bushes, kill them, using silenced pistols. Ron and David should kill the two others as they sleep in the guardhouse. We want to eliminate these four without arousing anybody. When Sharon hits the front door with the ram, all surprise will disappear, and we'll need to use speed and night-vision goggles to attack the others. Ron will handle the door guard, Jim and Tom, the cook. Steve and David will move immediately to the master bedroom and kill the last guard, but not Orzon. That's it."

Using surprise, darkness, and the vision goggles, the first part went without a problem. Tom and Jim quietly killed the two patrolling guards as Ron and David dispatched the other two outside guards in their beds. Half of the second part went well; Ron killed the door guard, Jim and Tom, the cook. Difficulty arose in the master bedroom, however, because the noise of breaking down the door woke Orzon's personal guard who fired at the door. Steve and David knew enough, however, to stay low on the floor, and were not hit. When they fired back to kill the guard, however, a stray round hit Orzon in the stomach.

David examined Orzon's wound and told Steve that Orzon was bleeding out from a gut wound and that Orzon was going to die within minutes. Steve tried to talk to him, but the colonel was very weak, so harsh methods were out. Steve was able to obtain only a few names before Orzon died. The team then took documents and left well before dawn.

Before Orzon died, he used the name of a Vietnamese contact, a Viet Cong leader named Quan, who had recruited Orzon and the Sayyaf for the theft. Orzon also said an agency officer named McMillian was Quan's contact for the operation, but Blevins could not make Orzon reveal who had masterminded the mission. The documents taken shed little light.

Blevins rendered a full report to his controller who signed off with one caveat. Blevins had to remove all references to McMillian from the report. That caveat puzzled and worried Blevins and his team.

For the first time, he had doubts.

CHAPTER TWENTY-TWO

On Friday evening, Bev and Hank walked to a restaurant at the west end of the semi-circular harbor where she lived. Swanky shops were on their left and expensive sailboats were docked on their right. Their restaurant was at the lower end of the harbor. It was on a second floor and had a panoramic window looking west at the setting sun. They could see across the mile-wide, calm inland waterway dotted with sail boats and water skiers testing mild March winds. The sinking sun shone on the sparkling water and created a shining path toward them. She seemed happy. The combination broke through his gloom and Hank forgot about Muslim terrorists and nuclear weapons.

"Where do your daughters stay when they come home?" she asked.

"They've been using my second bedroom, but Faith is talking about getting her own place near the bank where she has been offered a good job. Hope would then be able to stay at either place. I've been thinking about having a get together with you and them the next time they come home, but right now, they seem to enjoy the father-daughter, one-on-one stuff. Let's think about how we can work you in."

"It's your call," she said. "What did you give them last Christmas?" "A couple of these new portable phones, so they can call me anytime they want. These phones are really cool, and I programmed theirs with a speed dial, so they can reach me quickly and at any time."

"Can I be programmed, too?" she asked.

"Sure," he said. "Like the movie, you just pucker up and blow." "Tell me about El Paso," she laughed. "Why was it so bad?"

"The Vietnamese colonel was pretty sick," he said. "He's terminal and evidently, has only a few months left. That was sad. But he was well enough to talk about some Phoenix agents during an attack on an orphanage that I flew into during Tet. He claimed those guys had turned bad and killed an American during the attack. He also made a preposterous claim that some nuclear weapons had been taken from an American depot in West Germany by terrorists."

"Nuclear weapons again, and terrorists," she said. "That's scary. What did he say?"

"He based it on a rumor from a Filipino drunk. The guy was a retired colonel and had visited the colonel a while back. The guy claimed a terrorist gang from the Philippines had stolen the nukes, taken them to the Philippines, and sold them to Saudi Arabia. I was in the nuke business for a while, and that would have been a big deal everyone would have heard about. But I never heard anything. So the story didn't make much sense."

"That's for sure," she said. "Anything else happen in El Paso?"
"Only one thing unusual," he said. "On my way to the airport, that guy Blevins stopped me and questioned me about the dying Viet colonel. He also mentioned the theft of those nukes, so I reported Blevins to Washington. And then I thought more about how important the theft could be, and decided to call some guys I had known in Vietnam. They agreed to check things out, and so did my attorney, Paul Ruth, here, on Hilton Head. I gave him a full report for our file. He also has a F.B.I. contact who Ruth said is a good guy who would help."

"You called military people?"

He told her about meeting Bean and West during the orphanage attack and that Colonel Manh had been a boat person and met Colonel Orzon in the Philippines. How Orzon had come to see the Manhs in El Paso and, thoroughly drunk, had told a story about Muslim terrorists stealing nukes.

"It all seemed so absurd that I ignored it until Blevins stopped me and sort of corroborated it. That was when I decided to look into it."

"Why not just report it?"

"I really don't know. I suppose I just resented Blevins. But I'm going to drop everything unless Ruth, Bean, or West dig up something. The story about the nuclear weapons worries me, however, and would be important if true. I also was annoyed when Blevins implied Faith and Hope might be in danger, so I reacted. But I'm tired of it now. I'd rather be here with you. Missing nukes seem far away in another life."

He had his bourbon and she, her scotch. Soft music played overhead. His veal was thin and crisp; her snapper was soft and spicy. They lingered for a drink after dinner and held hands as they strolled back through the small crowd of evening shoppers and diners. She put on some soft music and they danced again. Made him feel good. Pretty soon, he picked her up and carried her to the bedroom.

Later, he looked at her as she slept. Beautiful. Everything was good. He was happy and satisfied.

Chapter Twenty-Three

She was still sleeping when he left early in the morning. Life was good. He prayed nothing out of the past would show up and ruin everything. He had a future now, and Bev was a part of it. Things quieted down, and by the time Gus Bean called him back, Hank had almost forgotten about him. The demands of everyday life had taken over, and he was no longer quite so angry at Blevins. He picked up Bean's call expecting little, and that's what he got.

"I didn't do well," Gus said. "It was a real effort, but I found two guys in army intelligence, a couple of military oxymorons. At first, they said they had contacts that could locate Elliott and McMillian, but then, they never called me back. When I called them again, they claimed the C.I.A. didn't answer their inquiry, said the agency folks were nervous and cautious. Said the Phoenix program was bad business and implied that it would be better for all concerned if we let the subject of Phoenix, Elliott, and McMillian die. Emphasized the Phoenix Operation was bad medicine, like the stuff I take every day. If I were you, I'd forget about this."

That smacked of worried government officials trying to cover up something. Hank always enjoyed a puzzle, and this one was starting to look like a good one. Bean's report appeared to be just what Blevins had said, "Leave this alone or somebody might get hurt." He didn't like the sound of that, but he still wasn't quite angry enough to get started again, so he shrugged and ignored the report. He didn't tell Ruth or Bev about Bean's call because there was nothing to tell. It was more than just a sin of omission. He was getting too old for games and all he wanted to do was enjoy his new life with Bev and his daughters.

A week later, Bill West called. At first, he joked about coming down to Hilton Head to play golf with a hawk. Then, like Gus, he changed his tone and became serious. "I spoke to three officers," he said, "one each from state, defense intelligence, and army. All three agreed to check on our targets. All of them were familiar with C.O.O.R.D.S. and were very much aware of the history of the Phoenix program. They sounded promising. When several weeks later I hadn't heard from any of them, I collared each separately and asked what they had learned. All three were nervous about the question. The state guy said that Waters was not listed in any department records and that there was no data about anybody with that name. He claimed that nobody named Waters had ever worked for C.O.O.R.D.S. Yet, you and I know that was not true. It was the same with the other two. Their C.I.A. contacts had claimed they couldn't talk about classified Phoenix operations. The net result from all them were the same; *nada*. One thing was odd about all three of them; they seemed afraid to talk to me. It was strange."

"Did you find anything about that Colonel Orzon?"

"Yeah," West said. "That too was odd. The state guy said Colonel Orzon recently died in a terrorist incident in the Philippines. Evidently, two rival terrorist groups were involved, but the reports were vague and unclear. Had a lack of details."

Orzon had told Colonel Manh that Sayyaf terrorists had stolen nuclear weapons from a depot in Germany. Now he was dead. Nobody could ask a dead man about the theft. Coincidence? He called Paul and brought him up to date, including the fact that Orzon had died, maybe at the hands of the Sayyaf. Who were the Sayyaf?

"Some were criminals that had been kicked out of the Philippines," Paul said. "They went to Saudi Arabia for a couple of years, and when they came back, they had morphed into terrorists who beheaded people. Not a good group to tangle with. If I were you, I'd stay clear of them. I recommend that you forget all of this, especially Waters and Phoenix. But if you're as stubborn as I remember, you might try the Freedom of Information Act. Before you do, however, there's something you should know. You remember Senator Tompkins?"

"The South Carolina senator?" Hank asked. "Of course. I went to see him when I was at the war college. He and his sidekick, Steve Powell, were interested in my thesis about Saudi Arabia and asked smart questions. They seemed like good guys."

"Tompkins has always been a good guy," Paul said, "and he is very interested in Hilton Head. He has a condo here and I do some work for him. He stays in touch. As a matter of fact, he called me a while back. Said he had seen a routine listing of ongoing intelligence operations. One was code-named 'Three Colonels.' The colonels were Manh, Orzon, and Kean. Your name caught his eye, but there was nothing more, no explanation. He knows we're friends so he asked if you were involved in some bad stuff. I told him you were clean. But the fact that there was even such a listing worries me. It means that, for some reason, you have come to someone's attention at the federal level. You should ease off on all this. The government can handle intelligence operations. You can't. Forget it before it gets worse."

"It may have gotten worse already if I'm on a government list with Manh and Orzon," Hank said. "And if it's gotten to Senator Tompkins's attention, politics is involved. I'd hate to think I'm on his bad list. Do you think the Freedom of Information Act would shed some light?"

"Probably not," Paul said. "I think you'd be wasting your time and money. It might even alert Senator Tompkins again, and you don't want to do that."

Paul was right. Senator Tompkins was a political power, someone Hank didn't want to cross, but if drugs, terrorists, and nuclear weapons were involved, Hank wanted to know how and why, no matter the risk. He thought about what had happened. All these separate government people were individually warning him to leave this alone or he might get in trouble. Why were they so concerned about the Orzon story, a fantasy told by a drunk? Such unity of concern might have come about if it was ordered by someone in a position of authority, someone who wanted to hide something important. If it's politics, Hank hated it. Always had. He told Paul, "Something else is going on. I smell a rat."

"Well, I smell an old fart who should mind his own business," Paul said.

Ouch. That hurt, but Hank still wanted to know more about stolen nukes in West Germany.

"If some weapons had been actually stolen, we could have asked Orzon about that. Except now we can't. He's dead. How? But no details. Convenient for anyone trying to cover up the theft of those weapons."

"You're joisting with windmills again, grasping at straws. You don't have anything to go on. I'm repeating myself, drop it."

Paul hung up. He was probably right, but there were a lot of coincidences about Orzon, nuclear weapons, and fake federal agents. Missing nuclear weapons were too important to drop.

He called Paul back and told him to try the Freedom of Information Act.

"Find out if Elliott and McMillian are connected to Waters and nuclear weapons."

This was the right thing to do. Let all the evidence come out. When he had all the information, he would know what to do. Paul was right.

Chapter Twenty-Four

As Hank waited for a response to the F.O.I. request, he continued to search for answers. Why did Manh want Hank to come to El Paso? Was it to finger Elliott and McMillian? When Bean and West had tried to check them out, both had run into brick walls. Their contacts at the C.I.A. and the state department had tried to distance themselves from Phoenix operations. It seemed odd. What was also intriguing was that Agent Blevins had been very interested in whether or not Waters had said anything at all to Hank on the chopper before dying. What did Waters know that so worried Blevins? Could Manh really be trusted? Why he was accusing members of the Phoenix team of killing Waters after such a long time? A conundrum.

Maybe Nung realized that his death would erase the memory of the killing. Paul's F.O.I. request might shed some light. Maybe he'd find out if Agent Blevins was really a government agent. As for Waters, when did state hire him? When did he go to Vietnam? And were Elliott and McMillian actually Phoenix agents? Where were they now? If they were C.I.A. agents in Vietnam, did they stay with the agency after the war?

Paul phoned.

"Our F.B.I. contact, Ted Storm, finally got back to me on the rumor of a theft of weapons. He got nowhere and thinks you should ask the Department of Justice those questions. He says Justice would be able to talk to Vietnam and deal with the agency, but as a private citizen, you cannot."

"I had considered going to Justice after I talked to Manh," Hank said, "but the whole story seemed so flaky that I had decided to drop it until Blevins stopped me. When he asked about Colonel Orzon and the nukes, he raised a flag that alarmed me. I was convinced that

Colonel Manh was not into drugs, so that wasn't why Blevins was hassling me. He wanted to know about Waters's murder or the theft of those weapons. If either of those had really happened, they were crimes that might get somebody into real trouble, even after all the years."

"But why would Blevins target you?"

"Maybe trying to frighten me. Murder and theft of nuclear weapons are serious subjects, and maybe the people involved are still around and want me to walk away. So when they saw me talking to Nung, they looked for ways to make me ignore what he said. And I might have done that if Blevins hadn't made those threats. That got me mad. If this was important enough to threaten harm to my family daughters, it just might be true. Where there's smoke, there could be something worse, maybe even Muslim terrorists running around with suitcase nuclear weapons. I really doubt that, but it still haunts me."

Paul and Storm wanted Hank to turn everything over everything to the attorney general and let the Department of Justice handle the problem. "Don't make a stink," they said. But he didn't want to make a stink, just find some facts, so he could decide the right thing to do. Paul did not sound optimistic about the Freedom of Information request. He pointed out that there were many exceptions to the act. He said that federal agencies don't have to give out classified data, and all internal agency practices were exempt. Personal files were off limits. Paul warned about such things, but Hank saw no other route, so it was worth a try. Had to be.

In mid-July, Paul called to say that he had an answer from state. It had taken four months, so long that Hank had almost forgotten about it. He was happy to be with Bev and his girls. He had three ladies now, a real family that kept him busy and his mind away from thoughts of nuclear weapons. He no longer had a burning desire to pursue terrorists.

"What took so long?" he asked.

"They asked me several times for additional information or clarification. Each request appeared to be nothing more than a delaying tactic, avoiding me."

"I'll come over."

"Don't bother. When you skip over the legal jargon and cut to the core, C.O.O.R.D.S. hired a Randy Waters in 1965, and he volunteered to be director of that orphanage in Vietnam. As you know, he died three years later. His body was shipped to El Paso for burial. No indication he had a family. That's all there is, nothing more."

It didn't make sense. How could state hire a convicted felon that had been in prison for assaulting a child and put him in charge of an orphanage full of kids just like the one he had assaulted? Something was missing.

"State's rules in third-world countries are less stringent," Paul said. "That's absurd," Hank said.

"It's also a fact."

Hank felt that if the story of Waters's hire ever got out, someone would hang. And maybe that was another reason they wanted to keep this quiet. Paul's report started him wondering again, and he found himself looking forward to seeing how the agency's reply might be different than that state had sent. Maybe the agency would eventually provide some answers, however lame they might be. It was a hope.

A month later, the C.I.A. did reply, and Paul told Hank to come over. "Here's a copy. Skip to page five for the substance; the agency hired a Jack Elliott in 1964. He went to Vietnam in 1966, but his rank, position, and duties there were classified, and still are. He was declared missing in action in 1969. His body was never found. The C.I.A. has a longtime policy of protecting the records of agents who die in the line of duty. I am inclined to think that is what they have done here."

"What do they say about McMillian?" Hank asked.

"A Charles McMillian was hired by the agency about the same time as Elliott. Again, the agency claims that his rank, position, and duties are classified, and thus, the reply does not address any of that. There is also no indication that he left the agency. If he is still with the agency, they would be even more reluctant to release any information about him."

"And if he's been there twenty-five years," Hank said, "he'd have to be in a senior position."

"True. Maybe even senior enough to have dictated this response."

That was worthy consideration. How could he find out if this was the same Charles McMillian, he had known a long time ago in Hawaii? He wanted answers and asked Paul if there was a way to get them. Who could help?

"That's up to you," Paul said. "You are the one that has raised the visibility of this situation and who might suffer the consequences. Your name was on my request. As a result, you must assume that many more people now know of your interest in these agents and the death of the orphanage director. Some people at the agency might not appreciate your inquiry, and they might respond negatively. In sum, barring the emergence of some additional data, such as the details of Elliott's disappearance, I recommend you lump them with Randy Waters as a dead file. To pursue it further would cost much more time and money than you'd want to shell out. To obtain additional evidence, for example, you might even need to go to Vietnam. That would be expensive even if it were possible, considering the fact that America's relations with that country are tenuous at best. In the present climate, such a trip would be out of the question. You would need a high-level state sponsor and a good Vietnamese contact just to get a visa. And apparently, you have neither. On the other hand, if you have a friend in a very high place, you might be able to twist a few arms at state or the agency. Lacking such, I'd drop it."

Hank was sure not going back to Vietnam. But then he remembered those two El Paso police officers who were with Blevins at the airport.

"Have you found out which officers were on duty when I was stopped?" he asked Paul. "We could start with them."

"Negative. No response from El Paso. They didn't even bother to answer my request. Come on, Hank. Get back to reality. Forget all this and get back to work. Make some money. Love your girlfriend and your daughters. Get a life."

"Aren't you concerned about the theft of those nukes?"

"You have no evidence that such a theft ever actually occurred. If we sent the story to the press, they would want proof, something you do not have. Go talk to Bev, and try to listen to her. Women always make more sense than you do. You tend to be too rash."

He did, and she was reluctant. "Don't push this," she said. "Cool it. Don't keep chasing ghosts. You and I are doing just fine. Please don't do something that might change what we have. It's too good to risk."

When he woke in the morning and found the sun shining, Hank decided Bev was right; he had been stupid. It was closed, finished, unless something turned up.

CHAPTER TWENTY-FIVE

Two weeks later, Le Trang called.

"My father passed away. He had told me several times how pleased he was with your visit. He said it meant much to him. I wanted you to know."

"I'm sorry to hear that he's gone," Hank said. "Was he in much pain?"

"The doctor said it was from natural causes, probably a heart attack. He was buried in the Fort Bliss cemetery. The military gave him a color guard, a rifle salute, and taps. It was a nice ceremony. Mother thought it was good of them to do it."

"It was. How is she doing?"

"She is very sad. They had been together for a long time, through good and bad years. They survived the Vietnam War, the capture of Saigon, and attacks by pirates at sea on their way to the Philippines. On the other hand, she is relieved that he will suffer no more. The medical examiner said his death was caused by a sudden, massive heart attack, not unusual in cases of those who have been exposed to Agent Orange, had a stroke, and were diabetic. Because he was probably sleeping when it happened, and because there were no signs of pain or struggle, he most likely went quietly and did not suffer at the end."

"What will your mother do now?"

"She still has her job in the public library, as well as a widow's pension and some medical benefits from social security and the military. We are searching for a larger place, so she can move in with us and not remain alone at the Cielo Vista apartments. She worries about being alone. Everything is too quiet and she jumps at the slightest sounds. She thinks that it is dangerous for there. She's afraid someone might accuse her, and the government might send her back to Vietnam, where she would be persecuted. She came from a country that for centuries has ignored the rights of its citizens. She has seen how badly and quickly such governments can turn on people. She doesn't want that to happen to her."

"Reassure her for me. She is here legally and cannot be deported. I will do anything I can to make sure your mother is treated well. If I can't, I have friends who can. I hope she will be able to recover and move on. Please keep me informed."

That evening at Bev's apartment, when Hank told her what had happened, she stopped making their drinks, turned around, held her hands to her face, with her eyes starting to tear. In a quivering voice, she said, "That is so sad. And think of her now. Alone in a foreign country at the end of her life, her husband gone, her former friends far away."

Hank held her. "She won't be alone," he said. "Her son is with her, and he's a good man. She has two beautiful granddaughters and friends at the library. I'll stay in touch with the boy in case she needs anything. She'll be okay."

He promised himself he would call and do what he could. Two days later, Faith called.

"Dad," she said, "a federal agent just stopped me." "What? How?" Hank asked. "Are you okay?"

"I'm okay. It just caught me off guard. A policeman approached me as I was leaving work. He asked me to get into his cruiser. There was a man inside, trim looking in a business suit. Said he was a special agent from some sort of drug enforcement agency and needed my help. He asked about drug use on Hilton Head, said if it was true his agency needed my help to stop it. When I told him I wasn't a user, didn't know any users, and hadn't seen any, he asked about Hispanic workers that might be drug gangs. I told him to ask the police or somebody else. Then he asked about Muslims, and I told him there had always been Black Muslims on the island, but they had never been a problem as far as I knew. When he asked if you were a drug user, I stormed out of the car."

"Did he hurt you?"

"No, but he sure pissed me off."

"I don't blame you. It sounds as if that guy Blevins is acting up again. Don't talk to him or anybody like him again. If anybody tries to contact you, clam up until Paul or I get there. I'll talk to Paul and the Hilton Head police. We'll try to make sure the cops don't let this happen again. Try not to worry."

He called Paul immediately and told him what had happened, "Remember how Blevins stopped me?" he said. "Well, this is worse. He's picking on my girls now."

"You're upset," Paul said, "and I don't blame you. But as always, you are too quick to take offense and jump to conclusions. Just relax. I'll also talk to the police and ask them for the name of the officer that stopped her. We'll follow up on this. It won't happen again."

Faith had not been attacked, Hank knew that, but she had been hassled. Why was Blevins doing this? Could it have anything to do with the fact that Nung Manh had just died? And why go after Faith? What was the connection? He had to find a way to stop this, anything he could, because he had to end it. He almost blew up a week later when Hope called from Clemson.

"An agent just talked to me," she said in a quivering voice. "I had just left my last class when my counselor stopped me and said an agent was in her office waiting for me. He said he was with immigration or something. Said his name was Green, showed a badge. Said he was looking into drug use at Clemson and wanted to talk about that. But he switched quickly to ask about you, drugs on Hilton Head, and gangs of Hispanics working on roofs and driveways. Said they might be Muslims. I told him there were lots of Black Muslims on Hilton Head. Then he asked if I used drugs or if you did. That made me mad and I stormed out."

"He claimed he was a federal agent?" Hank asked.

"Yeah. Asked about drugs and immigration. He had a badge."
"I'll call Clemson and tell them not to let that happen again."

He also called Paul and told him about Hope. This was getting worse. Another so-called agent, probably Blevins or someone that worked for him. Same questions about drugs or illegals. It was a pattern. A man claiming to be a federal agent used authorities to detain them and ask the same kinds of questions. It all started after he saw Nung Manh in El Paso, and it escalated when we sent the F.O.I. requests. There had to be a connection.

"Just because it started happened after you saw Colonel Manh," Paul said, "doesn't mean your meeting caused it. That's bad thinking. I don't think these are federal agents, neither C.I.A. nor state. I think you're just getting jumpy. Why would federal agents bother you and the girls? That does not make sense. Let's talk to Storm at the F.B.I."

Chapter Twenty-Six

The three of them met a week later at Riley's, and Storm started with his findings, "The bureau has no outstanding case on you or your family, no drug file or anything else. As far as the F.B.I. is concerned, you're clean, as is the family of Colonel Manh and his son."

"Well," Hank said, "just for the record, nobody in my family has ever been involved with drugs or illegal immigrants. So, why are we being hassled? What we can do about it?"

"What you can do depends on why you're being hassled," Paul said. "If those were agents working on a case, they had to follow up on everything, even the obvious. They have to pin down every loose end every bad lead. On the other hand, if they are really working a case, we need to know what and why they are coming after you. If we can find a case, we can make them drop it or go to court. If they aren't on a case, we need to know that, too."

"Let's find out if they are even agents," Hank said. "I have the phone number of the one who said his name was Blevins, in El Paso."

Paul put his phone on speaker and dialed. After three rings, an operator came on and said the phone had been disconnected.

"Nuts," Hank said. "That was worthless."

"No," Storm said, "that tells us something; real agents don't give out fake phone numbers."

"There's more," Paul said. "Because of the contacts with you, Faith, and Hope, we have a pattern. The agents always bring authority with them to reinforce their creditability. And they flash fancy I.D.s to make them look official. That way, they hope to look real and maybe trick you or yours into furnishing some information."

"And they always ask the same questions," Hank said, "about drugs and immigrants. I don't think they care about those things.

They use the questions make them look legitimate. The real subject is probably Vietnam, Waters, Orzon, or the theft of those nukes."

"Those agents are just trying to put pressure on you," Paul said, "through your girls."

"And if so, that again means they aren't real agents," Storm said. "I'll try to find out more about how this Colonel Orzon died," Storm said. "I'll put a full court press on him and see what comes out from under his rock. But I'll tell you one thing; if suitcase nukes were actually stolen, as he claimed, and the thefts were hidden, heads would role. There would be a major shakeup. People would go to jail. That could be behind the harassment of you and your family. I'll pin down the possibility of a nuclear theft."

"I'm with you on that, even if the story is a drunk's fantasy," Paul said, "but Orzon is not around now and can't help us. My expertise is with the law, and I want to pin down whether or not there is some legal action afoot concerning you. Let's find out if any government agencies are working on a case that might in some way involve Colonel Kean or his family."

"The F.B.I. is not," Storm said. "But go ahead and write letters over your letterhead to D.E.A. and the agency. Spell out the contacts, the time, and place of each. Say that you are Hank's attorney and ask for any evidence those agencies might have concerning him that could be used in court. I can reinforce your letters by making phone calls to my contacts at both. Since the F.B.I. has jurisdiction in such matters, I might stir up some response, especially if I refer to you as the representing attorney."

"I'll write the letters," Paul said. "You make the calls."

"And can you track down the guy named Steve Blevins?" Hank asked Storm.

"I'll try," Storm said, "but if he is really an agent, personnel information is very closely held in government agencies like the C.I.A."

"Okay," Paul said, "I'll talk to the sheriff here and warn him to be on the lookout for people that seem official and ask to see you or your family. I'll warn him that such individuals might be fakes, and if he works with them, I want to be called in. Hank, you call Clemson again and demand that the university offer the same protections to Hope."

"Okay," Hank said. "What else?"

"With these kinds of guys coming after you," Storm said, "I suggest that you all get concealed carry permits. Apply, buy handguns, and get some training. Have them always nearby."

"Are gun permits hard to get?" Hank asked.

"No." Paul shook his head and explained that on Hilton Head the process was fairly easy and barring anything unusual, most applications took about a month.

"I'm not so sure Bev, Faith, or Hope would want to carry a weapon or even have one around," Hank said. "Guns make them nervous."

"That's up to them," Paul said, "but they might think about having a weapon with them when they are alone at home. Try not to worry them. Just say it's a precaution."

"Guns in their homes won't sound like precautions to them," Hank said. "They'll just be afraid there's going to be some shooting."

CHAPTER TWENTY-SEVEN

Hank tried to relax, but he was always on the alert, even while resting. "Nothing more was going to happen," he told himself again and again. But his interior voice sounded hollow to him and told him to be ready for anything. Even with Bev, Faith, and Hope around, Hilton Head was not such a bright and happy place. And El Paso had its own problems. That became clear when Le Trang called. With anguish in his voice, he said his daughters, Kay and Samantha, had been kidnapped. He pleaded for help.

Startled, Hank stammered, "What on earth happened?"

"They didn't come home from school yesterday. After waiting for hours, I was about to call the police, when a man phoned us. He said he had our girls in Juarez. He put them on the phone separately to prove it. Kay was angry and defiant, but Sam was clearly crying. The guy cut them off pretty quickly, but had made his point; he has our girls."

"What did he want? Money?"

"He didn't say anything like that. Just told us to keep quiet and wait for his instructions. He said that if we talked to the police, he would punish the girls. He then repeated that he would be in touch, and hung up."

For a second, Hank was too shocked to respond. Then he recovered. "That's terrible. How are you doing? Is Nancy okay?"

"She hysterical and crying. Wanted me to call you. Said you might know what to do. Do you think you can help?"

Hank almost panicked, thinking what he would do if Faith and Hope were ever kidnapped. Then he said, almost ordered, firmly, "Call the police. Do it right after we hang up, while everything is fresh in your mind."

"They said they would hurt the girls if I did that."

"They may hurt your girls, no matter what you do. Criminals like these might do anything. You can't depend on them. You need to call the cops. But first tell me everything you remember, including that guy on the phone."

"The girls usually ride the buses, public transportation. And they always come home right after school. When they didn't show up, I was about to call for help. That was when that thug called and said he had them. He didn't ask for money, just said to shut up and wait for instructions. I think they are in Juarez. But should I really call the police?"

"You should. Kidnappers are like cockroaches. They hate the light of day, and they don't like the cops. Call the police right after we hang up. I'll talk to my attorney, Paul Ruth. He has years of experience in these kinds of things. He's licensed in Texas. He'll know what to do. I'll be in touch soonest."

Hank immediately called Paul and gave him the facts.

"You were correct," Paul said. "The police can handle this. You should not get involved. The police have the experience and the means. They know the territory, and will do it right."

"But I want to help. I know how the Trangs are suffering. I would be devastated if Faith and Hope had been kidnapped. I need to do something."

"No, you don't."

"I know you. You think you want to help, and on one level, you do. But in reality, you just want action. You're too aggressive. Always have been. Just sit back and let the police do what they do best."

Hank hung up and thought for a long time about El Paso, the Trangs, and Juarez. Then he knew what he had to do. He called retired Sergeant Jenkins, who had been Hank's right-hand man when Hank commanded a battalion in the 82nd Airborne Division. Jenkins knew how to handle stress. After a few pleasantries, he told Jenkins about the kidnappings and said he wanted to help, "I'm thinking that a few of us might go down the El Paso, offer moral support, and look around in Juarez. What do you think?"

"I've got a better idea," Jenkins said. "I've kept in touch with a bunch of our guys who are retired in Juarez. They're good men. I'll tell them what happened, and I'll bet they'll be happy to look around for us. They'd be able to look around better than we could, and then if they find anything, we could go down there."

"That's why you're a master sergeant," Hank said, "and I'm just a colonel."

Jenkins said he would be in touch and hung up. Several days later, he called back, "We're in luck. Our guys have lots of friends in Juarez, hundreds of them. To protect themselves from the drug cartels, some time back, they organized an informal network to alert and warn of trouble, sort of a gigantic neighborhood watch. They know what's going on everywhere in Juarez, even in the poor barrios. I'll tell them the facts about the kidnapping. And I'll bet they'll do what you want. But most of all, they want you to come down to Juarez for a reunion. By then, they'll have looked around and can brief us. I recommend we go."

"Let's do it!" Hank said, a new energy in his voice. "I'll get the plane tickets for next week. You tell them about Sam and Kay and set up a meeting. Give me a few days to make some arrangements and pave the way."

Hank arranged with his firm to meet the El Paso doctors again, made reservations at the Marriott, cleared out his calendar, let Faith and Hope know, and called Paul, "I'm going down to El Paso to help Le and Nancy."

"No, you're not," Paul said, "you're going down there to get in trouble."

Hank ignored Paul and called Bev to tell her about the trip.

"I want to go with you," she said. "I want to hold Nancy's hand." "I'm afraid that's not possible," he said. "This will a hectic business trip. But I'll tell Nancy what you just said and hug her for you. When I get back, we'll go over to the Bahamas for a weekend. Make more memories."

Then he called Le back and asked for an update.

"A detective named Geaches came to see us," Le said. "He's a good man about your age. Has plenty of experience. He's sympathetic because he has daughters the same age as Kay and Sam. I trust him. He contacted the border police and they remembered the crossings. He told the newspaper people, and our story is being published in all the papers and on television. The girls' pictures have been on Juarez T.V. and in the papers in El Paso. I worry that the kidnappers will react in anger to that."

"Try not to worry," Hank said. "You did the right thing. I'm coming down to El Paso next week with a friend. We'll talk about everything. Tell Nancy we'll try to do more."

CHAPTER TWENTY-EIGHT

Hank and Sergeant Jenkins flew Delta to El Paso, arriving at the airport where Hank had last seen the infamous Blevins. Jenkins went to meet his contacts in Juarez, and Hank drove to the Trang's place, an apartment above their shop. Le said he had good news and bad.

"The bad news is that that those scum punished me for going to the police by taking lewd pictures of Kay and mailing them to me. Said they'd do the same or worse to Sam if I don't cooperate with them. I'm worried."

"What's the good?" Hank asked. "They freed Kay," Le said.

Hank sat back, shook his head, and clapped his hands, "What the hell happened?"

"She just showed up at the border," Le said, "and after a doctor checked her out, Geaches brought her to us. She's a strong kid in pretty good shape but shook up mentally."

"And the crooks just let her go?" Hank asked. "Just like that? No money?"

"No money," Le said, "but she was told to give us some messages, mostly false, to indicate that dad and mom were into drugs. We're supposed to pass the messages on to the newspapers to mislead the coverage. There was also a real message; they want me to set up a computer contact with Colonel Quan, who led the attack on the orphanage. He was a major back then. Evidently, he's a big-shot colonel now and involved in some sort of international operation. If I won't help them, they say they'll take it out on Sam."

"Can I talk to Kay?" Hank asked. "Sure," Le said. "I'll get her."

When Kay came in, she seemed subdued, as if she had been crying. Hank asked if she was up to telling him what had happened.

"I'll try," she said. "I think I'm okay now. The day they grabbed me was an ordinary day. I was alone after school, just walking toward my usual bus stop when a black sedan stopped beside me. A woman wearing an I.N.S. jacket got out and asked me to get in the car. When I said I wouldn't, a man got out and forced me into the back seat. I tried to resist, but he was too strong. They tied me up and gagged me. At the border, they told the agent I was being deported and gave him some papers. The agent seemed sort of dubious, maybe because of my being tied up, because he studied the deportation papers for a long time. Then he copied the one with the judge's signature, took some other notes, and finally let the car through. Once we were in Juarez, they blindfolded me. And after about a twenty-minute ride, they put me in a house with a woman guard."

"Was Sam there?" Hank asked.

"The kidnappers said she was, but I never saw her. We were in separate rooms. When they released me, they said she would be kept there as a prisoner as insurance for some things they wanted my father to do. Most of the time, the woman guard was with me in a bedroom. When she went to the bathroom or took a nap, a man came in to replace her. I was never alone. They never mistreated me, except when they took those horrible pictures."

Kay put her head down and quietly sobbed. When she straightened up and was able to look at him again, Hank asked, "How did you get free?"

"They drove me, blindfolded, to the border. Then they took off the blindfold and set me free. I just walked to the crossing, said who I was, and the guards let me cross."

Hank turned to Le and Nancy and said, "Those pictures were bad, but think about what kind of people these guys are. They are probably the ones that killed Ahn and I'm starting to think they might have had something to do with Nung's death. They could just as easily have done the same to Kay. I don't know what those scum are after, but we should give thanks that Kay's out of their hands. Count your blessings."

"I can't," Nancy said. "Sam's still a prisoner,"

Hank shook his head, sat back, and considered Nancy's anguish. What could he do to help Sam? It looked bad. He had to work out something.

"That's not all," Kay interrupted. "There's more, but you must promise not to tell anyone about the rest. If you do, the guy that took those horrible pictures said he would retaliate by doing even worse things to Sam."

"Tell me about the more?" Hank asked.

"Two things," Kay said. "First, they gave me some fake data that I was supposed to use to make it look like Nung and Ahn were involved in drugs, so that drugs would appear to be the cause of anything that might happen to the Manhs. That was just a diversion for the second set of instructions. As Dad told you, they want him to act as a computer link for someone called Quan in Vietnam."

"What kind of a link?" Hank asked.

"I have no idea," Kay said. "But I remember you told us that the agent at the airport wanted to talk about Vietnam. Maybe that's the connection."

She's right. Blevins did bring up Vietnam. There had to be a connection. But what?

"But we think he wasn't really a government agent," Le said.

"I would hope he wasn't any kind of an agent," Hank said. "I don't like the idea of our government being involved in murders to cover up something going on in Vietnam."

Then he asked Kay, "Do you know where Sam is being held?" "No," Kay said. "I was blindfolded when we went there. But I did hear one thing. Two thugs were talking when they thought I was asleep and they mentioned the man who was in charge of the kidnapping. He wasn't one of the kidnappers, but he was in charge, and they were afraid of him. His name was Blevins."

Shocked, Hank stood and paced in disbelief. Blevins again. He didn't believe it. What on earth was going on? Drugs, kidnappings, Vietnam, and nuclear weapons. Everything seemed to lead back to this guy Blevins. Who was he?

"If I ever find those thugs," Le said, "I'm going to make them pay." "That's not your job," Hank said, calming a bit and sitting down.

"You'd just get in trouble. Let the police, the law, and the courts do their thing. If you interfere, you'll make it more difficult for everybody." "Maybe so, but if the kidnappers hurt Sam, I swear I'll never stop until I find them and when I do, I will not take it easy on them. I'll take a gun and use it."

"Not a good plan," Hank said. "You're a student, a family man, a computer nerd. You've fought your way up on the mental route. These criminals have always taken the physical way, killing and maiming their paths through the slime. They've probably done this kind of thing before. They'll be prepared for you to come after them. They thrive on violence and guns. They're psychotic freaks. You wouldn't have a chance."

Le looked at Hank for a time in silence. Then he conceded, "All right, I guess I understand but I want to do something. I can't just sit here. What can I do?"

"Sergeant Jenkins is meeting with some of my former troopers that now live in Juarez. They have developed good contacts all over the city, sort of a big neighborhood watch. We hope they can find Sam for us. If they do, I plan to take some help over there, pin the bad guys down, and call in the police."

Le jumped up and tried to hug Hank, saying, "I want to go into Juarez with you."

"Not such a good idea," Hank said. "We need you safe and sound. Your job is to take care of Nancy and set up a communications system for my guys over there."

Then he outlined the concept; first to find Sam. Then they would keep the place under surveillance while notifying the Juarez police. That way he could bring Sam home without violence that might harm her or anybody else. And they had to find a way to bring the El Paso police into the net.

"I can do that," Le said. "My contact, Geaches, is a good man. I'm sure he'll help."

"Okay," Hank said. "I'd like to talk to him, and I also want you to get a permit to carry a gun. For defense only, in case the kidnappers retaliate. And under no circumstances are you to meet with the kidnappers. Most of all, you must never go into Juarez. Those thugs might set up a trap. But you should set up a recorder on your phone, in case they call you back."

"Will do," Le said. "Although I don't think Nancy will want a gun around."

"That's up to you," Hank said. "I need to go to the Marriott now and talk to Jenkins. I'll call when I know more about our Juarez contacts. Call me at the Marriott if you get more news."

Hank checked in at the hotel, got cleaned up, and went down to the bar to wait for Jenkins. As he nursed his bourbon, he tried to make sense of Blevins's recurring appearances. When the guy had stopped Hank, he had asked about Colonel Manh, drugs, immigrants, nuclear weapons, and Orzon. Now he had apparently ordered the kidnapping of the Trang daughters. He might have had something to do with the death of Nung Manh. If Nung's body could be exhumed, maybe that would answer some questions. He resolved to talk to Le's detective contact, Geaches, and see if the body could be examined. It looked like progress. While he was still considering the situation, Jenkins appeared.

"What news?" Hank asked, rising to shake hands and order drinks. "All systems are go," Jenkins said. "The guys remember good times, jumping with you at Fort Bragg, and they want to help. They just need more details about the two daughters and when and how the kidnappings happened. I said you would come over with me the day after tomorrow and fill them in. In the meantime, I plan to get in touch with some of our guys in the states who might want to come and help out."

"Good," Hank said. "Tell them I'll reimburse their costs. For my part, I want to meet with this Detective Geaches to see what kind of support the El Paso police can give us. It looks like we're a go for now. Let's work out the details; transportation, weapons, and communications."

Just as Paul said, Hank was where he wanted to be; back in action.

Felt good.

Chapter Twenty-Nine

That evening Le called and said Detective Geaches was coming to the Trang's place at noon the next day. He suggested Hank come over for lunch and meet him. Geaches turned out to be middle aged, short, overweight, and wearing a rumpled suit. On the other hand, his handshake was firm and he made good eye contact. "Geaches," he said, "but you can call me Grumpy."

"One of the seven dwarfs?" Hank asked.

"Yeah," Grumpy said. "I used to be much taller, but years of police work wore me down to a pint-sized dwarf. You can see the result."

Hank liked him. He radiated confidence and competence. "Glad to meet you, Grumpy. I'm Hank Kean, but you can call me Peachy. Can you bring us up to date on what El Paso is doing about the Trang kidnappings?"

"It's on the front burner with us. You can count on that, but I'm not so sure about the Juarez police. Sometimes, they seem lazy and don't appear to want to help. Maybe some of them just don't like us gringos. There's bad, because the ball is now in their court since Kay proved the bad guys are in Juarez. I just don't see much fire in the Juarez belly. What's your interest in all this, Peachy?"

"I served with Colonel Manh in Vietnam, and I want to help his widow and family. Some of my paratroopers from the 82nd Airborne now live in Juarez, and I'm in the process of contacting them. They were good men, I trust. I'm hoping they know something I can use to find Samantha Trang. Maybe pay the bad guys a visit."

"I'm not sure I like the sound of that," Geaches said. "This is police work, not combat, even if firearms are being used. Police work different than what soldiers do. Your guys might jump in too quick and muddy the waters. They should back off and just let us do our jobs."

"I'm not about to interfere with what you and the El Paso police are doing," Hank said. "But I look at it like you. I think the Juarez police might need some help my guys could provide."

"I never heard you say that, colonel. We never had this conversation. But I really want to help Le, Nancy, Kay, and Samantha. That's why I'm here."

"If you want to help, detective," Le said. "Tell me how I can get a gun."

"A gun?" Grumpy asked.

"Yeah, you know, one of those things that go bang." "Why do you want a gun?"

"The kidnappers may come at us. So, how do I get one?"

Geaches took a hard look, first at Le, and then shifted to Hank. Quizzical. Then he answered, "It's easy. Anybody not a felon can buy a gun. The problems come if you don't know how to use one or if you carry one and go someplace where that's not permitted. Say you pick up your daughter at school and are stopped for a traffic violation there. If the officer decides to search your car and finds a handgun, you'll go to jail, without passing go."

"I won't carry a gun," Le said, "but I'm worried about someone breaking in here and attacking Nancy when she's alone. So I want one down here at the store and one for Nancy upstairs. Do I need a permit or training?"

"Not required. The right to have a gun at home in Texas is well established. But if you carry one around, that's different. The courts don't like that. But if you really want to get a gun, just apply for a permit and take a course. That way, if you fire your weapon in your store and injure someone, even a robber, you could show you knew what you were doing and be better able to defend yourself in court. If you shoot somebody, a judge will have to determine if you acted legally. If you have taken a qualified course of instruction, maybe he wouldn't bring charges against you. He would think that if you had studied proper use, you probably knew what you were doing. The court would want to know you were actually in danger, and that you had to defend yourself. But if you shoot somebody, make sure they are inside your place. That way you could claim defense of what English law says is your castle. If the guy falls dead outside on the front steps, the jury might not believe you were actually defending your castle. So be sure to drag him inside."

"Drag him inside? Are you serious? That's crazy talk." "That's why they call me Grumpy."

"Okay, Grumpy. I'll try to be careful. What's the drill?" "Get a license, pay a fee, and take that short course." "You really sound like you think this is a bad idea."

"It is a really bad idea. Innocent people get hurt by guns in homes."

"But we're not dealing with innocent people. These are kidnappers."

"That's right. And I've seen this before. Believe me, you are the innocent ones who would get hurt, not the kidnappers. Evaluating what they have done so far, I conclude that they are experienced and professional. If that's so and they decide to come after you, they'll hit you when you least expect them. And they'll come at you fast and in force, armed with much more firepower than any handgun you can buy. And they'll laugh at your pistol as they kill you."

"How can you be so sure that these crooks are professionals?" Hank asked.

"We talked to the border patrol agent who stopped the car that had Kay in it," Geaches said.

"The three adults with her, two men and a woman, had on jackets and caps with logos. They had papers that seemed to show that they were in the act of carrying out a court-ordered deportation. Subsequent examination of the papers showed that they were forged but in correct form, and the signatures looked real. The one of the judges, who usually signs such orders, was particularly good. Only a search of court records proved the papers were actually false. The whole thing was carefully planned and neatly done. These are professionals."

"Why would professional people target my girls?" Le asked.

"We still don't know that," Geaches said. "We talked to kids who were with the girls at school that day, as well as their teachers. Nobody could shed any light."

"What were you looking for?" Nancy asked.

"We asked about trouble at school," he said, "with boys or drugs, anything that might help. I know you said that neither boys nor drugs were involved, and I believe you. But negative answers help eliminate dead ends."

"If all you have are dead ends," Nancy said, "what are you going to do now?"

"We're pushing as hard as we can with the authorities in Juarez," Geaches said. "The Mexicans police are pretty much a mixed bag, but sometimes they help. It just depends."

Nancy began to cry and hurried to the kitchen to fix lunch.

Hank then asked if Geaches could get the names of the troopers that had stopped him at the airport.

"That way," Hank said, "we can ask them why they were working with that Agent Blevins. Maybe somebody ordered them to help him. If we know who that was, we might find a higher up involved in something big."

"I can check the duty roster," Geaches said. "When I find out who they were, I'll question them. It should be easy."

"Great," Hank said, "but here's something harder. I want to have Colonel Manh's body exhumed. Kay told us that Agent Blevins was in charge of the kidnappings. When I was last in El Paso, he questioned me about Manh, drugs, killings, and nuclear weapons. The coincidences make me think he might somehow be involved with Colonel Manh's death. If the body could be examined, we might find out if dirty work was involved."

"To exhume a body," Geaches said, "takes a lot of firepower. Your chances are small. But I'll give it a shot."

Geaches then got a call to check out an accident that involved a death. He left after promising Nancy he would push the investigation and stir up the Juarez police.

When he was gone, Hank told the Trangs that Geaches looked like a good guy they could trust to put on a full court press to free Sam. He hoped he was right, but there were too many questions and too many loose ends.

He was worried.

Chapter Thirty

"Why would criminals go after my family?" Le asked. "If they are as professional as Geaches says, they'd know we don't have money for ransom."

"The kidnappers want us to think it has to do with drugs," Hank said. "But Kay told us that drugs were a diversion. What really interests me is that these guys want to set up a link from you to Colonel Quan. I think Blevins has some sort of role in this. My attorney is talking to the attorney general in Washington to see if he can dig up anything about the abductions and border crossings by Blevins's men. And if Geaches locates and questions the policemen who were with Blevins when he stopped me, maybe we can make some progress."

Hearing the desperation in the Trangs' voices, Hank tried to sound hopeful. He promised to call Paul that same afternoon to see if any federal agency had responded to his queries or Storm's calls.

"We'll get going," Hank promised.

Paul sounded hopeful, "I think we're making progress. I can tell when I'm getting straight answers or someone is twisting or distorting the truth. D.E.A. is adamant in denying they were in any way investigating you or your family. I think the guy that stopped you was bogus, like the ones that stopped Faith and Hope. I'll update your file, but I'm convinced the F.B.I. and D.E.A. are not after you or the Manhs. Storm thinks all this might have something to do with something more important, maybe those missing nukes. He's looking for the connection between the nukes, the fake agents, and the Manhs. He has a theory, but there are gaps in what he's found so far. He had to dig really deep to get what he has, but here it is; you were correct when you said that in the sixties and seventies, we had hundreds of those small nuclear weapons in a depot in West Germany. There was a strong movement both in Germany and here at home to get them out of there. It worked. The president issued the order to bring them back to the U.S.A., and that was when the shit hit the fan. When the receiving depot made a meticulous inventory, it showed that two of the nukes were missing. Extremely good fakes had been substituted at the storage depot in West Germany. Storm's still working out exactly how that happened, but a sergeant, a colonel, and a general were apparently interrogated, fined, reprimanded, and retired early after signing papers that would put them in jail for a very long time if they ever talked to anybody about the theft. Storm's optimistic he can find more."

"I can't believe that I never heard about those thefts," Hank said. "I still think it could be some kind of administrative screw up, rather than a robbery. A nuke theft could never have been covered up. It would be too big a deal. If there was an order to cover it up, that order would have to come from a very high level, maybe even from somebody in the White House. It wouldn't make sense unless someone important had a plan to use those bombs for something our government wanted to do, something covert, with international implications."

The idea was intriguing. That could be why government agents were stopping Hank and his family. It might be a coordinated effort. "How would the government use those things?" he asked. "What could possibly coordinate such an effort?"

"That's what we're trying to find out," Paul said. "It would be helpful if that Colonel Orzon were still around to interrogate."

"Maybe the reason he's dead," Hank said, "is part of the cover up." "The idea of a massive concealment of stolen nukes gained traction with Hank. It made more and more sense. And it was more and more important for Storm to find out how the nukes were stolen and who did it. If it was a terrorist gang from the Philippines, as Orzon had claimed, then Storm had to discover who helped the thieves. Finding them had to be a priority effort." "Do we have a plan?" Hank asked.

"Storm will continue to work on who masterminded the nuclear weapons theft," Paul said. "I'll keep your master file up to date and out of reach from anyone trying to destroy it. The rest is up to you.

Pressure that Detective Geaches in El Paso. Work with Juarez any way they'll let you. Smoke out the kidnappers. See if they and Blevins are connected to someone in the Philippines. Hope the kidnappers make a mistake with Samantha."

"That's not enough. I want to do more for the girl." "Like what?"

"Maybe take some troopers and go into Juarez after them."

Paul almost exploded. Then he unloaded on Hank, "I knew it. That's just like you, certifiably insane with a crazy idea. Acting on impulse. And in a foreign country. If you didn't die in such an effort, you'd be hauled into court and sent to prison for a long time. Either in Mexico or here. You think like a soldier. You think this is a war. But it's not. The authorities should handle it, not a washed-out military retiree."

"Spoken like a liberal wimp. It looks like war to me."

"That's because you're too aggressive. I see it in everything you do, even on the golf course. Especially there. Time and again you try an impossible shot and end up in the water. That's why I always beat you."

"You have a short memory about who wins. I can always count on you to three-putt your way around the course because you're a weak-kneed dreamer. If we just sit around and wait for the kidnappers to act, something bad is going to happen."

Both were silent for a moment, thinking. Then Paul continued. "Something worse will happen if you take an army into Juarez and shoot somebody. Maybe even Samantha. Your claim that you are helping Le and Nancy is just an excuse. What I hear is the hawk in you talking about acting hastily and impetuously. Get back to your peachy side. You've got a life back here, a woman who loves you, and daughters who need you. Shape up."

He abruptly hung up.

Hank was left staring into space and hanging on the horns of his self-made dilemma. He knew the Trangs needed help, but Paul was right; this wasn't just about Sam. There were others involved;

Bev, Faith, and Hope. And Jenkins had called men from his old battalion. Some of them were on their way to El Paso. They believed in him and would go into danger in Juarez if he asked. That might be too much to ask. He couldn't do that. Paul was right. He ought to drop the idea. But if he gave up now, he would have failed many people, not just Le and Nancy Trang, although they would be devastated. Samantha would be lost. On the other hand, if he took those men into Juarez and screwed up, hell would pay. Sam might even be injured. He had to work this out.

CHAPTER THIRTY-ONE

After a sleepless night tossing and turning at the Marriott, Hank was still undecided when Le Trang called and made the decision for him.

"Ahn has been killed," Le blurted out. "It happened last night. I'm at her place now. The police are here. They have blocked off her apartment, but I saw everything."

"Calm down," Hank said. "Tell me. Slowly, so I can understand you."

Le was quiet for a moment, evidently gathering his thoughts. Then he started again, a little more collected, but still agitated. "I tried to call her this morning as usual. When she didn't answer, I went over and found her. She was in bed and she had been shot. Blood was everywhere. I called 911 and while I waited, I looked around. There were strange boxes all over marked 'Philippines.' They had white packets in them that looked like some sort of powder. When the police came, they kicked me out, so I called Geaches and you."

"Hang tight," Hank said. "I'm on my way."

When Hank got there, Le and Geaches were in a police cruiser. Geaches waved for Hank to join them. Geaches was behind the wheel, Le on the passenger side, and Hank in the back seat.

"When did you see her last?" Geaches asked. "Sunday at church," Le said.

"She has other kin here?"

"No, just me and my family. What's that white stuff in those boxes?"

Geaches paused for a moment, then he turned, and gave Le a hard look. "How do you know what's in the boxes?"

Le hung his head and then said, "I screwed up. After I called 911 and you, I opened a box. I know I shouldn't. And now, my fingerprints will be on that box. I didn't touch anything else."

Geaches shook his head in disgust.

"You're in trouble," he said. "But do those boxes look like something you've seen before? Are they Ahn's?"

"I've never seen anything like them. They don't belong to her. What's in them?"

"Don't quote me, but it looks like hard stuff. Maybe crack. The police lab will test. Let's go look around your place."

"Sure. Just let me call Nancy."

"I'd rather you didn't give her any warning," Geaches said as he started the cruiser. "We need to do this without giving her advance notice. I'll bring you back here later."

What did "no advance notice" mean? Whose side was Geaches on?

"If you're looking for cartons like these containing drugs," Le said, "you won't find any at my place. Nobody in my family is involved with drugs, never have been."

"It sure looks like your mother was involved in something," Geaches said curtly.

"That's just not possible," Le said as he turned to look helplessly at Hank, who nodded, rolled his eyes back, and gave him a thumbs up.

"Do you have handguns?" Geaches asked.

That was a really cruel question. This was tuning out badly.

"We have licensed guns," Le said, "just like Colonel Kean recommended. We took a course in handling them. We got them because we might be danger from the drug gangs."

"Drugs again," Geaches said. "What a surprise." "Why did you say that?"

"A while ago," Hank interrupted, "I was stopped and questioned by an agent who asked me about the Manhs doing drugs. I told him the Manhs weren't involved."

"Interesting," Geaches said, turning back to Le. "When were your guns last fired?"

Geaches is really piling it on. And unnecessarily.

"Are you suggesting I killed my mother?" Le asked. "That's a terrible idea. Why are you acting like this? I thought you were our friend."

"I'm pre-empting any questions about you," Geaches said, "doing you a favor. I'll make a record of the fact that I made a surprise visit to your place and found no drugs and that your pistol had not been fired. That way, nobody can later come along and raise doubts about you. In domestic deaths, the best suspects are always family members, but I'm going to clear you in advance, I hope."

Hank sat back and smiled. Le shut up.

They drove to the Trang apartment in a strained silence. When Geaches searched the place, he found nothing that he could connect to drugs or the murder. He looked at the Trang's guns, and concluded they had not recently been fired. The Trangs were in the clear. As he left, he said, "You are now no longer persons of interest. Keep it that way."

CHAPTER THIRTY-TWO

All that night at the Marriott, Hank tossed and turned thinking about the murder of Ahn Manh. El Paso had become a dark place more dangerous than the jungles of Vietnam. He could almost hear Quan's soldiers coming through the orphanage fence to blow up his memories. Blevins was everywhere. He may have been involved with Ahn's death. Hank couldn't back away. He had vengeance on his mind. After breakfast, Geaches called to report the names of the officers who had been with Blevins at the airport. They were Jones and Killen. Geaches said he had started the process of checking them out.

"Let's search the Manhs's apartment," Hank said. "Who knows what we'd find?"

"The police have done that," Geaches said. "It's a crime scene." "Try to get us access, soon, before somebody cleans it out."

"I suppose that shouldn't be too hard. I'll make the request."

Hank went to Le's place to tell him that Geaches was trying for clearance for them to go to the Manh apartment. While waiting, Hank stressed again how important it was to keep Kay away from reporters following up on Anh's killing.

"There is a lot going on," Hank said. "The kidnappings, Colonel Manh's death, and now Ahn's murder. They might be able to confuse her and somehow turn up the Vietnam connection. That would put Sam in danger. Tell the reporters that she's a minor, and that additional questioning might do permanent mental damage. If they still insist on getting some answers and their pressure becomes too intense, you can release a statement. Let's work on one."

Ahn's killing had made up Hank's mind; he would go with Jenkins down to Juarez and see what they might be able to do for Sam. As the idea of taking action began to firm up, El Paso skies seemed to brighten a bit, and he dismissed the earlier warning Paul had given him. He would actually be doing something pro-active, instead of waiting and reacting. He was back where he really wanted to be, in a fight, in action again.

Geaches called back with approval to go to the Manh's apartment. Said his lieutenant had not been happy about it, but had agreed. The visit was on. They could go in and remove any personal stuff. Because the apartment was technically still a crime scene, Geaches had to accompany them. They would meet at noon. In reality, the Cielo Vista management must want to put the place back on the market, and that probably had facilitated approval. When Hank and Le arrived, Geaches was waiting. Inside, they found the place a mess, most likely because the police had taken it apart while searching for drugs, and nobody had bothered to clean it up.

"Let's take a look around," Hank said, "and gather the personal effects. Look for anything that seems out of place."

Personal effects were all Le wanted because the furniture belonged to the Cielo Vista. So they looked for pictures, personal papers, financial stuff, clothing, and things like that. They were actually helping management to put the place back on the market. They found no reason for the lieutenant to have delayed them. Hank wondered why he had.

"I have no idea about that," Grumpy said. "At first, I thought he just didn't want us snooping around and maybe finding something that would make him look bad. But that really didn't make much sense. What could we possibly find?"

"Has he also delayed on our request to exhume Manh's body?" Hank asked. "Maybe an autopsy would show that he was murdered like Ahn."

"I'll press him."

Le and Hank gathered items, showed them to Geaches, and loaded the stuff in their car. After an hour, when they had found nothing out of the ordinary, Geaches received a call and had to go to a robbery scene.

"Now that he's gone," Le said outside, "I'd like to talk about those boxes I opened before the police arrived. I wonder if they had anything to do with Orzon. He was from the Philippines."

"Maybe the bad guys are trying to fabricate a connection," Hank said. "They could plant doubts, get us thinking, and lead us in the wrong direction."

Before Le could answer, a small, frail, white-haired lady came out of the next apartment and walked slowly up to them.

"Mister Trang," she said to Le, "I'm Pat Wilson. I live in the apartment next to Nung and Ahn. You and I have met."

"Sure, Mrs. Wilson, I remember," he said. "What can I do for you?" "You can tell me if this man is with the police."

"He's not. He's Hank Kean, a friend we knew in Vietnam. He's helping me clean out personal things that belonged to Father and Mother."

"In that case, I want you to come in my place. I have something important to tell you, and it would be better done inside."

In the apartment, Mrs. Wilson lost no time.

"Before I say anything more," she said, "I want you to know that I will never repeat this to anybody. If the police ever question me about what I'm going to tell you, I will deny everything. Do you understand?"

"Of course," Le said. "What is it?"

"As you may remember, I live here alone, ever since Mr. Wilson has been gone these many years. My eyes are now so bad that I can't read too much and I can't do the crossword puzzles anymore, so I just watch television and look out the window. I stay back from the light because it hurts my eyes. Nothing much happens during the day, just things like delivery people and men working. It's mostly quiet, what with the children being at school and other occupants gone off to work, but the day Colonel Manh died, something caught my eye."

"Something unusual?" Hank asked.

"Yes. That day, two men drove up and parked right in front. They just sat there for a time and then got out and went to Nung's door. Both of them were wearing some sort of uniforms. I think they were pest control, because their van had a decal on it. That wasn't unusual, because we have a lot of cockroaches here. I couldn't tell if they went inside the Manh's apartment, but they were there long enough to have gone in. I couldn't see for sure. After a time I saw them get back into that van and drive away."

"And that seemed odd to you?" Le asked.

"Yes, later, when the ambulance came and took Nung's body, I remembered those two men. But what happened a few weeks after, the night Ahn was killed, was really odd. You see, I don't sleep very well. I suppose that's because I don't get out very much during the day. I'm alone, and I nap in front of the television a lot. So frequently, during the night, I can't fall asleep. And my eyes are tired, so I don't read. I just sit there in the dark and look out my window. It's quiet and still. I like it that way. After a while, I can go back to bed and sleep. I almost never see anything out my window at night, but I did two nights ago, the night Ahn died. After midnight, I saw a dark van drive into the parking lot. Two men got out. They were dressed all in black and they moved very carefully as if they were looking around. That was what caught my attention, them acting so sneaky. I got concerned and sat real still hoping they wouldn't see me."

"What happened then?" Hank asked, now more interested in her story.

"One of them went to the Manh's front door while the other went to the van and opened it. Four more men got out, all dressed the same. Some were carrying boxes, and they all went to Ahn's place. That was when I realized that two of those men looked just like the pest control people that were here the day Nung died. After a while, they came out and drove away."

"Did you hear anything?" Le asked.

"No, but I don't hear so good these days. I didn't know what to think until the next day when the police and an ambulance came and I learned Ahn had been killed. Somebody had shot her."

"And you never told anybody?" Hank asked.

"No. And I never will. If those men ever find out I saw them, they will come back and kill me, too. So I'll never repeat this story. Never."

"I understand," Hank said, "but could you describe those men?" "Only the ones I saw the day Nung died, not the others that night." "What did they look like?" Hank asked.

"They both looked the same; in their thirties, white males, trim, clean. I couldn't see the others that night. It was too dark. But they weren't Hispanic. They were gringo. Clean shaved, looked like bankers, not like any pest control men I've ever seen around here."

When they left Mrs. Wilson's place, the two sat in the car for a while, and Hank said, "From her description, one of them could have been Blevins. She was almost describing him."

"And from what Kay told Nancy and me," Le said, "she might well have been talking about the guys that kidnapped Sam and her."

"Do you believe that old lady?" "Why would she lie?"

"Maybe someone told her to." "That doesn't make much sense."

"Nothing about this makes any sense." "Well, what do we do with her information?"

"Put it on file and store it in memory. Keep it to use later when we have Sam safe or have permission to exhume Nung's body."

"Store it? Shouldn't we tell somebody?"

"She would deny everything. Let's just list her as another reason to push Geaches to get permission to exhume your father's body, and find out if he was murdered. Wilson backs up Kay's report that she had heard the kidnappers claim they had killed him. It's not a kidnapping now. It's a gang of crooks involved in murder and conspiracy that might involve the Pentagon, the C.I.A., Vietnam, and nuclear weapons."

El Paso was indeed a dark place.

Chapter Thirty-Three

That afternoon, Hank and Jenkins went to Juarez to meet three of their former troopers. They met in a small *cantina* off the main drag in a part of the city where tourists almost never went. The three had already finished their first beers, and they seemed genuinely happy to see Hank. Firm handshakes all around. One, apparently the leader, was trim and fit. The second was a large bearded man, and the third was small and grim.

"They have a problem with names," Jenkins said. "They want to remain anonymous."

"That's *verdad,*" the leader said."If our names get out, we won't be *simpatico* anymore. We would lose trust we have built. People don't like the idea of anyone helping gringos come down here and make trouble. We have built a large watch system based on the trust people have in us. We cannot risk that by having our names in the paper."

"We don't mean any disrespect," the bearded one said. "We were good serving in your battalion. Jumping with you, *jefe,* was always a pleasure."

"Thanks," Hank said. "We'll respect your wish to remain anonymous." Privately, he named them Boss, Beard, and Grim.

The three raised their near-empty glasses in a salute, Hank ordered another round with nachos, and the little reunion got going. The conversation was loud, half in English, half in Spanish. It began with reminiscences about parachute jumps, good and bad, and then it moved into the present. At first, Hank was worried about attracting attention but he soon realized nobody around them cared. He then relaxed, drank his beer, and went with the flow.

"So, exactly what can we do for you?" Boss asked.

"I'm looking for six men and two women," Hank said. "They're bad guys, maybe murderers, who kidnapped two American teenage girls. These guys are gringos, and we think they're holed up here in Juarez. The men are middle aged, not kids. They're white, clean shaven, and most definitely not Hispanic. They're in a small house somewhere, probably in a poor or middle-class part of the city, trying to hide under the radar."

"Then finding them will be easy," Beard said. "In a poor barrio, they'll stand out. The people in those places watch for drug dealers and cartel hit men. They're alert to watch for strangers. Finding those girls should be a piece of cake."

Hank did not think this could be a piece of cake at all. Were these guys for real?

"How can that be?" he asked. "Juarez is a large, sprawling place, with millions of people. Looking for six men and two women would be like finding that needle in a haystack."

"*Nada*," Boss said. "Years ago, when we came back home here, the drug gangs and cartels ruled everything. The police took money from them to keep quiet, so we looked for a way to protect ourselves. I don't mean with guns, though we got those, too. We cut Juarez into twenty-five parts, and appointed one of our guys as contact in each part. Those guys set up a watch in each zone, finding people who wanted to help in every few blocks. Over these last ten years, people began to realize they could report anything to us and we would never tell anybody their names. So, if we decide to help, you find these bad hombres, we *puedo* can."

Hank sat back and considered the concept. If these three were for real, they were exactly what he was looking for. He needed to convince them to help. Before he could say anything Grim asked, "Why should we care about two kidnapped girls?"

"It's personal with me." Hank replied. "These guys kidnapped the daughters of a friend of mine. They roughed up one, took nasty pictures of her, and sent her home to her parents with demands about some sort of contact in Vietnam. They told the parents to comply or they would take revenge. When the parents called the cops, the gringos killed the kids' grandparents."

"Killed the grandparents," Boss said. "Were drugs involved?"

"I don't think so," Hank said. "I think this has something to do with Southeast Asia. I really don't know much about that, but I know that little girl still in their hands is in trouble."

"A sex ring bringing Asia girls?" Beard asked.

"Probably not," Hank said. "They let the one girl go free, the one they'd taken the bad pictures of. Sent her home with a message. They want the father to work for somebody in Vietnam. Said they'd punish the second girl if he didn't do it."

"I don't like the sound of Vietnam," Grim said. "Never did."

"Me neither," Hank said, "but the thing that really bugs me is that the kid they're still holding is only thirteen. The parents are really worried, especially the mother. The girl they freed is a basket case about the pictures the bad guys took. The family is frightened. The father says he wants to find the kidnappers and rough them up."

"I don't blame him." Boss said, "but if we find them, what happens?"

"Then we'll stake out the place," Hank said, "and call in the police." "If the *policia* don't help," Beard asked, "what would you do?"

"We might have to storm the house," Hank said. "I don't want to do that. Might hurt the girl. I just want to find her and take her home. We'd need to do that without shooting. We don't want to take a chance on hurting her. But we will need firepower, just in case. You got any?"

The three huddled for a time to discuss the question. Hank quietly waited them out.

"What if those crooks spot you?" Boss asked.

"We may need guns to take them down and then bring the girl back across the river," Hank said. "There may some rough stuff if that happens. Do you think you can help us?"

They huddled again. Then they shook hands, and then Boss said, "We will help."

Triumph. He reached across to high five. "I'll buy the next round and we'll drink to it."

The leader then asked Hank how much and what kind of equipment he needed.

Now we're down to the nitty and gritty. He leaned forward to quiet them down, get their attention, and focus on the operation.

"Sergeant Jenkins is rounding up five guys who were in our battalion and are now retired. I'll have communications equipment and night-vision gear for them. We'll come across in a van. From you, we need the location, some firepower, guides, and a place where we can watch those thugs until we can bring the authorities. What would the firepower cost?"

"About five hundred apiece," the leader said. "You might also want something to break down *la puerta* rams, that wouldn't cost much."

"I'll bring the cash when we next meet," Hank said. "Thanks for your help."

Walking back to the car, Jenkins clapped him on the back, "You're back in command."

He wasn't so sure. There was too much unsettled. Too much could go wrong.

Chapter Thirty-Four

The next morning Hank deposited a check for $7,000 to First El Paso, and when he met Jenkins for lunch at the Marriott, the sergeant had the names of five former troopers from the 82nd who had agreed to come help. All were master sergeants, had served in Vietnam, and spoke some Spanish. He went over the names.

"You must remember Morales. He was always aggressive. Even if the weather for a jump was doubtful, he wanted to go. Of course, you remember Gomez. He was your driver, a former company clerk. He was always careful and meticulous, wanted everything perfect. Alvarez was from New York, a real loud mouth, could always be heard in a crowd. Velasquez was a fighter, in a bar or behind the barracks, it didn't matter. He just wanted to hit someone. The last one, Gonzales, worries me. Although he volunteered, he didn't seem eager, was too quiet. All in all, I think these guys were bored in retirement and wanted to be on a mission again."

The next day, they gathered with the five at the *café* near the Trang apartment, and Hank briefed them about the kidnapping of the Trang girls into Juarez, the deaths of Colonel and Mrs. Manh, the nasty pictures of Kay, and the Vietnam angle.

"Murder, kidnapping, Vietnam, and abuse of kids!" Morales said. "Those guys are really bad pricks. Let's go after them."

"We might be able to do just that," Hank said. "Some of our guys now living in Juarez are tracking down where the bad guys have the little girl. If they can find the kidnappers, I want us to go over, pin the pricks down, and call in the Juarez police."

"A piece of cake," Alvarez said.

"Offense is better than defense," Velasquez said. "Let's go."

"I have some ideas about that," Hank said. "But first, I want you to know that this is really dangerous. If the Juarez police catch us, we may be in a Mexican jail for a long time. If there's shooting, any of you or the girl could be hurt. And even if we bring her back safely, we may be in trouble with our state department. So I want you to know that if any of you don't want to take the risk, you can back out at any time. There will be no stigma, no problem or anything like that. If you walk away, I'll understand. This could turn out badly, and if you don't want to be a part of it, that's perfectly okay. I have checks for all of you, whether or not you go."

"And leave that little girl in the hands of those murderers?" Morales said. "Not a chance. You got a plan, Colonel?"

"Not much of one really," Hank said, "but a Russian general once said that any plan well executed is better than no plan at all. So here's an idea of what we might do; if our troopers find the place, you'll go over and meet our men there. I'll be with Le Trang here and in contact with you by radio. When you know where Sam is being held, you'll tell me so I can activate the authorities to rescue Sam and pick up the bad guys. You'll all have weapons, night-vision devices, and radios."

"What if you can't get the Juarez police to do anything?" Gomez asked. "Or what if the kidnappers move the girl?"

"Those are the real problems," Hank said. "Anything could happen, and probably will. That's why I need you, soldiers that have been in combat and can adjust to handle change. We may have to take down the bad guys or follow them if they move. I don't want shooting because Sam might get hurt. We have to be flexible."

"Looks like a night jump on a hostile drop zone," Alvarez said.

He took a deep breath and wondered if he really could send these guys into Mexico when and if Jenkins's contacts found where Sam was being held. There were many risks. On the other hand, how could he not? The kidnappers were killers, had shot Ahn Manh, and maybe killed Nung. Le and Nancy Trang were being torn apart, just as he would be if Faith and Hope had been kidnapped. And he wasn't going to do anything rash. His men would simply find Sam, stake out the place, and call him so he could notify Geaches and activate the Juarez police. He would stay in El Paso on the radio and have Geaches use his contacts to corral the bad guys. If it worked out as planned, Sam would be free and the kidnappers would be in a Mexican prison. He would live up to his commitment to the Trangs, and he would be okay with Bev. He didn't want to take any chances and lose her. She had saved him from a slow death.

He was taking action. Things were looking up. He might have a life after all. Paul wouldn't like any of this, but Hank thought he saw a light at the end of the tunnel. It looked like they were finally making progress. It depended on those guys in Juarez finding the house where Sam was being help. Could they do it? He heard his mother's voice reading to him, "When the sun was running, it was lovely. The air dazzled and the clear water sparkled."

But the sun wasn't running yet in Juarez.

CHAPTER THIRTY-FIVE

In a few days, Hank had the money in hand, secured the radios and the night-vision gear, and rented a van. He was ready. He felt alive again. Maybe the sun was shining after all. A week later, Jenkins got word from Boss that the neighborhood watch in an isolated barrio had found the kidnappers. Hank rushed to tell Le and Nancy. She cried with joy.

He withdrew $5,000 in hundreds. He and Le loaded the night-vision gear and the radios. Things were falling into place, and he made some decisions. If the kidnappers moved Sam, he would order his men not to attack. To avoid getting Sam hurt, they would just follow the kidnappers discreetly and stake out the new place.

Le briefed him about the radios.

"These are first class headsets, top-of-the-line stuff, easy to wear, and crystal clear. We can all talk to each other. They are an easy fit and look like the earphones all the kids wear. The night-vision goggles are small. They look like big sunglasses. They are battery powered and will fit well with the radios."

Reassured and loaded, Hank went to meet Jenkins for final planning now that they knew where Sam was. They met with their troopers to go over the plan.

"We've got a good concept," Hank told them, "but I want to go over everything now, to look for holes. We need to be prepared for anything. So listen up."

They watched him with big eyes and concentrating, just as they always did before a parachute jump. They knew that when they jumped out of that plane, mistakes could kill. It would be the same, going across the border and engaging those killers. Morales was eager, as always. Gonzales looked worried. Gomez was pensive. Velasquez sat forward, ready to hit someone. For once, Alvarez shut his mouth. Hank and Jenkins would evaluate their various responses after the briefing.

"Here we go," Hank said. "I have a van, an unremarkable vehicle that won't attract any attention by police or kidnappers. It's plenty big enough for you and your equipment. It won't really be involved in the operation. We'll just use it to get into position and follow if the bad guys move."

He went over the entire plan in detail, with Jenkins occasionally chipping in. It took the better part of an hour. Then he made the final and most important point.

"The worst case is you might be tempted to fight to rescue the girl. I don't want you to do that. You can't do anything that might backfire and hurt her. So if there's even a hint of trouble, I want you to abort. You'll cross over tomorrow and meet our guys, the ones that found where Sam is being held. They'll lead you to a place where you can load the guns and rams in case you need to knock down some doors. I'm going to give each of you some money, for expenses and to carry over the border for our guys there. After you load the gear, you'll go to a surveillance house where you can keep track of the bad guys while I call in the Juarez police. Then you'll bring Sam home. That's it."

"What if we're spotted before the Juarez police arrive?" Gonzales asked.

"You can't let that happen," Hank said. "You have to stay concealed. Only move at night. Stay off the radios. Be quiet. Don't attract attention. Be cool."

"If we have to grab her before you can get the police to us," Gomez asked, "how would we get her out of dodge?"

"Just walk her across the river like any other illegal," Hank said. "Hundreds cross that way every day to work and return. There's no reason you can't do the same. Once you get to the river, Gomez can take the van back across the border alone while you cross. I wouldn't think that would alert anybody."

"How do we find a place to cross?" Gomez asked.

"Our Mexican buddies," Hank said. "Just like they'll take you to surveillance positions and act as lookouts, they'll lead you to the best place to cross."

"What if the Juarez police won't or don't come?" Gonzales asked. "That's the worst problem you have," Hank said. "I don't like the idea of attacking to grab Sam just because it looks like the kidnappers are going to move her. An attack then would be a sudden, last minute thing, done in haste. If you have to grab her, I want to plan that carefully and work out the details. If they move her, you should just follow, without being seen."

"Are you telling us," Morales asked, "that under no circumstances will we attack and try to grab Sam?"

"No," Hank said. "Something may come up that would force at attack. I don't know what those circumstances could be, and we need to think that out. But if you decide to attack, the best time would be a couple of hours after midnight when your vision gear and surprise would be on your side. The six of you should be able to take out four sleeping guys and two women. You'll have guns with flash suppressers and silencers. But I want to emphasize that your guns are only for self-defense, as a last resort, not for an attack that might hurt Sam. You need to have the guns ready, because those crooks will be well armed, and you may have to react. So if you decide, for some reason, to go in, you should do it late at night, about two o'clock when the guards are most likely sleeping. No guns. Hit hard and fast. Surprise and awe. Overpower them. You know the drill. Do you have questions?"

"Are you, Colonel, really okay with this?" Gonzales asked.

"I've got concerns," Hank said, "especially with the possibility that you might be discovered and have to shoot in self-defense. That's why the best plan is to simply find the bad guys, secure the location, and turn the capture over to the Mexican police."

"That wouldn't be any fun," Morales said.

"If you screw up and Sam is hurt," Hank said, "that really wouldn't be any fun."

As they talked, he realized most of them were primed for action. The majority of them were fighters. It would be tough to stop them from going. They wanted to punish the bad guys. He needed to think more about that.

"Will our Mexican friends be armed?" Gomez asked.

"They always are," Hank said. "Nine millimeters like ours. But they're worried about being seen helping gringos, so they don't plan to use their weapons except in self-defense. They're just going to be your lookouts. But if a fight starts, you'll have the night-vision stuff going for you. You'll have the initiative, surprise, and combat experience as your advantage."

"What about the radios?" Gomez asked. "How do we get them across the border?"

"Easy," Hank said. "They look just like the headsets the kids wear all the time to listen to music. When you go over, Le should be broadcasting loud music, something like Ranchera. If a border guard stops you, just turn up the volume."

"How strong are the doors of the house?" Gonzales asked, concerned and cautious.

"The Mexicans say the doors are really flimsy and only secured by light locks. They'll have two Ram Stingers for us, for the front and back doors. If you decide to attack, do the front and back at the same time, on my radio signal. You'll break down the doors and be inside before those thugs know it."

"What do we do with any guards we capture?" Velasquez asked. "Tie them up," Hank said. "I'll notify the police. Let me ask you; now that you've heard what might happen, do any of you want to back out? If you do, there will be no recriminations. No stigma. I'll just give you your money and you can leave."

When nobody answered, Hank said, "Okay. That's it. Be careful what you wear. You need to look like old farts out on the town, not a raiding party. Pack a small bag for your dark clothes and gloves."

"The old fart part will not be a problem," Jenkins said. "That's what we are. We'll wear basketball shoes like everybody else. We'll have on white tee shirts when we cross, but we'll pack black jackets in some suitcases together with swim trunks and other stuff that will look to a searching border guard like we're on vacation."

"We can rely on our Mexicans," Hank said. "They'll know a good surveillance place and where to cross the river if you need to get Sam over. One of you could then drive the van back alone. If you have to cross the river, take your weapons with you in case somebody's waiting on the other side. I'll be there to alert you to any danger. I'll be in a van with Le Trang and stay in radio contact with you the whole time. When we join up, I'll take you to the Trang's place."

He looked around for more questions. Finding none, he said, "Okay, you go tomorrow. I'll give each of you $500 then. It's for the Mexicans. I don't want to alert the border guards by having the entire amount on somebody, so I want each of you to carry part. I'll also give each of you a check to cover your costs."

"I don't need money to rough up some bad guys," Morales said. "That will be fun."

Not if we're caught. That wouldn't be fun at all.

After the men left, he asked Jenkins how he thought the meeting had gone.

"I was watching the men carefully," Jenkins said. "On balance, I think they're okay with the plan. Gonzales is worried, but that's his nature. Velasquez and Alvarez would rather attack the kidnappers than wait for the Juarez police. We'll need to hold them back, so they don't do something stupid. Make sure that the Trang guy knows what we're doing and how to contact Geaches if we need to call in the Juarez police quickly."

All systems are go, Hank thought. But no plan ever survives the first contact with the enemy. He had to be ready for anything. Hank decided he needed to check in with the home front, so he called Paul and had him update their file with the death of Ahn Manh and the request to exhume Nung's body. He omitted telling Paul about the plans he had arranged for the troopers who had come to help. Paul would be out of his mind if he knew what was about to happen.

He then called Bev to see how she was doing.

"Thank goodness you called," she said. "I miss you and was getting worried because I hadn't heard from you. What's going on? How are things in El Paso?"

"Lonely," he said. "And I have some bad news." He could hear her gasp.

"Don't worry. It's not about me, but a few days ago Ahn Manh, Le's mother, was murdered. Some goons broke into her apartment and shot her."

"Oh my God," she said. "Poor Nancy. First the kidnappings and now a murder. How is she holding up? And Le. First his father, and now Ahn. Do the police know who killed her?"

"We have a witness who saw some guys looking around her place just before this happened. We think it was the same thugs that kidnapped Kay and Sam. Those guys might have had something to do with Colonel Manh's death. We have put in a request to exhume his body and find out if he had been murdered."

"El Paso is a terrible place," she said. "Please come home."

"I'll be there before you know it," he said, "but we did have some good news. The kidnappers released Kay. She's home and doing as well as could be expected. The kidnapper sent her home with a demand that Le work for them with Vietnam."

"Vietnam? What's that all about?"

"That's one of the things I'm still working on. That, and the fact that our guy Blevins is working with the kidnappers. I'm trying to figure out how he fits in."

"Blevins again. I really hate him. He's always bad news." "Try not to worry. How are you holding up?"

"I keep busy at work. And to stop worrying about Blevins and moping about your absence, I set up an outing a few nights ago at Riley's. Faith, Hope, two of my hairdressers, and I got together. It was fun. Your daughters are really great gals, and they seem to have accepted me. I enjoyed it. We talked about you, had a good meal, and toasted life. After supper, Hope and the hairdressers went to the bar to check out some guys who had been making eyes. But Faith has a new boyfriend, a guy from her bank, so she behaved. And I have you, so I was good. Come home soon."

"Say hello to Faith and Hope. Tell them I'm okay and will see them soon."

CHAPTER THIRTY-SIX

That evening at dinner at the Marriott, Jenkins waited only a few minutes before saying he and the guys had a problem. It was clear, "We want you down in Juarez with us."

Hank had sensed that would come, and he had given it plenty of thought. "I want to control things from here in case you need backup," he said. "That way I'll have flexibility. I can either come over with a response team if I'm needed, or trigger Geaches and the Juarez police."

"We know that," Jenkins said, "but the men came after me when you weren't around. They said they would feel better if you were in Juarez. I would, too. It was always better when you were in the plane when we jumped. I always wanted my commanders with me in Vietnam. Leaders need to be at the front, not safe in a bunker behind the lines. Think about it."

Hank knew that was right. Gonzales would be the first to drop out if Hank didn't go down with them, and if Gonzales dropped out, others might follow. He understood. The toughest decision down there would be to attack if they had to secure Sam. And it might have to be a snap decision. Jenkins could do it, of course, but somebody might be hurt, and Hank was the one who would be responsible. So he should be on the spot, not trying to make a tough call over the radio. If his guys backed out, he would never have another chance to get Sam.

"You're right, of course," he told Jenkins. "I'll go. The van's big enough for us all."

When Hank went to the Trangs to pick up the gear, he told them he was going across, and Le immediately asked to go with him.

"Not a chance," Hank said. "You have to control things from here. You need to handle the radio, and make sure you can get in touch with Geaches quickly when I tell you we've found Sam. It's important. Be ready to react."

They were to meet their hosts at the same *cantina* just before noon the next day. They wore basketball sneakers, dark slacks, and white polos, as if they were headed into Mexico for fun. The night-vision goggles were in their bags, together with gloves, swimming suits, and dark jackets. They had not shaved for two days and looked scruffy. They were listening music on the headsets. Just seven buddies headed for forbidden fun in Juarez.

When they pulled up to the border, a proactive border guard waved them to a stop. Gomez opened his window as the others chattered happily away, half in Spanish, half in English, some singing mostly out of tune.

"You guys got papers?" the agent asked.

"We've got better than that," Gomez said, handing over military identification cards that showed they were retired United States soldiers. "We're the good guys."

The agent looked at faces, comparing them to the cards. He saw the suitcases.

"Planning on staying long?" he asked.

"No," Gomez said. "But we've got some extra clothes and stuff just in case we stay over or go to the beach for a swim. You want to see?"

Shaking his head, the agent asked, "What's with the headsets?"

"Ranchera," Morales said, taking his headset off. He held it up and raised the volume, so that the agent could hear the music. "You like music?" Velasquez asked. "Then listen to this." He and Morales began to sing loudly and badly out of tune,

"Tu eres mi vida, mi cielo. Sin ti yo no puedo vivir. Porkay tu ojos muy negro, paloma mia, mi maten a mi."

"They're already drunk," the agent said to Gomez. "Are you sober?"

"Yeah," Gomez said, "but not for much longer." "Where are you headed now?"

"To the closest *cantina* with cold beer and nachos," Gonzales said.

The agent handed back the I.D. cards and stepped away.

"Try not to get into too much trouble," he said as he waved them through.

They drove off happily singing and pulled up beside the Mexican van at the appointed hour. The leader got out to greet Hank and Jenkins.

"I've got the money," Hank said.

"And I have your gear," Boss said. "But we can't make an exchange here. Follow us."

In fifteen minutes, during which Gomez and the others became completely lost, they pulled into a small, wooded, empty park. Boss and Beard emerged to unload the pistols, nine-millimeter Berettas, each with a seventeen-round magazine. Boss also unloaded two Sting Rammers.

"Seven of you?" he questioned. "I got six pistols."

"Our driver won't need one," Hank said. "And here is $3,000. Is that enough?"

"Plenty," the leader said. "My guy is at your surveillance house just across and down the street from where the gringos have the girl. Follow us."

"How in the world did you find her?" Hank asked.

"Easy," he said. "Over the last ten years, we've built up a really efficient network. I have contacts in every barrio, and each of them has a number of residents that help. Over the years, we've established a system that works. They help us by warning about cartel killers. We help them by keeping their names out of it. They trust us. The gringos you want have tried to stay inside, away from scrutiny, but our people know what's going on in their barrios. They spotted the bad guys easily, especially when we saw two white girls who seemed to be prisoners."

"Are there four men and two women with them?" Hank asked.

"No," Boss said. "Two of the men and a woman left a few days ago."

That didn't make sense. Unless they were so confident after they let Kay go that thought they could handle Sam with two men and a woman. They probably thought that with fewer of them they'd be less conspicuous. But that was going to make it easier for his guys.

"Let's go," Boss said. "I'll take you to your lookout house, but I won't stay around. I don't want to attract the gringos' attention. The other one you met before is inside to brief you. When we get there, unload quickly, quietly, and get inside. Go with God, *amigo*."

Gomez followed Boss into a poor barrio. The streets were only partly paved; beat up, cracked, and rutted. The roads were narrow with old cars and ancient trucks parked all over the place. Boss turned into an alley, narrow and cluttered with all sorts of junk that blocked access. They stopped behind a run-down shack that badly needed paint.

Hank was concerned. They needed to drive the van carefully through there. Anything could happen. We might not even get through. And we don't want to stir things up by having a wreck that alerts the neighbors. Inside the frame house were four main rooms, a living room, an eating area, a kitchen, a bedroom, and a bathroom. The place had a flimsy front and rear door. Inside, Grim waited with a scowl.

CHAPTER THIRTY-SEVEN

Everything had fallen into place. The dark clouds were gone and bright weather lay ahead. All systems were go. As Hank's mother would say, "The grass was green, the sun dazzled and at night the coyotes barked and howled at each other in the hills."

Hank smiled. *Good things are going to happen.* He crossed his fingers.

He shook hands with Grim and the guys all did the *tanto gusto* thing, laughing as they did, but nothing got a smile from the ever-scowling Grim. He just nodded and led them to a table on which were a diagram of a house and a small map of the neighborhood.

"This is a layout of the place where they have the girl," he said. "As you can see, it is the same as this one, exactly. Twenty years ago, the same contractor built all the casas in this area. Every one is the same. We think the girl is in the bedroom on the left in the rear."

He pointed to the diagram, "Here, next to the kitchen. One guy stays in the kitchen, watching her room and the back door at the same time. Just as you see in this *casa*. The other man watches the front rooms. The woman mostly watches the girl. They take turns napping. We know they have electricity, like us, because we see lights at night. They don't have air conditioning, because their van once brought them new fans."

"It's hotter than hell here," Alvarez said. "Even with these fans."

He pointed to several large ones, all just pushing the heat and the dust around.

"I think that's why several of the guards left," Grim said. "They couldn't stand it. I don't think I can take it here much longer either. Take the girl home so I can leave."

"We'll be out of here soon," Hank said, "Just as soon as we get the Juarez police here."

Grim laughed and said, "Better not wait for the Juarez police. They may never come. Usually the bad guys pay them off."

My God, he's right. If that's so, we may be forced to grab Sam. Bad as that might be, it might be the only way. Nevertheless, he would try the police first.

"Here's a pretty good small map of these streets," Grim said. "The one you see in front of us runs between the two rows of casas."

He pointed to theirs and Sam's across the street, "It is fairly straight, but full of pot holes, poorly parked pick-up trucks, and trash. The alley behind her house is even worse. Don't even try to drive through it, especially at night."

A night approach on foot would be as bad as a foot patrol in the jungle of War Zone C in Vietnam. He started sweating worse than the heat had already made him. "What kind of activity goes on over there?" Hank asked.

"At first there was some," Grim said. "But since that one girl left, almost *nada*. Every few days, a van come by and drops off things like larger fans and some supplies. They rotate people. Aside from them, there is very little traffic, almost none after midnight."

"How do you know Sam is in there?" Hank asked.

"The neighbors saw two girls go in," Grim said, "but only one come out."

If they brought in supplies and rotated people, they don't keep a car there. If one showed up to do anything more than drop off supplies, they were probably about to move Sam. He decided to have Le tell Geaches he had located Sam, even though he hadn't actually seen her. He wanted to see how the Juarez police reacted. There were risks to that, because if Juarez was working with the kidnappers, they might alert the bad guys to get out of that house. That might force a confrontation. He decided to take that chance and called Le.

After waiting and watching a hot and anxious twenty-four hours, Le called back.

"Grumpy says the Juarez police won't move unless we have actually seen Sam. We're on hold."

Damn, he was in a bind; if the Juarez police tipped off the kidnappers, they would move. And he didn't really know if Sam was in the house. "I realize we can see the front door from here," he told Grim, "but what about the rear? Could they have taken Sam out that way?"

"I don't think so," Grim said. "We see both entrances to the alley."

Hank gathered his sweating team around him. "The Juarez police are an unknown," he said. "They're either working with the kidnappers or they're just plain lazy. It looks like we have to rescue Sam on our own. And we need to do it tonight before the Juarez police interfere. I've been resisting this because there might be shooting, and one of us or Sam might be hurt. So if any of you want to back out, just say so. No stigma. Just take the van and go home."

"Not a chance," Morales said. "I'm ready to end this. Go after those thugs."

Gonzales looked down and tightened his fists. This was crunch time for him. Then he looked up and said, "I'm in." The rest of the men nodded. It was a go, and it had to be tonight.

"Okay," Hank said. "Two teams, front door and back. I'll control from the van. I'll give the signal when you're in place and ready. Hit the doors with the rams. Radio silence except to abort. Shoot only in self-defense. Move out in time to be in attack positions two hours after midnight. You've done this before. You know the routine. Any questions?"

Seeing none, Hank turned to Grim, "Have your van join us at midnight." For the first time, the man actually smiled.

Jenkins, Gomez, and Gonzales were the front team; Morales, Velasquez, and Alvarez the back. They dispersed to plan and prepare. After an hour, Gonzales and Jenkins came over to Hank.

"We have a problem," Jenkins said. "Gonzales wants out."

"I'm sorry, but I'm rusty," Gonzales said. "I haven't done anything like this in a long time. I might shoot somebody in the confusion, maybe one of our own. But I don't want to ruin everything. So I want to stay in the van on the radio."

"I'm okay with that," Jenkins said. "Gonzales in the van, and you with me on the front."

That would work.

"Okay," Hank said. "I understand, Gonzales. No problem. You take the van and handle the radio. I'll need your pistol. Jenkins, you tell the others. It's okay. No recriminations. I'll let Trang know we're going in after midnight. Be ready."

During the next few hours, occasional questions came up.

"Why don't we bring one of the crooks home for questioning?" Velasquez asked.

"I want to," Hank said. "I'd like to sweat one of them and find out who's behind all this. But that's a bad idea. We have to keep this quick and simple. That won't happen if we try to take a prisoner back with us. And eventually, we'd have to release him, and he would identify us. I don't want that to happen, so we'll concentrate on freeing the girl and getting out of Dodge. We'll leave the guards tied up, I'll tell Le to notify Geaches. We take no prisoners across."

"What if we have to shoot a guard?" Gomez asked.

"If that happens, it better be in self-defense," Hank said.

Hank and Jenkins summarized, "Once we have Sam, the Mexicans will lead us to the river, and if they can't, we have a map. Remember to drive carefully. Don't attract police attention."

"We got us a plan," Jenkins said.

"Okay," Hank said. "Dark jackets, caps, and gloves. Check the night-vision gear and your weapons. No rounds in the chambers until we get to the house. Then seat a round and take off the safety. Each weapon should be set to fire only three round bursts, no sprays."

"Don't worry about gunfire," Grim said, smiling now that he was getting out of the heat. "Happens around here all the time. Nobody will pay any attention." Then he took out the rams. Each cylinder was about two feet long. "You've used these things before," he said. "They're spring loaded. Just grab them by these two grips and swing them so this end hits the *puerta* right next to the knobs. That's where the locks are. The whole door will shatter."

"Okay, men," Hank said, "listen up. We move in radio silence. But if anybody sees anything that looks wrong, anything at all, use your radio. I'll make the decision if we need to abort. We should be in attack positions about thirty minutes after leaving here, but that's not important. Just take your time. Be ready after midnight. I'll click twice to let Gonzales know when to start a thirty-second count. We'll hit the doors on zero. Right after that, Gonzales and the Mexican van should come to the front of the house, keep the engines running, and stand guard. When we get Sam out, we'll follow the Mexicans to the crossing. Once there, we'll give back the rams. If we lose the Mexican van, we'll use our map. We'll cross, take everything with us, and send the gear back later. After we're across, Gonzales will drive to the border alone in the van and meet Le Trang on the other side. Any questions? Speak now, or shut up."

Hearing no response, he gave the go ahead. Told himself he was doing the right thing, but God help him if Sam was hurt. He couldn't let that happen.

Chapter Thirty-Eight

Hank, Jenkins, and Gomez moved down the front street while Morales's group went into the alley. Goggles made everything dark and green, but Boss had been right. This was a poor neighborhood. Houses were wooden, badly painted, one-story shacks with no garages. Cars were parked haphazardly on the dirt lawns and in the street. Only a few streetlights were not broken. Sam's house was the third. Each step took him into unknown territory. An ambush could be anywhere. Each house could hide bad guys. Every parked car was an obstacle. On patrol in Vietnam, he had been aware of constant danger, but this was worse. He broke into a sweat, took several deep breaths to shake it off. Once he heard a sound like someone had moved behind a nearby truck. He tightened and almost radioed abort. But he tried to relax, and his team reached the target house. Even if he aborted now and pulled his men back, rifle fire could break out in the darkness. It was too late to stop. Momentum had taken over. He saw Jenkins poised and in position. Gomez had his ram ready. No more doubts. He signaled Gonzales that his team was ready. Morales did the same. Gonzales started the count.

His mother had read from her favorite poet not to "go gentle into any dark night." She was right. As Gonzales neared the end of the count, Hank tightened his grip on his pistol, took the safety off, and put a round in the chamber. Gomez raised his ram.

Gonzales counted, "Two, one, zero."

Bedlam broke out as Gomez hit the door and stepped aside. Jenkins crashed through and stumbled. Turned to his right. Hawk followed, turned left. In his haste, he fell over the broken door. That turned out to be dumb luck because shots from the darkened room went over him and missed. From the floor, he fired a burst at the dark-green shape. Then all movement stopped. Noises came from the rear of the house, and then silence. Gomez went to the guard in the front room. Hank headed for the bedroom.

"Where's the woman guard?" Morales yelled. "I can't see her. Anybody see her?"

"No!" Gomez shouted from the front. "Not up here. What about the back?"

"We've got a guy under control here, but I can't find the woman."

Hank went to Sam's room. She was curled up under covers and crying.

"We're friends," he said. "I'm Colonel Kean. Where's your guard?" "Bathroom," she said. "With a gun."

"Okay, Jenkins, secure the guards. Velasquez take Sam out front to our van. Gomez, stand on the right of the bathroom door, Morales to the left. I'll do the talking."

When the two were in place and Jenkins had verified the other guards were secure, Hank went to one side of the door and called, "Your friends are done, lady, and we have Sam. You can die in that bathroom, or live. It's up to you. If you crack open the door and slide your gun out on the floor, you'll be safe. I guarantee that. Otherwise we're going to start firing through the door and I can't guarantee anything. It's your choice."

No answer, nothing but silence.

"Ten seconds, lady. Then we start shooting."

He signaled Jenkins to make sure Sam was outside, and then he fired a three-round burst high through the door.

"See that, lady," he said. "If I don't hear from you in ten seconds, we'll fill that room with lead. Ten, nine, eight, seven, six, five, four..."

"Stop," a voice from inside called. "I'll throw out my gun." "Okay," he said. "Open the door slowly and slide it out."

The lock clicked, the door cracked open, and a gun slid out on the floor.

"That's good, lady," Hank said. "Now lie face down with your hands in plain view."

Gomez and Morales were poised with weapons ready to fire as Hank knelt and slowly pushed the door open. A woman faced down. He let out the breath he had been holding.

"Sam's with Gonzalez," Jenkins said, "but we have a problem, the front guard is dead."

Hank realized he had hit the guy when he'd answered fire. "I was the shooter," he said. "I'll take care of it. Let's get out of here. I'll call Le to send the Juarez police."

He went to the van and took a shaking Sam in his arms. "It's okay, honey," he said. "You're going home."

As they cautiously followed the Mexican van down the street, no lights went on. Nobody came out and stared at the vans. No trucks moved. He couldn't see anybody watching from a window or paying the slightest attention. The first part of the operation, the most dangerous part, was over. Now they had to get Sam to Nancy. She was huddled in his arms, apparently unhurt. A wave of exhilaration swept over him, and he almost cried out in relief. It was as if he had rescued Faith or Hope.

CHAPTER THIRTY-NINE

Crossing the river might be a dangerous time for the group, the only big hurdle left. Hank said a silent prayer that there were no bad guys waiting for them on the other bank. He would cover Sam and pull back. And even if they made it to the Trangs, it wasn't over. He had killed a guard and had broken more other laws than he could imagine. Paul might abandon him. Bev would feel he had let her down, and he might be alone again. That would end him. This thing was not over, but the road to this particular hell had been paved with good intentions.

When they were several blocks away from the house and seemed to be well on their way to the river, Hank radioed Trang. "Are you there, Le?"

"I am," Le said. "I heard everything. Is she safe?"

"Completely. I'm hugging her now. We're headed for the crossing." "Thank God. But I've got a problem. When I left the apartment to come to the rendezvous about an hour ago, a black sedan followed me. It stayed behind me as I went through El Paso and out onto the Interstate heading west into New Mexico. When I turned off the highway and onto McNutt Road, the sedan did, too. When I stopped north of where you're going to cross, the sedan stopped behind me. The people in the sedan made no attempt to get out or contact me, but I suspect that there are several of them. If I leave my van and head down to the river, they could seize the van or hit me in the field.

Then they could ambush you as you wade across. What should I do?"

"Where are Nancy and Kay?"

"They're in our apartment with the doors locked. They were not to let anyone in, and Nancy was to keep her pistol ready. I think she's listening to us now. Can you hear us, Nancy?"

"I can," Nancy said. "Is Sam okay?"

"She's fine," Hank said, "but that black sedan could be a problem. They probably reported that you went out to McNutt after midnight. That undoubtedly alerted their controllers to the fact that something out of the ordinary was happening. Did you call Geaches?"

"I did," Le said. "He wants to help. What should I we do?"

"Go back to Nancy and Kay. Tell me if that sedan follows you. We'll cross over when we can, but you should call Geaches now and tell him we're on our way. Tell him about that sedan following you and ask him to come meet us out on McNutt."

"Got it. I'm headed home, and so far that sedan is following me." "Call Nancy when you're near her, so she can let you in quickly." "What now, Colonel?" Jenkins asked when Hank got off the radio. "It's possible that nothing's wrong," Hank said. "The cops might have just been told to keep an eye on Le. Let's see what the situation looks like when we get to the crossing."

The Mexican van led them out the west side of Juarez and in fifteen minutes, they pulled off onto a dirt side road. After five minutes of bumpy travel, they stopped in an open lot, and Hank could see a band of water shimmering in the twilight, just a few hundred yards away. The Mexicans got out and searched the area. Finding nobody, they came over to Hank's van.

"All clear," Boss said. "Ready to cross?"

"Let me call Le," Hank said, "and see what's going on." "I'm in the city," Le said. "And the sedan is still behind me." "Can Nancy hear us?"

"I can," she said.

"Be sure to let Le in fast, so nobody can stop Le and ask him what he was doing out on McNutt. Both of you get upstairs and lock yourselves in. Call me when you're safe. Make sure Geaches is headed for the crossing. Tell him when you are safe."

"I will," she said. "Please don't take any chances with Sam."

"She's right, guys," he told his group. "We have to keep the kid safe, but that's no reason to delay. We can't stay here. We'll have to cross now."

"Roger that," Jenkins said.

"What's the crossing like?" Hank asked Boss.

"The river here is about a hundred yards wide," he said. "On the other side, you'll be about a mile from McNutt Road in a fairly open field that has a little cover. Because of the drought, the river is shallow now and easy to wade, although the bottom could be slippery. I've never seen people fall into the water while crossing if they took care."

"Okay, guys, listen up," Hank said. "We can't wait. Someone might have already gone to the house and talked to that woman we left. They might already be looking for us. So we have to go now. Spread apart and move with weapons ready for a fight. Have rounds in the chamber, and keep the night-vision devices on. That might give us an edge if somebody is waiting on the other bank. Radio silence."

"Agreed," Jenkins said. "We'll send the stuff back later." "Gonzales," Hank said, "leave for the border as soon as you see us safely across. Try to get to the meeting spot as soon as you can without being picked up for speeding. Take off your dark jacket, cap, and gloves, but keep your headset on and monitor our frequency. We'll leave the rams here but take the guns and goggles with us."

"Do you really think you should try to cross now?" Gonzales asked, always cautious.

"We have no choice," Hank said. "The bad guys or the cops may be on the way, and if they find us, we and our Mexican friends will lose more than just Sam. Let's get ready. I'll carry Sam on my back. Remember to spread well apart. Keep your weapons dry and ready. Jenkins, you lead. I'll have my hands full carrying Sam."

"Is the river shallow?" Jenkins asked Beard.

"Right now, the water is knee deep with little or no current," he said. "As you heard, the dirt bottom has a few pebbles and enough mud to be slippery. Just go slow and take care."

"Okay, guys, we have to get going," Hank said. "It got a little rough back there, and I may have to pay for that. But you guys are in the clear. Keep Sam free and unhurt. That's what we wanted to do. It's time to cross."

"*Bueno suerte,*" Boss said.

"We couldn't have done it without you."

"*Denada. Vaya con Dios.* Give her parents our best." "You were great, *amigo,*" Velasquez said.

It was time to get moving. "Even after we cross," Hank said, "we need to stay well spread out. And as we move through the field to the road, take it slow, just like on a patrol. When we reach McNutt, I'll keep Sam with me and you guys find places where you can see cars coming but be well out of sight. I'll get in touch with Gonzales by radio, but it's always possible for him to be delayed at the border. My guess is we'll have to wait at least an hour for him to reach us. Don't worry if he's not waiting for us. Le Trang has talked to Detective Geaches, and he's on the way. If Gonzales doesn't show, we'll just wait for Geaches."

"There's no need for Gonzalez to stay here until you cross," Boss said. "We'll hang around to cover you until you're over. He can leave now."

"Great. Gonzales, get out of here."

"Wilco," he said and with a big grin, he ran for the van.

"We appreciate everything," Hank again told Boss. "You guys are above and beyond."

"We're 82nd Airborne," Boss said. "All the way, always."

"Let's stay in touch," Jenkins said as everybody shook hands. "Roger that," Beard said. "Just like old times."

"Saddle up, men," Hank said. "Once in the water, stay apart, move slowly, and focus on the far bank. If shooting starts, fire a full clip."

"Now you're talking like the Hawk we know and love," Morales said.

Hank felt worried, not loved. If some bad guys were waiting on the north bank, it would be a catastrophe. Even if he got Sam across and to the road, that black sedan could be waiting. Instead of feeling triumph, he felt trapped. But Sam's safety justified anything that could happen to him later. Now he had to cross, be ready to fight, and get her home to Nancy.

Chapter Forty

They moved to the bank and tested the water. The Mexicans took up firing positions. Then Jenkins stepped cautiously into the river. "It's colder than I thought it would be," he said, "and slippery. Take small steps, feet wide apart."

"Try not to shift around too much," Hank told Sam as he hoisted her onto his shoulders. "I'd hate to lose my balance, slip in this mud, and dump you in the water."

"I can swim," she answered.

The river was a little over seventy-five yards wide where they were crossing with a sluggish, barely moving current. Toward the middle, the depth of the water increased to just over Hank's knees. They were then at their most vulnerable point. Hard not to tighten up and prepare to duck anticipated fire from the dark bank they were slowly approaching. Had to hold to a slow pace, putt one foot after the other and not slip. After ten tense minutes, however, they reached the other shore without incident. He set Sam down, safe in friendly territory. Waved to Boss, Beard, and Grim back on the south bank. Good guys. He owed them. His goggles gave him a green view as they waved back and headed for their van.

He took a deep breath, let out the tension, and smiled at Sam. Felt better than coming back from a jungle patrol. No ambush, no booby traps, no snipers, at least not yet. Safe across and headed for the meet on McNutt Road. Didn't see that far, however, just a few yards into the shadowy field in front of them, the view dark. McNutt about a mile straight to their north.

His group waited for his signal, but he took his time looking for an initial path and searching for any signs of an ambush or movement. Saw no movement, but snipers and ambush patrols stayed quiet and still as they waited. He had plenty of time before Gonzales could cross the border, get through the city, and come for them. No need to rush. Better to move deliberately and be careful not to screw up after having made it this far. This had to be easier than taking a tough golf shot over water to beat Paul. He was ready.

"Move out," he whispered into the radio. "Go slow, stay near cover, and watch for any movement in front of you. If you see anything suspicious, hit the ground. Try to stay near concealment. If there are any bad guys up near McNutt, they might have vision goggles."

"They would have been on the bank of the river," Morales said. "How would you know, dumb ass?" Velasquez said.

"When we get out of here, I'm gonna whip your butt." "You and what army?"

"Shut up, you two," Hank said. "The world could be listening. The next thing you'll hear will be rifle fire. You want that? Radio silence. Knock off the chatter."

They spread out and moved north. Jenkins first with Hank not far behind and Sam holding onto the back of his belt. After that, all they heard were night sounds. Too quiet. Where were the crickets? Thar worried him. Moving through that dark field with Sam close behind was difficult. No defined path. The little group made too much noise. Anybody could hit them without warning. The attack could come from anywhere to their front. A hint of dawn helped.

"Stay behind me, Sam," he whispered. "Hold on tight. I'll go slow.

Don't want to stumble, fall, and make noise." "I'm okay," she said. "I don't hear anything."

"It's too quiet," he whispered to her. "There ought to be some night sounds, crickets or birds, something, but there's nothing. I don't like it."

He could hear Gomez to his left, and the other two on his right. From the little he heard, he could tell they were doing a good job of staying about even with him, yet spread out. Old soldiers never forget. That's how they get to be old soldiers.

When they seemed to be well across the field to McNutt, a vehicle came down the road from the direction of El Paso. Under a street light, a white vehicle with *POLICE* painted in blue on its side. When it stopped right about where he thought Le Trang might have been about a half hour ago, they could see it had blue lights on its roof.

"Hold up, everybody," Hank whispered into his radio. "We've got company. Find some cover and freeze."

Hank and Jenkins were too close to the road. They had been leading and were less than fifty yards from the south edge of the road. Easy to been seen. Thankfully, they were in bushes and could kneel down, well concealed. Two policemen got out of the cruiser, walked to the edge of the road, and began sweeping the field with flashlights. They looked familiar, but not friendly. Had to stay in the shadows, quiet, and see what they did. Doubts rose. Questions formed. Why were they here? Who sent them?

He wondered.

Chapter Forty-One

After about fifteen minutes, the two troopers got back into the cruiser, and Hank whispered into his radio, "Gonzales, where are you?"

"I'm just west of El Paso," Gonzales answered, "well past the border and headed toward you, maybe ten minutes out. How're you doing?"

"Not good," Hank said. "We've got police visitors here. Le, what's your situation?"

"I'm in the apartment with Nancy and Kay."

"Call Geaches again. Tell him I'm with Sam in the field just south of McNutt, where you must have been when we last spoke, and I need help. Two cops are parked right near us. They stood on the edge of the road for a while, searching with flashlights. They're back in the cruiser now, just waiting. Something about them reminds me of those cops that stopped me at the airport a few months ago. I'm going to keep my guys out of sight in this field. You stay with Nancy, but tell Geaches to get here fast."

"I'll tell him," Le said. "But is Sam all right?"

"She's fine, and we're going to keep her that way. Those cops haven't seen us and I don't want to give anybody an excuse to start shooting."

No matter who sent those two, it looked like they intended to remain there in the cruiser, waiting for something, or someone, maybe hoping they caught him bringing Sam across the field. They were still in the cruiser with windows closed, air conditioning on. Buttoned up like that, they wouldn't hear him use his radio.

"Listen up," he said. "Stay right where you are. We'll wait for Gonzales or Geaches. Whatever happens first, don't start shooting. When Geaches gets here and we move in, hide your guns in your back belts under your jackets. If the cops get their hands on those guns, they'll have a link that would place us in that house in Juarez. We'll have to get rid of the weapons as soon as we can. If the cops get out and start shooting, don't answer fire. They might be trying to provoke a response that would show where we are. I don't want to start a fight with some policemen that might be bad apples. We have to wait for the cavalry."

"How long do you think that will be?" Jenkins asked.

"Not too much longer. Gonzales says not more than ten minutes. Just stay quiet. Don't worry. My guess is those cops aren't going to risk coming out into a dark field at night. Maybe at dawn they'll come at us, but not now. By then we'll have help."

Gonzales radioed, "I'm on McNutt and must be pretty close." "When you get here," Hank said, "you'll see a cop cruiser on the road. Stop well back from it and stay in your car. We need you as a witness to whatever happens. Just park and watch. When Detective Geaches arrives, make contact with him. Sam and I are well hidden in the field not far from the cops. We can hear everything."

"I just talked to Grumpy," Le reported. "He's almost to you."

Hang tight. Now was not the time to screw up. Better days lay ahead. Then Gonzales's van appeared and stopped well back as Hank had instructed. Gonzales turned off his headlights and one of the cops got out and walked cautiously toward the van. The other and stood by their cruiser. About fifty feet away from Gonzales, the cop stopped with his hand on his weapon and called out, "Get out of that car, slowly and keep your hands where I can see them."

Gonzales exited very deliberately, hands high, and faced the cop. "Who are you?" the cop asked, pistol now drawn.

"Master Sergeant Gonzales, U. S. army retired. I'm a combat veteran, master parachutist, highly decorated, and honorably discharged."

You can say that again. How would the cop react? "What are you doing here?" the cop asked.

"Detective Geaches of the El Paso police department is a friend of mine," Gonzales said. "He called me and told me to come and meet him here."

"He's not here," the cop said.

"He told me to wait for him. He said he was just behind me and moving fast with blue lights on. He'll be right here, and you can ask him about me."

Hank looked down the road where Gonzales had come. No blue lights.

"I don't believe you," the cop said.

There was something very familiar about that cop. "Why would I lie?" Gonzales said.

"Why would Geaches tell you to come here?" the cop asked.

"I have no idea," Gonzales said, "but I didn't want to disobey a police detective."

The headlights of a car appeared on the road behind Gonzales. The vehicle was coming at high speed with blue lights flashing. The cop facing Gonzales holstered his weapon. The car arrived quickly, skidded to a stop beside Gonzales, and Geaches got out, leaving his blue lights flashing. Before anybody could say anything, Hank heard him call out in a loud voice, "Jones, get over here. Killen, you stay where you are. Both of you shut up."

Jones and Killen, the cops from the airport with Blevins. This was starting to get good. Could be quite a show. Only Blevins was lacking to make it a full house.

When both officers were in front of him, Geaches asked, "What's going on?"

"We had a report of an illegal crossing," Jones said.

Geaches took off his hat, wiped his brow, and put his hands on his hips.

When he finally spoke, it was with sarcasm and anger.

"That is the dumbest thing I ever heard a cop say," he almost yelled. "You must think I'm an idiot, and that pisses me off. How long have you been on the force?"

"Three years," Killen said.

"In those three years, how many times have you been sent to the border late at night because of a report of an illegal crossing? Think before you answer."

"Never," Jones said after a pause, "until tonight."

"Well, I've been in the department, here, as a cop and now as a detective for almost twenty years. During all that time, I've never been sent to the border, never, because of a report of an illegal crossing. It makes me think there's something else going on. Why don't you tell me what that is?"

Gonzales called out, "Detective Geaches, I'm Sergeant Gonzales, 82d Airborne Division."

"And I'll bet you know a Colonel Kean," Geaches said.

"You got that right," Gonzales said. "He asked me to come here and help."

"And what's that on your head?" "A radio."

"I'll bet you are in touch with Colonel Kean. Where is he now?" This was a critical moment.

"In the field south of us," Gonzales said, "just north of the river." "I'm calling this in," Jones said.

"No, you're not," Geaches said. "I'm the senior officer here, and that gives me the right to make decisions and give orders. Do not move. Do not use your radio. Stand there and shut up."

"My lieutenant told me to report any crossing," Killen said. This could go bad fast.

"He's not here," Geaches said, "and I am. This is an active, emergency situation. Procedure calls for obedience of the authority at the scene. I'm that authority, and if you disobey my order, I'll make sure you get a reprimand, maybe even lose your badge."

"The lieutenant will take care of us," Jones said.

"Now I want you to understand what I'm about to tell you. Pay attention because your future depends on it. I need to make sure you know what's really going on. A kidnapping has taken place, one that involved taking minor children across an international border. That's a serious federal offense. I suspect that the fact you were sent here is somehow connected to that kidnapping. If you disobey my orders now and help the bad guys, no state police lieutenant will be able to keep your sorry asses out of a federal pen. And you know what happens to cops in those places. Do I make myself absolutely clear?"

Well done, Grumpy. What would the cops do? "Yes, Detective," Jones said, after a pause.

"Good," Geaches said. "Now shut up. Here's what's going to happen; Gonzales is going to tell Kean to come in with the girl. I'll take her into custody, and I'll assume full responsibility for doing so. I'm going to put her and Colonel Kean in my car. If there are others, Gonzales will transport them. Do not follow us. Just do your job. Watch the border. Do you understand?"

"Yes, Detective," Killen said, this time more quickly.

"Okay. Gonzales," Geaches said, "tell Colonel Kean to bring the girl in."

Gonzales spoke into his radio and Hank rose with Sam beside him.

"Follow me, men," Hank whispered into his radio. "Hide your weapons. When you approach the cops, hold up your hands to show you're not armed."

"They're on the way," Gonzales told Geaches.

The group emerged from the darkness and as they came into the lights of the cars, they took off their night-vision goggles and caps. Hank came out first, with Sam beside him. He went to Geaches and shook hands.

"This is Samantha Trang," Hank said. "These other men are ancient leftovers from the 82d Airborne Division and Vietnam. Sam has had a bad time, and we want to get her to safety and her parents as quickly as we can. She needs to see a doctor A.S.A.P."

"Okay, Colonel, you and Sam get into my cruiser," Geaches said. "Have your men follow us in Gonzales's van. As for you, Jones and Killen, you stay here and do what you say you were ordered to; watch for illegal immigrants crossing the border. Got that?"

"Yes, Detective," Jones said, even more quickly. "Let me give instructions to my men," Hank said.

He gathered the group around him and spoke quietly.

"When you reach El Paso, break off from following us. When you see no cops behind you, find a sewer and dump those guns. Then go to the airport and get out of here."

"Will do, Colonel," Jenkins said. "It's been fun. Let's do it again." "Never will be too soon," Gonzales said.

As they headed for the Trang apartment, Hank radioed Le, "Sam's safe. She and I are in the cruiser with Grumpy and headed toward you."

Then he turned to Geaches.

"Those two cops are the same ones that stopped me at the El Paso Airport two months ago when all this started. I'm sure of it."

"I know," Geaches said.

"What will they do now?" Hank asked.

"For a time," Geaches said, "they'll just sit there, think about what I said, and try to decide what to do. Eventually, they'll call in a report of contact with me and you. That will start a reaction. We need to have Sam home before somebody decides to try to find us. My guess is someone will come out to the Trang place. We need to be inside and locked up tight. Your guys better get to the airport and head for home."

Hank got into the back seat and held Sam's hand. He and the men had done it. The dark night had shifted, and there seemed to be a dim light in the east.

CHAPTER FORTY-TWO

As they neared El Paso, Geaches kept the police radio on to see if Killen and Jones reported Sam's crossing. Hearing no such call, he questioned Hank, "I take it you guys came across the river from finding Sam in Juarez?"

"You take it right," Hank said. "I got some old soldiers together, located where Sam was being held, took her from the bad guys, and brought her across. We were supposed to meet her father on McNutt, but when he saw he was being followed, he went home."

"There was shooting," Sam said.

"Please don't say anything more, Sam," Hank said. "We need to be very careful until we see if Detective Geaches is on our side. We don't want to compromise anybody."

"I'm trying to decide which side right now," Geaches said. "If there was shooting, as Sam said, and somebody got hurt, the Mexicans will be very angry, especially if some gringos were involved. If you and your men shot somebody, not only will the Mexicans be angry, so will our state department, and you would be in big trouble. But if all you did was go over to Juarez and pick-up Sam, I think you might be okay. The EL Paso D.A. will decide that."

Hank did not like the way this was going. He tried to shift the subject. "Those two cops back there were the ones that stopped me on the way to the airport. The agent, who was with them back then, was named Blevins, and he was the one that masterminded these kidnappings. Maybe Blevins found out Sam had been rescued and sent those two cops after us."

"I don't think so," Geaches said. "I checked them out. I think they're just pawns, dumb as skunks, easily manipulated. They will eventually call in the fact that you came across with Sam. That's why

I want to be in the Trang apartment before an El Paso police lieu-tenant shows up, shoves me aside, and takes over. If we are already in the apartment, he couldn't take Sam. There would be too many witnesses. The newspapers would raise a big stink if he took her from her mother and father right after she came home and before she had a chance to recover. After all, she was kidnapped and her sister had been sexually assaulted. The heat would be too much. But my guess is that you, Colonel, have stepped in it big time. You need a good attorney and some high-priced help, or you're going to be in serious trouble with a long time behind bars to think about tonight."

Hank still wasn't quite sure where Geaches stood, but one thing was clear; Sam was free. His men were headed for the airport, and he had to call Paul soonest.

They drove in silence until they approached the Trang apart-ment. "Call Trang," Geaches said. "Let him know we're here."

As Hank radioed Le, Geaches turned on his blue lights.

"Just a precaution," he said. "If the bad guys are watching, we don't want them to start shooting and then deny they knew we were the good guys. Extra insurance I hope we don't need."

When they arrived, Geaches took a good look around before he let them out. Le and Nancy stood by the open front door. As soon as the cruiser stopped, Sam ran to them.

"That's worth a lot," Hank said.

"Worth you spending time in prison?" Geaches asked. "I need to make some phone calls."

"Better do it fast. The El Paso district attorney is going to pull you in, and he's going to make you wait as long as possible before he lets you make that call. My guess is that he may come for you tonight, because when Jones and Killen finally get up the courage to call in a report, some big wheels will start rolling. The duty officer will call the chief, and he will in turn brief the D.A. The D.A. will immediately authorize your arrest. My guess is that the police will show up here in an hour or two. You'd better make your calls before they come. Where are your sergeants now? What did you tell them to do?"

"They're on their way home."

If the El Paso police were going to pull him in, Hank had to get Paul here as soon as he could. The El Paso skies had turned dark again. The light he had seen in the east was gone.

In the apartment, Geaches cautioned the Trangs, "Let nobody in, especially reporters. Don't talk to anybody, except your attorney. If you're pressed, keep saying, 'No comment.' If the police pull you in, say you need your attorney present. Most of all, insist that nobody talk to Sam unless you or your attorney are with her."

"You can use my attorney, Paul Ruth," Hank told them. "He's licensed in Texas. I'll get him down here to help. If Geaches will drive me, I'm going to the Marriott now to call Paul and ask him to come down here to represent me. If I tell him what happened and how you really need him, I think he will represent you at little or no cost."

"Please ask him," Le said. "We need all the help we can get."
"Let's get to the Marriott," Geaches said, "before the cops come for you."

CHAPTER FORTY-THREE

On the way to the Marriott, Hank questioned Geaches, "Why would the El Paso district attorney try to make a case against me? All I did was go into Juarez and bring back an abducted, traumatized little girl. People are going to love me when they find out she's free."

"The D.A. will be pretty mad," Geaches said. "You've made him look inept and weak, and no elected public figure ever wants to be made to look like that."

"But the media will play it up that Sam's free."

"That's the best shot you have. The D.A. won't want to look like he's punishing a hero the people are applauding, so he might be forced to take it easy on you. Push that angle if you have a chance. But you've got other problems, much more serious ones. That guy Blevins and the people he's working with are the ones you need to worry about."

He was right. Hank was more and more concerned about Blevins. First at the airport. Then at Bev's place. Now he was with the kidnappers. And by bringing Sam home, Hank had put himself right in Blevins's crosshairs. Hank could only imagine how Blevins had reacted when he found Sam gone and one of his men dead. No, Geaches was right; Jones and Killen were the least of Hank's problems. How would Blevins retaliate?

"Do you think Blevins has a mole with the El Paso police?" Hank asked.

"Probably not," Geaches said. "But someone sent Jones and Killen out to McNutt to find you. High priced help is somehow involved, not those two dummies. And that high-priced help is what is going to come after you."

"So you think I'm in big trouble?" Hank asked.

"That depends on what really happened in Juarez tonight," Geaches said. "I don't suppose you'd like to tell me about that."

"Have you read me my rights?"

"No. I haven't," Geaches said. "I'd like to help you, and if I read your rights, you might clam up. I can't help if you cut me off. I don't want that. As it is now, anything you tell me can't be used against you, unless you lie, but it might make it easier for me to help."

"Okay then, here's the gist; I recruited the men, organized the raid, and funded the operation. I led the attack, during which, unfortunately, we killed a kidnapper. I brought Sam back across the river and returned her safely to her parents."

Geaches was silent for a minute. Then shook his head and took a deep breath and almost screamed at Hank, "You killed somebody! Who in the hell do you think you are?"

Hank had no easy reply. He sat back and thought of Nung's death, probably a murder. Ahn being shot and Kay being abused. Rescuing Sam had been an imperative after Geaches said the Juarez police might be part of the problem. He had fired in self-defense.

"When they opened fire," he said, "I had to shoot back. Those guys were killers. I have a competent, reliable witness who saw them at Nung's place the day I believe he was killed, the same men that showed up the night Ahn was shot. And if we can exhume Nung's body, I'll be able to prove he was murdered."

Geaches calmed down a bit and was silent for a time. "Any other bombshells you want to unleash on me?"

"Nope," Hank said. "That's the essentials. So, what do you think will happen to me?"

"I think Paul Ruth better be the really good attorney if he's going to keep you from going to trial. But if the D.A. does put you in front of a jury or allows you to be extradited to Juarez, the rescue of Sam might help you beat the rap. If you ever visit Mexico, however, and are picked up, even for a minor offense, you'll be in jail for a very long time. Your trial here would not be the worst of this for you. Far worst is the fact that those people who contacted the El Paso police about you are a different kettle of fish. I think they'll come after you and your girls outside of a court of law. And that's where your real problem lies, because those people will be like Blevins, only worse.

I'll do everything I can to help, but my guess is that my captain will decide that I'm biased. He'll cut me out of the El Paso loop on this case. One thinks I know for sure; he will want to see you very soon, maybe even tonight, and when he has you in front of him, you'd better have your super-duper attorney with you, or you'll go to jail pre-trial."

Those last words hit Hank hard. Jail. Not to be with Bev, Faith, and Hope for a long time, maybe years. And even if he beat a trial, Bev and Paul would not be happy with what he had done in Juarez. And if Geaches was right, the bad guys might be coming to Hilton Head guns in hand to retaliate. He didn't want Bev, Faith, and Hope to be put in jeopardy. He couldn't let that happen. He clenched his fists tightly. He had made a mess. This was looking more and more like the stupidest night of his life.

CHAPTER FORTY-FOUR

"You did *what*?" Paul asked when Hank called.

"Some of my former soldiers and I rescued Sam," Hank said. "She's home with her family now, shook up, but okay. I need you here soonest. The El Paso police are looking for me."

Then Hank summarized what had happened in Juarez with his men and explained that the local police captain was sending some troopers after him. He pleaded for help.

"Did you say that weapons were involved?" Paul asked. "Yes, we had to—"

"Stop right there," Paul said. "The government is now monitoring domestic telephone calls. Anybody could be listening, and anything you say might get before a court. The government wants information. Just answer to my questions. First, where are you now and what's your exact situation with the El Paso police?"

"I'm at the Marriot, and Detective Geaches says that the police will be coming after me very soon. He says his captain will want to interrogate me about what happened in Juarez and how we got Sam home. Geaches says I'll be put in jail pending a bail hearing."

"Stay where you are," Paul said. "Were the police involved in the rescue?"

"Two cops were waiting for us where we forded the river to bring Sam back. They tried to arrest us but thankfully, Detective Geaches stopped them. Geaches is on our side. Le Trang was monitoring our radios. He sent Geaches to help, and Geaches says I'm in big trouble. I need a good lawyer. That's why I called you. Can you come to El Paso?"

"I probably shouldn't, but I think I can be there by early evening. Right now, listen carefully to me. If the police pick you up and read you your rights, refuse to answer any questions, any at all, until I get there. Tell them I am registered in Texas. And even if they don't read you your rights, you should still remain silent. Take the fifth. Delay any cooperation as much as you can. Your goal is to slow things down until I can discuss this more fully with you. That's important. Do you understand? And one more thing; it is essential that neither Le Trang nor Sam talk to a reporter. If the police want to question the girl or her family, make sure they demand to have me present before they answer any questions. Until I get there, they should clam up, remain silent. Now, have you told Bev, Faith, or Hope what happened in Juarez?"

"No. I wanted to talk to you first."

"Okay. I'll call Faith and Hope, but you call Bev now. Tell her as little as you can. Just say that somebody could be listening and taping the call, and that anything you say could be used against you. I'll try to be in El Paso by supper. With any kind of luck, they'll let me see you pretty fast. If they do, you probably won't have to spend more than one night in jail. Just try to slow the police down until I arrive."

Hank thought about Ruth's warning and considered carefully what he could tell Bev.

She answered quickly.

"Where are you?" she asked. "What's going on?"

"I'm in El Paso," he said, "safe and sound, but I have a problem."

He quickly summarized the situation and ended by warning her that although Sam was safe, there had been opposition during the rescue. Some violence and legal complications he couldn't tell her about over the phone because Paul said phones could be tapped. He was quite concerned about that and told me to say as little as possible until he could be here as my attorney.

"He's headed for the airport now to come to El Paso."

"You aren't making sense," she said. "Why do you need an attorney?"

"There are people who think I might have been involved in Sam's rescue. I can't tell you anything more, because someone like Blevins might be listening."

"My God, Hank. Are you serious?"

"I am. But Detective Geaches, from the department down here, is on my side. He says there is so much sympathy for Sam Trang that no jury in Juarez would ever convict me for anything I might have done to free her. Paul thinks the same thing, but he told me not to answer questions, any at all, until he arrives. He thinks he can keep me out of jail."

"Out of jail? You are crazy, Hank Kean, certifiably insane, out of your mind. What did you do? What could you have been thinking of?"

"I was thinking of how I might feel if Faith and Hope had been stopped, questioned, or even kidnapped like Kay and Sam. I was thinking what pressure Le and Nancy Trang were under. I knew how bad those kidnappers were. They murdered Ahn Manh and might have killed Colonel Manh. So I had to help Sam, but let's not talk about that now. I just wanted to tell you that Sam is safe and I am okay."

She was quiet for a minute, then said, "I love you. Please come home safe and sound."

Then she hung up. He might be in deep trouble with the El Paso cops, but he treasured the support of the people he loved. He needed them on his side.

Chapter Forty-Five

When the phone in his room at the Marriott rang, Hank had had just three hours sleep and he was still groggy, not sure where he was.

"Hawk here," he answered, "this better be important." "This is Grumpy, and it's important."

"Did you really have to call this early?"

"You're damn right I did. You'd better wake up fast because two cops are on the way to pick you up. I warned you. They're supposed to bring you in to see the captain. He and I had an early morning meeting, because someone told him that I picked you up out on McNutt. He's mad as hell about that and I'm in hot water. He's gonna cut me out of the loop on your case. The cops coming for you don't have a warrant, but I recommend you cooperate and come in with them. If the captain has to go to a magistrate and get a warrant, he'll be really pissed. That wouldn't help you when you face him."

"I'm going to refuse to go with them."

"That's your call, but you'd better be ready to deal with an angry police captain who just might put you in jail, without letting you make any phone call at all."

Twenty minutes later, a loud knock sounded. When Hank opened the door, with the chain still in place, he found two large policemen waiting for him.

"Colonel Kean, please come with us," one said. "Am I under arrest?" Hank asked.

"No, Colonel, the captain just wants to talk to you, and he wants it now."

"Well, I have some things I need to do. Tell your captain that I'll come to the police department voluntarily by mid-afternoon. A few hours won't change anything. I'll be there after lunch. I want to be helpful, and I will be, but I know my rights. So, if you have nothing more for me, I'd like to get some things done. If you keep on delaying me, I'll blame the delay on you."

Hank then closed and locked the door. He had only a few hours before they would be back with a warrant, so he packed his gear and checked out. He left his bags with the concierge and sat down in the lobby, headed either to jail or South Carolina.

When the cops came back just after noon, they had a warrant and Hank was still searching every newspaper he could find for news of any shootings or kidnappings in Juarez. He had found nothing even remotely like what had happened.

They read his rights, handcuffed him, and hustled him not gently to a squad car. In twenty minutes, they had him at police headquarters. In a small room they sat him down, chained by his ankles to the floor. Then they stood by in silence. They waited for what seemed like an eternity, and then a scowling captain entered.

"Okay, smart guy," he said. "What the hell went on in Juarez last night?"

"Plenty," Hank said. "I want to see my attorney, Paul Ruth."

"Look, smart ass, I'm investigating the kidnapping of one of my citizens, and I want your cooperation. What happened over there?"

"I don't want to make a statement or answer any questions without my attorney present. Someone might misunderstand or twist anything I say. If you're arresting me, I need my attorney. He is licensed in Texas, and he also represents the Trangs. He has advised them and me not to make a statement until he arrives. He's on the way here on Delta as we speak."

"Lock this smart ass up," the captain said as he stalked out.

A policeman marched Hank to the jail block, where he found that his cell was small, dirty and stank of urine and vomit. When the bars clanged shut, the sound echoed in the empty cell block and resonated in his mind. He was alone again, absolutely on his own this time, and the consequences of his actions in Juarez had become very real. He had never spent time in jail and the situation hit him hard. He hoped Paul would arrive soon because a Texas storm worse than a Vietnamese monsoon had pulled Hank under water.

Ruth was true to his promise and by seven that evening he arrived. The El Paso Police Department had verified that he was licensed in Texas, and he was allowed to meet with Hank in a conference room.

"Do not discuss anything here," Paul said. "These rooms are wired and they're watching us now. We'll talk more in detail later, but for now, I want to draw up a statement we can release to the press. So don't talk. Just write and I'll read and edit what you say. Let's do everything with very little discussion. First you should identify yourself and describe what happened last night. Do not incriminate yourself any more than you absolutely need to."

As Hank began to write, his hand was not steady. This had become too complicated.

Chapter Forty-Six

The two of them worked carefully and after a little over an hour, they had what Paul thought was an acceptable statement. He asked to see the captain. In about fifteen minutes, they were taken to him. He scowled from behind his desk as they handed him the following statement:

"My name is Henry Wilson Kean. I am an honorably retired colonel of the United States army, a citizen of the state of South Carolina. I met a Colonel Nung Manh in Vietnam in 1968 while serving in the war there. A short time ago, I learned that the colonel and his wife his wife were living in El Paso. Since then, he has died and his wife has been killed. I also learned that their granddaughters had been kidnapped and that one of the girls was still being held, perhaps in Juarez. The father of the kidnapped girl is Le Trang, a legal Vietnamese immigrant and a graduate of the University of Texas. He is living in El Paso and running a local business. I contacted some of my former soldiers in the 82nd airborne division and asked if they would help me rescue Samantha, Le Trang's daughter being held somewhere in Juarez. They agreed and we located the house where Samantha was being held. Last night, my men and I went to Juarez to that house and freed her. Neither Samantha nor any of my people were injured in the rescue. Because we didn't know if the kidnappers might be watching the city border in Juarez and might try to recapture Samantha, we decided to bring her back by crossing the river. To enlist the aid of the El Paso police, we notified an El Paso police detective when and where we would be crossing. We also asked him to provide transportation. He did that and escorted us to Sam's parents. She is now trying to put this deplorable experience behind her. The family asks that everyone respect their privacy and give their daughters a chance to heal. I would like to thank the El Paso Police Department for their assistance in this matter. I request that you refer all questions to my attorney, Paul Ruth."

The captain leaned back in his chair with a sneer and said, "This is bull shit."

Paul stood up and paced as he answered tersely, "That is a legal statement, which can be used in court. As the Trangs's attorney, I authorize you to release it to the media. Before you do, however, I want make a few points absolutely clear. To start with, your evaluation of this statement reveals a bias that I will use if Colonel Kean is tried or made the subject of an attempt to extradite him to Mexico."

The captain sat straight up and Hank moved aside to be out of the line of fire as Paul continued, "If you consider Colonel Kean to be a subject of interest in the kidnapping of Kay and Samantha Trang, you are being absurd. It is equally absurd to think he killed Mrs. Manh or was involved in the death or Colonel Manh. What happened in Juarez is a different matter. You obviously do not know anything about that, or you would not have asked Colonel Kean for the details, and Juarez is well out of your jurisdiction."

The captain stood up and glared at Paul. Hank sat upright. It was show time.

Paul continued, "We will vigorously fight any attempt to extradite Colonel Kean to Mexico, and we will note your stated bias as we do." The captain started to interrupt, but Paul stopped pacing, raised his hand, and continued, "My client is innocent of wrongdoing, but I have made a record of your efforts to discredit him. If you do not desist, I will fully inform the El Paso newspapers and television news of your behavior so that the citizens who are now rejoicing because Samantha Trang is free will know of your many attempts to smear Colonel Kean. I ask that you free him now. If you do not release him, I want a bail hearing so that I can make your bias known."

The captain leaned over, hands on the desk, and glared at Paul. Hank watched with interest as Paul sat dawn, took out a yellow pad, and prepared to note the captain's response. The captain paced in silence for a minute. Then, he sat down and said quietly, "Go back to the holding cell."

In the cell, Hank was upbeat, saying that Paul had been brilliant, but Paul wrote "We bluffed, but this isn't poker. We are not out of the briar patch just yet. That captain is calling the D.A. and the judge who signed your warrant. He wants to know how to proceed."

Three anxious hours later, an officer came for them.

"The captain wants you to talk to the press," he said. "Let's go."

In a room packed with reporters, the captain made an opening statement, "Samantha Trang was freed from her kidnappers early this morning. Colonel Kean, a retired United States army officer, organized the effort that brought her back. His attorney will now read his statement."

Ruth then read the prepared text and said he would not take questions because Colonel Kean was a person of interest in what happened.

"Is Colonel Kean under arrest?" a reporter asked the captain. "No, but he wouldn't come in to talk unless we had a warrant."

"If Kean rescued that little girl," another reporter said, "my readers are going to want to give him a medal, not send him to jail."

"They don't know all the facts. It's a case in progress."

"My Juarez source tells me there was some shooting over there last night," a different said. "The source also says an American was killed. Do you know anything about that?"

"I have no facts that would substantiate that," the captain said. "If you have information you should give it to me. I want names and other specifics. Juarez has not notified us of an American being killed there last night. If that actually happened, the state department and I would like to know how you know about it."

"Can we talk to the girl or her parents?"

"They have asked that their privacy be respected," the captain said.

"You're giving us very few details."

"That's because I have very few," the captain said. "If you want more, you're going to have to do what reporters are supposed to do; dig them out for yourself. And if you find anything that is in any way connected to the rescue of Samantha Trang, I want to hear about it from you before I read it in the newspaper. If someone tells you that an American has been killed in Juarez, get me the facts, not rumors.

I made copies of Colonel Kean's statement for you. That's all, ladies and gentlemen. Go home. It's past your bedtime."

When the reporters were gone, the captain told Paul that Kean could go. "I may press charges," he said. "But now, I'm tired of both of you, so get the hell out of here."

When he dismissed them with a wave of his hand and a scowl, he was not a happy camper.

Hank took a deep breath of fresh air. He was a free man, for now.

Chapter Forty-Seven

As they headed for the Trang apartment, Hank congratulated Paul. "You handled that captain masterfully. What do you think his district attorney and the judge told him?"

"The facts," Paul said. "You can't be tried for anything in El Paso, and anybody who tried to extradite you would be crucified by public sentiment. Just make sure you never visit Mexico again because they will be looking for you. If they catch you, they will put you away for a long time. Now, I want to know what actually happened when you rescued Sam."

Hank told him the full story, from recruiting his soldiers, to finding the house where Sam was being held, and the attack.

Paul was silent for a minute. Then he stopped the car and with face reddened turned to Hank, "You are completely nuts, a raving lunatic. I could never defend that. And even if you escape the Mexican government, I suspect that if the full extent of your involvement reaches our state department, the F.B.I. may come looking for you, and Ted Storm will no longer be an ally."

"I have a bigger problem that the F.B.I.," Hank said. "Agent Steve Blevins and the people he's working for are a much more important threat."

When Paul recovered enough to drive on toward the Trang place, Hank spelled out the times he, Bev, and the Trangs had encountered Blevins.

"He seems to be everywhere," Hank said, "and he, apparently, has some very powerful help. That's what I'm worried about now, not the Mexican government nor the state department. Blevins is the bigger threat because he's a killer. Did Storm find out if Blevins is actually an agent?"

"Personnel files of agents are off limits," Paul said. "We need to take precautions."

They talked about what might have happened to the woman guard Hank had left tied at the house, and who might have found the dead guard; the Juarez police or Blevins. In either case, Hank was sure that Blevins would retaliate for Hank rescuing Sam and killing the guard.

Paul just shook his head and shrugged.

"I can't help you with Blevins," he said. "But we can warn the Trangs to home school their daughters and to be prepared for the media blitz coming their way when the news of Sam's rescue gets out. I need to write out statements they can give out, and rehearse Le and Nancy."

Hank then remembered that his name had come out during Sam's rescue. The woman guard would tell Blevins that Hank had been there. "Blevins knows my name," he told Paul. "He's already been to Bev's apartment. He might come after Faith and Hope now."

"I suppose that's true," Paul said, "and he might come after Bev again. Let's take the red eye back to Hilton Head and set up a defense. Where's your gear?"

"Packed, ready to go, and with the concierge at the Marriott."

Just before midnight, they arrived at the Trang apartment and knocked on the door for several minutes. Le finally opened it, keeping the chain in place. When he saw them, he broke into a wide grin.

"Come in, Colonel," he said, double-locking the door after they were inside. "And welcome, Counselor. I feel better already. What a relief."

Upstairs, Nancy enthusiastically welcomed them, hugging Hank. "Come in, come in," she said. "Let's celebrate."

"Where are the girls?" Hank asked. "How are they?"

"They're in bed," she said. "This thing has exhausted them. Sam still cries, but they're both safe, because of you. We can't thank you enough."

"My men were just as important," he said.

"Of course," Le said. "They were great to take such a risk. And you, Mr. Ruth, we appreciate that you came to help us."

Nancy made coffee and brought out some cake left from dinner. While she was preparing everything, Hank told Le about the police captain and the media.

"Reporters will come after you," Paul said. "The most important thing is that none of you should ever make a statement, either to the police or especially to the media about Sam's rescue unless Hank, Detective Geaches, or I are present. The only exception would be for your daughters to give a description of the kidnappers to the police, to assist in the investigation. If they do, one of you should be with them. You must make sure that Colonel Kean's name is not brought up in connection with the rescue."

"And Le, you need to prepare for the possibility that the police may pull you in for questioning," Hank said. "If they inquire about the attack, you must request for one of us to be present. Most of the time, just answer, 'No comment,' pleading that you are concerned about the possibility of a future attack against your family. In reality, you do not want to say much of anything. Just plead ignorance. Worse problems will arise if the prosecutor insists on questioning your daughters or either of you. If that happens, Paul or I should be present. Just as important, the girls must not say anything about the rescue to their friends. That is going to be very difficult, I know, because I have two daughters and they love to gossip and impress friends. But it is very important they not say anything."

"But it is also important to enlist the aid of Detective Geaches," Paul said. "He's valuable. Tell him everything. Hank tells me he is a good guy. Ask him about additional police protection around here. Set up home schooling for Kay and Sam. Lock your doors. Keep a loaded pistol handy. Operate only from your shop. Don't make house calls. Don't even think about going into Juarez. You actually know what to do. It is pretty much common sense. But I want to emphasize that the media are not your friends. They only want a sensational story. And be careful about the El Paso police. Grumpy is your only real friend there. If you get a call from one of the bad guys, or if it's only a suspicious call, tell Grumpy."

"I'd especially want to know if somebody tries to talk to Le about using his computers to contact anyone in Vietnam," Hank said. "That has something to do with all of this. If you hear the name Blevins, it should set off an alarm."

"Now, I have to get back to Hilton Head," Paul said. "Maybe Storm or I can line up some help in Washington."

"And I need to get back to work," Hank said. He needed to see Bev, Faith, and Hope. The reunions might be difficult when they find out what happened in Juarez. He couldn't hold back. He had to tell them. Bev was going to be very unhappy. Faith and Hope would be shaken. An awkward combination of pleasure and pain, sun and shadow. Anything could happen. As much as he wanted to see them all, a night mist prevented him from seeing the future. He would need to be at his best to survive the next few days.

"Keep it simple," he told himself. "Take the initiative, but be careful. It would all work out."

He crossed his fingers. This would still be too complicated, but he had to clear the air, if only to keep the women in his camp. Many problems were on the horizon. He had to keep everybody informed, and safe.

CHAPTER FORTY-EIGHT

The redeye flight to Atlanta was dismal. The airline simply wanted its plane back at Atlanta, and it cared little about those who rode it. As soon as the craft was airborne, cabin lights went off and service disappeared. In the almost empty plane, Hank and Paul stretched out on several seats under blankets for the three-hour trip. The layover in Atlanta before an early flight to Savannah was a complete waste. There was not enough time to find a place to sleep, and there was nothing but fast food to eat. Hank was tired and looked forward to being home, seeing his ladies, getting some rest, and figuring out what to do next. Bev met the flight. Her eyes were red, as if she had been crying. Her hands shook.

"What's wrong?" Hank asked, taking her in his arms.

"Blevins came back," she said, almost crying. "They were waiting for me when I came home from work, and before I could shut the door, they forced their way in. The same group. That creep Blevins said it was an emergency. Said one of his agents had been killed in Juarez, and that you did it."

Oh my God. That bastard got here first. Shaken, he and Paul led Bev to a Delta Connection conference room with comfortable seats and gave her a cold drink.

"Blevins said I had failed," she sipped a soft drink and then continued, shakily, "and that I had lied to him, but I told him that he was the one that had lied when he said you were a threat to the country, and I would be doing a service to America if I worked for the agency and trapped a criminal. He meant you."

Was Blevins actually an agent with the C.I.A.? Was there an ongoing agency operation involving Vietnam, nuclear weapons, and Saudi Arabia?

"That's how I knew he was lying, Hank." She continued with more confidence. "You are not a criminal. You're a combat hero. You proved it by risking your life to save that little girl from that bunch of thugs. So I told him then that you were the honest one and that I knew he was lying about everything."

Not only a liar, but also a killer. She was lucky to be alive. "What did he say then?" Hank asked, fearing the answer.

"He said you were a killer. That's how I knew he was lying. He had killed Ahn Manh and maybe her husband, too. When I said their deaths were a waste because they were just harmless old people, he lied again. He claimed they weren't harmless, but significant threats to the United States. Then he went on to accuse me of knowing you were going to El Paso to kill that agent. But I knew that wasn't true; you were going there to help some friends. You did exactly that. You saved that little girl."

She sniffled a little, drew back, but kept on.

"But he said I had concealed your trip to El Paso, deliberately kept him in the dark. Said if I had told him what you were going to do, he would not have lost a good agent. He said there was blood on my hands, and that he would have to retaliate against you and us."

She put both hands to her face, covering her eyes.

"I told him that if blood was shed, it better not be yours because I would go public through Paul. He then said I was talking crazy because I'd fallen for you. I'd fallen, all right, but I wasn't crazy. He then asked if I would help him in the future. Said I would be working on something with severe national consequences. I asked him if there were national consequences when you saved a child in Juarez. He then said the darned most insane thing. Said that nuclear weapons were involved. He contradicted himself, because before he had said that other people, not you, were involved with nuclear weapons, and that you were interfering with them. So I told him he wasn't making sense, was changing his story by claiming you were working with bad people that had their hands-on nuclear weapons. I said for him to prove it, and he said he couldn't give me the details, because they were highly classified, but the interests of the United States in the

Middle East and in the acquisition of nuclear weapons by Iran were both at play."

Oh my God. Nuclear weapons and the Middle East again. He had to find out who this Blevins was and who he was working for.

She stopped, composed herself, and then continued, "I asked if you were working with Iran and he claimed that the opposite was true, that you were interfering with an operation to arm Iran's enemies, maybe Saudi Arabia, to stop Iran's nuclear program. I couldn't understand what he was talking about. And that's why I don't trust him. So I told him he was talking non-sense and that I didn't believe him."

Thank God, she's here in one piece.

She continued, "That's when he said that if you continued to interfere, you would go to jail and that I might take a fall myself because I knew too much. Said there would be retaliation if I didn't help him. I asked if that was a threat and he said no, it was a fact and a warning that if there were leaks, the consequences would be severe. Said he could not permit any leaks. That too much was at stake. At that point, I knew I was in deep trouble, and I asked him if he would kill me. He said nothing was off the table."

Hank put his arms around her and they went to her car. They sat in the back seat while Paul drove and Hank tried to figure out what he could do to protect her and his daughters. He needed help. He'd press Ted Storm about Blevins, but high-powered help from Washington would be even better. He had met Senator Tompkins after he had written his thesis on Saudi Arabia. He had gone to the senator's office and talked about Saudi Arabia to the senator and his chief assistant, Steve Powell. He liked both of them. They would help now.

"Who's Powell?" Paul had asked.

"Tompkins's top assistant," Hank had said. "He's a black attorney, sort of a rugged Sidney Poitier. Intelligent, asked the right questions. Firm handshake. Looked me right in the eye. A straight shooter, I liked him."

Hank thought about that meeting. The senator had called Hank to Washington to talk about Hank's thesis on Saudi Arabia. Both he and Powell had asked many questions, not only about Hank's ideas on desalination but also about Saudi society in general. In fact, they had asked more questions about the Saudi royal family than anything else. They both had shown great interest. They'd been very friendly, and Hank was sure they were the high-powered help he needed. He resolved to make an immediate appointment to see them.

Chapter Forty-Nine

Paul dropped them at Hank's place and headed home. When Hank opened the door to his apartment, he stopped cold—there was trash everywhere, drawers opened, and contents spilled on the floor. Cushions thrown about. Bed mattress askew. His desk was opened and its computer smashed. He held Bev back.

"I need to call the police," he said. "We can't go in. I want the cops to look for fingerprints and other evidence. The crooks might have left a trap for me or something. Let's go to your place. I'll call the police there and come back to meet them."

At Bev's, he arranged to meet a detective at the apartment at ten o'clock. Then he called Paul to keep him in the loop.

"Don't feel like the Lone Ranger," Paul said. "My apartment was also struck. I'm going to my office now and find out if they hit me there, too. Let's lunch at the Seacrest near Bev's place and compare notes."

While Hank waited for the detective at his place, he called Ted Storm at the F.B.I. to see if Storm had anything on Blevins. Storm answered quickly. "That's a coincidence," he said. "I was just about to call you. I have news about Saudi Arabia. But you first, how can I help?"

"Agent Blevins has shown up again," Hank said. "Have you dug up anything about him?"

"Zero," Storm said. "He's not in the F.B.I., and C.I.A. personnel files are classified. The news from Saudi Arabia is a bombshell; they've just donated an atomic weapon."

As he started to explain what had happened, a detective arrived with a forensics team and Hank had to hang up after promising to call Storm back for a full explanation.

The detective searched and his team went through Hank's apartment for an hour, looking for fingerprints, clues, and anything that might identify who had ransacked the apartment. They bagged a few items, took some notes, and left. Hank then called Storm and got a fuller account of the Saudi explosion. Then he headed for Bev's place, the Seacrest, and Paul.

At lunch, Hank found a common denominator to the invasion of his and Paul's places; the only items taken were the hard drives to their computers. Of much greater interest was Storm's account of the nuclear explosion that had taken place in the Empty Quarter of Saudi Arabia, without advance notice, the Saudis had set off a fusion device in a place where nothing or nobody would be harmed. The only evidence the United States had from that event was obtained from analysis of the nuclear cloud that formed; the signature indicated that the device was one of the two that had been stolen from the American depot in Germany. Countries surrounding Saudi Arabia, especially Iran, were in an uproar.

"Colonel Orzon was telling the truth," Hank said. "The Sayyaf or somebody did steal those devices and delivered them to the Saudis. Storm didn't know if Blevins was involved, but the story was not the product of a drunken imagination, it actually happened. This is way above our pay grades. I'm going to ask for a meeting to tell Senator Tompkins what has been going on. I've met him before while I was at the war college. He and his assistant were friendly and very interested in what I told them about Saudi Arabia. The senator said he wanted to meet again and learn more about the Saudi royal family. I'll use that to set up a meeting."

"And I am going to sit down with the detectives from the Hilton Head police," Paul said, "to go over the ransacking of our places and firm up a system to protect Bev, Faith, and Hope."

"If Blevins was the one who trashed your places," Bev asked, "how did he know you and Hank were working together?"

"The female guard we left behind when we rescued Sam," Hank said, "must have heard my name. I'm sure he knows Paul is my attorney. He must have sent someone to search our places, looking for any records we had made about our contacts with him. That's why they took our computer drives. He wants to know what we know and where we have stored it. Blevins is worried and I'm sure he will retaliate."

"If you see Senator Tompkins," Paul said, "give him my regards. He has a condo here on Hilton Head, and I have done some work for him. I think he's a good guy. Ask him to get the feds on our side. He has plenty of clout in Washington, exactly what we need to prevent Blevins from doing more damage. That thug and his gang may come after any or all of us. We need to be alert, set alarms, and have pistols ready."

"I want nothing to do with guns," Bev said.

"I understand," Paul said, "but at least you could always turn on your apartment alarm system, whether you're at home or out. Hank can drive you to and from work. The police will be watching your place."

In bed at his apartment that night, Hank tossed and turned trying to figure out what Blevins was going to do and what he and Paul could do to prevent more trouble. He arose without any brilliant ideas.

CHAPTER FIFTY

Hank had work to do. Call Washington for an appointment with Tompkins. Call Clemson on Hope's safety. Long hours at his office. His clients needed help.

Late one evening, a call came in.

"I need to speak to you, Colonel Kean," a male voice said. "We have a common interest in what happened in Juarez. You acted badly, and I will punish you very soon."

"Who is this?" Hank asked.

"I lost a good man, a friend, at your hands in Juarez," the man said. "I will balance the scales. Your daughters won't be safe until I do. The Trangs will not be able to operate their business. Yours will suffer."

"I thought I recognized your voice, Blevins," Hank said, "but all this is your fault. You are the one responsible for that agent's death. You caused it by kidnapping the Trang's daughters to Juarez. I just responded to what you had done. But for God's sake man, why did you have to kill Colonel and Mrs. Manh?"

"I swear I was not involved in the Manhs's deaths."

"Don't play games with me. Who but you would kill them?"

"How would I know? There could be many reasons. The Manhs may still have enemies in Vietnam. Vietnamese have long memories. Colonel Manh may have been dealing drugs."

"You know that's not true. You didn't kill them over drugs."

"We may need to talk about that later, after I deal with my man's death."

"Does this have anything to do with Colonel Orzon? And what do you know about the recent nuclear explosion in Saudi Arabia?"

"Those are completely different subjects. But they raise the risk and put an entirely new aspect on what I will do next."

Then, Hank heard only silence for some time until the phone disconnected.

He immediately phoned Paul.

"Blevins just called and told me he would balance the sales because I shot a friend of his in Juarez."

"Get going and make that appointment with Senator Tompkins as soon as possible," Paul said. "Time is of the essence. Tell him the whole story from your first contact with Blevins, to Juarez, to his call just now. Don't hold back. Tell him everything about Juarez, especially your role in shooting that agent. And be sure to tell him that Hope is at Clemson. Tompkins is a graduate. And emphasize you are a republican."

"Is this political?"

"Everything in Washington is political."

Hank saw brighter days ahead. With a senator on his side, maybe he'd be able to get some answers. He felt a cloud lifting. But how would Blevins retaliate? And against whom? He decided to double the protection for Bev, Faith, and Hope.

In Washington, Blevins assembled his team to issue their marching orders.

"David was a member of this team for twenty-five years," he said. "He saved my ass many times. I owed him. All of us loved him and we will not let his killer go unpunished. Kean actually killed a member of my team, so I am going to kill two members of his. Here's how we'll do it. I will lead Tom and Sharon to take out Bill West in Virginia. Ron and Jim will eliminate Gus Bean up in Massachusetts. I'll brief Tom and Sharon later, but here's how I want you to handle Bean. He had a stroke that severely weakened him. We have been watching his house, and he never leaves, except to go to the hospital. His wife takes care of him. Every day after noon, however, she goes out to shop and just take a break. Apparently after lunch, he takes a nap in front of the T.V. while she is gone, almost two hours. The quickest she has ever returned was still over an hour. Sharon has given us a satellite view of the house. Close behind it are some woods. You two get to those woods before Bean's wife leaves. As soon as she's out of there, cross the back yard and enter the back porch. Wear hats pulled low and high collars so if anybody sees you, which they won't, they still won't be able to identify you. On the porch, put on gloves and cover for your shoes. Open the back door quietly, and I think you'll find Bean sleeping in his lounge chair in front of the television. One of you hold him down while the other smothers him with a pillow. He won't be able to offer much resistance. When he's gone, lift him out of the chair and hit his head on the coffee table. Make it look like he got up, stumbled, and killed himself when he hit the edge of the table. One of you go to the refrigerator and find something like an olive to stick down his windpipe. Make it look as if he choked himself, tried to jump up, and fell. Muss up the place a bit so it looks like that's what happened. Go out the same way you came. You should be in the house less than fifteen minutes. Do it for David. Any questions?"

Seeing none, he turned to Sharon and Tom.

"Go to West's real estate office on a Wednesday. Tell him you want to buy acreage out in Rappahannock County. Say you live in a town house near Tysons Corner and work for Lockheed-Martin in the district. You feel cooped up in the town house and want some land to build on. You can't get away from work during the week, so make a Sunday appointment to spend the day looking for acreage. Take a picnic basket, so it looks like you're just going out to enjoy the day. On Sunday, show up and have West drive you. Leave your car locked at West's place. Sharon, you wear a bug so I can hear what's going on and be able to track you. When you're gone, I'll use my key to take your car and follow. When you get to a remote place, shoot West and I'll pick you up. Take West's watch, money, ring, and other stuff to make it look like a robbery. Any questions?"

Seeing no reply, he continued, "Let's get this done in the next two weeks. I want Kean to know everything he does to us will have immediate consequences."

"Why don't we just kill Kean?" Ron asked.

"He has powerful protection," Steve said. "He's made records we can't find, records that would be damaging if published. He's got some powerful friends we can't alienate. So we have to stay away from him. But we can go after those around him and make him feel the pain. So that's what we're going to do."

They left to carry out his operations.

CHAPTER FIFTY-ONE

A week later, Hank called to ask Gus how Waters had treated the male and female children differently at the orphanage. When Mrs. Bean finally answered, she said, "Gus is dead."

"I'm so sorry," Hank said. "I knew he was sick, but how did it happen?"

"When I came home from shopping," she said, "I found him on the floor. I couldn't wake him up so I called 911, and the medics came right away. The police were with them. They took him immediately to the emergency room."

"Was he already dead?"

"I think so. But they pronounced him dead at the hospital."
"Was there an autopsy?"

"Yes. The coroner said that he had choked on an olive that they found lodged in his windpipe. They guessed that he woke up and went into the kitchen for a snack, and when he came back with an olive, it went into his windpipe. When he could not breathe, he jumped up, fell, and hit his head on the coffee table. He died from a resulting heart attack. There was an open wound on his forehead that matched some blood on the edge of the coffee table. The coroner ruled accidental death."

"Do you believe that?" "No."

"Why not?"

"If Gus ever woke up from his after-lunch nap, he never got up and went to the kitchen for a snack. He just stayed in his recliner and watched television until I came home. If he ever had to get up, it would have been because he had to go to the bathroom, but he would not have gone to the kitchen because he wouldn't have been hungry."

"So you don't think it was an accident." "I'm suspicious."

"Why?"

"Gus hated olives."

At the first chance, Hank brought Paul up to speed.

"Blevins threatened to retaliate," Hank said, "and I think he just did."

He then told Paul about the autopsy and the olive.

"How would the kidnappers have known about Gus?" Paul asked. "When all this started, I called Gus because there is an intelligence unit near where he lived. That unit had been working with Gus in Vietnam. I asked if he had connections with some of their guys that had served with Operation Phoenix. When he said he knew several, I asked him to see if any might know anything about Elliott or McMillian. He said he was sure they would, but when I called him again a couple of weeks later, he said he got a strange response. His sources had been optimistic at first, but when he finally reached them, they had become guarded and negative. They wouldn't tell him a thing. I think that when his sources talked to their contacts at the C.I.A., the agency told them not to say anything about Elliott and McMillian. What's more, I'll bet the people Gus contacted told the C.I.A. that he was the one who was asking about Phoenix. That's how his killers found him."

"Are you suggesting the C.I.A. killed Gus?"

"Not necessarily, but I'm leaning that way. Of course, there could have been a leak. Stuff happens, but I'm going to ask Senator Tompkins about the agency, Waters, and Phoenix. Do you remember how you described the kidnappers as powerful, efficient, and organized? To me, that sounds a lot like a description of the C.I.A. And if I'm right, I'm probably next on Blevins's hit list. The best protection I can get is to have Senator Tompkins on my side. That may protect me, especially if we have all this recorded in our file. I'd also like to know if the Pentagon has a record of Waters's service. I'll ask Bill West."

"Why do you think Waters had a military record?"

"I think my family knew a soldier named Waters in Hawaii a long time ago."

"I'm going to call my father and see what he remembers. Maybe it's the same guy."

"Better do it soonest. Blevins may be coming your way."

"He won't touch me. He knows we have a file on him. I think he realizes you'll make that file public if I'm attacked. I think they don't want to risk that."

"And I think you're nuts." "Join the crowd."

Chapter Fifty-Two

"Bill, I need some help," Hank said when he called West. "Do you think some of your Pentagon buddies can dig up the records of a soldier named Randy Waters who was a private at Schofield Barracks in Hawaii about 1948? He may have been tried for desertion or assault and spent time in prison at Leavenworth."

"Maybe," West said. "All such records are kept somewhere in the bowls of the Pentagon. The problem will be to find someone who knows where everything is down there. Who's this Waters anyway?"

"A guy that sexually abused a child. A man with that name was the director of an orphanage in my area in Vietnam. He was wounded in an attack on the orphanage during early Tet. I diverted my chopper there and tried to take him to the army hospital at Cu Chi, but he died on the way. I'd like to find out if he's the same guy my father knew in Hawaii a long time ago. There was a scandal about him back then and if he's the same guy, I'd like to know how he got into Nam."

"Was he in the military in Vietnam?"

"No, was working with C.O.O.R.D.S. as the director of that orphanage."

"Okay, I'll see what I can do I can't make any promises. I'm sure you understand that the Pentagon people have other things to do."

"I do understand, but please give it a shot."

It was some time before Bill called back. In the interim, Hank had talked to school authorities at Clemson again about protecting Hope, and he had once more for an audience with Senator Tompkins. Clemson assured him they were as concerned as he was about Hope's safety and had increased surveillance by campus police and her guidance counselor. The senator's office said he was very busy but would make room for a meeting as soon as he could. The Hilton Head police had increased surveillance, and more police cruisers were seen around Faith's apartment. Things were progressing, although Bev remained worried.

"I can't take much more of this," she said. "Everywhere I go I think I see strange men following me, not ones wanting to buy me a drink. This has got to stop."

Hank tried not to stay late at the office. Occasionally, he drove Bev to and from her shop. At his apartment, he made sure his pistol was close at hand and that the alarm system was activated. Finally, to his relief, West called back.

"Some army personnel guys dug up a file on a Randy Waters from 1950. Waters enlisted in 1947, but by 1948, he was a deserter at Schofield Barracks. He was caught and convicted of assault against a minor. Sentenced to fifteen years, he spent ten at Fort Leavenworth."

"He must have been let out on probation," Hank said.

"That's right. He did. He then went to Texas and worked at a sporting goods store in El Paso, a place that sold camping goods, fishing gear, and guns. He was on his best behavior and never missed a meeting with his parole officer. There is no indication he ever got into any trouble. He may have let off steam in Mexico because back then, it was easy to make frequent day trips to Juarez, but the Mexicans never reported him. After he served his parole, he was released from supervision. There are no other entries. As far as the military is concerned, Waters simply disappeared after that."

"If he's the same guy, I'm amazed that he ended up in Vietnam working in the C.O.O.R.D.S. program and supervising young children."

"There was a need for many different people in Vietnam."

"But how could C.O.O.R.D.S. put a guy from prison in charge of kids?"

"I am never amazed any more at how Washington can screw up.

The only thing they seem to be experts at is spending our money." Hank recalled that the C.O.O.R.D.S. operatives were volunteers, as were Phoenix teams. He asked Paul if the director of an orphanage in Vietnam would need to have some sort of degree to be accepted in the program, not be just a nothing who simply volunteered.

"As I recall," Paul said, "the demand was so great and the volunteers were so few that almost anybody was accepted. Remember that the orphanage was in an active war zone."

That didn't make any sense.

"Who would put a guy who had been convicted of child abuse in charge of an orphanage?"

"That's the way Washington sometimes works," Paul said. "But it's absurd," Hank said.

"It's also a fact."

He had to keep a clear head and not let Washington take charge.

CHAPTER FIFTY-THREE

On Wednesday afternoon, Blevins took a cab to a mall near Bill West's Reston office and listened through Sharon's bug as she and Tom entered West's place. Bill's receptionist welcomed them, offered coffee, and asked them to fill out a form for basic information. When they finished, she reviewed the form before leading them into Bill's office.

"Bill, this is Sharon and Tom Moore," she said. "Here's their questionnaire. They live in McLean and are looking for acreage."

Blevins had looked the pair over before they went. Tom had dressed for the occasion, wearing dark blue blazer, red tie, and khaki trousers. He had on a class ring and a Rolex. He looked prosperous. Sharon helped because she was an attractive woman of indeterminate age. With short, blond hair and blue eyes, she was showing some wear and tear but still appeared younger than her acting husband.

"Acreage?" Bill asked. "What did you have in mind?"

"We live near Tyson's Corner," Steve heard Tom say. "Our place is a perfect location. I take the underground into Washington and get off just two blocks from my office. It's an easy commute, less than hour. I love it, but our townhouse is small and we feel cooped up. We'd like to get away now and then. Could you find about twenty-five acres for us?"

"To build on?" Bill asked.

"Not right now," Tom said. "Later, we might want to build a retirement place. But for now, we're thinking about camping on the weekends."

"I want lots of acres," Sharon said. "And I want to plant trees all over the land. White Pines or something like them that would grow fast and be beautiful. I'd like some hills, not just flat land. I want a place with a view."

She was a hoot, Steve thought, *and as always, she was doing a great job.*

"Is such land available?" Tom asked.

"Not unless you go about an hour west of Tyson's Corner to Clarke, Warren, or Rappahannock County."

"An hour west sounds perfect," Sharon said. "Can you check the listings?" Tom asked.

"Something off the beaten track," Sharon said. "Hilly but not too steep."

"Maybe," Bill said, "but land out there can run two thousand an acre or more."

"Price is not a problem," Tom said. "But I agree with Sharon, we want a view."

"You say you live in McLean," Bill said. "What do you do?" "I consult for Lockheed Martin."

"We'd need most of a day to get out there and have time to look around," Bill said. "Can you take a full day off?"

"No," Tom said. "I'd prefer a Sunday."

"That sounds fun," Sharon said. "I could pack a cooler, and we could have a picnic. I'd love to see the region, even if we can't find exactly what we want at first. It would be fun to get away now and then."

"I agree," Tom said. "We'd take several trips. I'd hope to find something sooner or later."

"I could pick out several sites that might meet your expectation," Bill said. "I'll make sure they're still on the market and available to view. Can you be here by eight this Sunday?"

"No problem," Tom said.

"I'm so excited," Sharon said.

That Sunday, Blevins waited at the mall as Sharon and Tom drove to West's office. They arrived promptly at eight. They were casually dressed with comfortable shoes and warm coats. They carried a substantial cooler and agreed to ride with Bill and leave their

Cadillac in his lot. By eight-fifteen, they were headed west on Route 50.

Sharon's bug worked perfectly. Blevins could hear their conversation clearly.

"Why not take Route 66?" Tom asked. "It's bigger and faster."

"It's also in an overbuilt corridor," Bill said. "Not the kind of land you're looking for. On the road we're taking, you'll get to see more of the country and have a chance to size up how much development is taking place. If you ever buy some acreage, you could then use Route 66 to get there faster."

"Did you find some really good land for us?" Sharon asked. "Clarke County is filled up and a little pricey. But Warren County to its south has one good offering. Then Rappahannock County farther south has several good sites. We'll take Route 50 to Warren and look at that land. Then we'll take Route 340 down to Rappahannock County and look at those places. In that county, there are several good pieces on Route 231, a beautiful, remote, back road that I think you'll like. From there, we'll take Route 66 home and you'll see the difference from Route 50 we're on now."

Blevins heard Tom immediately reject the Warren site.

"Too busy, no view," he said. When they turned south to Rappahannock County and found Route 231, a two-lane winding road down a valley of farms and cattle, they were ecstatic. Bucolic was Sharon's description.

"This road looks perfect," she said. "Small and remote." "And look at those perfect hills to the west," Tom said.

"Here's the first site," Bill said about ten minutes later as he turned off the road and drove slowly east up a gravel and dirt road and stopped by a crude gate with a worn "For Sale" sign nailed to it. He had the combination to the lock and opened the gate. Then they walked about a hundred yards into a deserted vale surrounded by trees.

"This one's thirty-five acres and has a slight hill to our east that gives you a view of Old Rag Mountain to the west. Because it's a little remote, it's priced at two thousand an acre. I think the seller would bargain."

"It's perfect," Tom said and Blevins heard three muffled shots. "He's done," Tom said. "Let Steve know while I set the scene."

Blevins had been following in their car and when he arrived, Tom had taken Bill's wallet, watch, and ring. He had tossed the rest of the contents of Bill's pockets onto the ground. With Blevins's help, they stripped the radio, C.D. player, and tape deck from Bill's car. Not bothering to lock the gate, the three of them drove slowly back to Route 231, carefully scanning the area for onlookers. Before entering Route 231, they verified that Bill's car wasn't visible from the road. By noon, they were on Route 66 and headed east.

"Well done," Blevins said.

CHAPTER FIFTY-FOUR

On Wednesday, Hank called Bill West again with questions about Waters's personnel record. After many rings, Mrs. West answered in a quiet voice. When Hank asked to speak to Bill, she hesitated and then said Bill had been killed during a robbery Sunday. Shocked, he offered his condolences and asked if she could talk about it.

"It's not easy," she said, "but you were one of Bill's friends, so I'll tell you what I can. Last week, he made an appointment with a Tom and Sharon Moore to show them acreage in rural counties about an hour west from here, Warren and Rappahannock. The appointment was last Sunday, and he was to spend the entire day with them. When he neither returned nor phoned by evening, I called the police. At about noon the next day, two policemen came and said a body had been found on Route 231 in Rappahannock County. I went with them and identified Bill."

Then she started crying and Hank said he would call back later. "No," she said. "In a way, it helps a little to talk about it, breaks open the dam. And Bill always spoke so highly about you. So I'll try to tell you what I know. The police checked surveillance cameras at Bill's office, and they have pictures of a couple arriving Sunday morning. The couple and Bill got into his car and drove away. A few minutes later, another man came into Bill's parking lot and drove off in the Moore's car. The police think this was all planned and that the man then followed Bill's car, maybe with a tracking device. They have put out a bulletin about the robbery and attached pictures of this Tom and Sharon Moore. Our lawyer can tell you much more. I'll tell him to expect your call."

The attorney was receptive and had more information.

"Bill's secretary had interviewed this Tom and Sharon Moore," he said. "She described them completely to the police. When the police checked the data they provided, they found no people named Moore in the town houses they listed in McLean. Nobody named Tom Moore works for Lockheed Martin in Washington. As for the sheriff's suggestion that robbery might have been a possible motive, Mrs. West says that Bill might have been carrying no more than two or three hundred dollars with him. His watch was a Rolex, and that might be worth a thousand to an illegal. His ring had a good stone worth maybe five hundred. The stuff taken from his car might get two hundred. So the total take to a thief might come to three thousand dollars, more or less. In my opinion, that's a small haul for murder and such a complicated operation. Bill's credit cards were taken, but before we cancelled them, they had not been used. A second car was involved in the operation, and we found its tracks near Bill's car at the murder site. This was carefully planned, and I doubt that such a complicated scheme would be set up just for a few thousand dollars. There has to be something I'm not seeing."

"Maybe they didn't start out to kill Bill," Hank said, "but got off track somehow and had to kill him, maybe when he started to fight. Do you have copies of the photos of the man and woman? I'd like to show them around."

"I'll send them to you."

"Please stay in touch," Hank added. "I'll do whatever I can to help, and I have assets I can tap to pursue this. I want to attend any services and send flowers."

When Hank reached Paul and filled him in, Paul immediately reacted, "I agree with West's attorney. This was too complex an operation to have been a simple robbery. There were at least three people involved, guns, selection of a site, and some sort of tracking device for the getaway car. If it was robbery, the crooks would have used those credit cards quickly before they were cancelled. Something more is going on, pardon the pun, and I don't think it was a jealous husband. When you get those surveillance pictures, send them to Le Trang and have him show them to Kay and Sam. I think we should look at this as a possible retaliation for what happened in Juarez when one of Blevins's men was killed. There may be a connection to Blevins, Waters, Manh, or Orzon, not just a simple robbery."

They kicked it around for a while, and as they did, Hank wrote out a time line, starting with Blevins at the airport. Then Nung Manh and Orzon. Then the deaths of Ahn and Nung. Then the kidnappings. Bill West had known Nung Manh in Vietnam. And Hank had used Bill to track down Waters at the Pentagon. That was where the bad guys could have gotten Bill's name. Certainly, the agency could have been alerted, and that may have been how Blevins knew the names of everybody Bill had tasked for information. Hank had started a file after meeting Blevins in El Paso, and it was becoming larger and more valuable.

"Add Bill's killing to that file," Hank told Paul, "and link it to Blevins and the death of Gus Bean. It all fits together, and that file is why they took our computer hard drives. Make sure Ted Storm has a copy. Keep my copy up to date, and give copies to several people we can trust. Make sure that my contacts with Senator Tompkins and Steve Powell are in the file. It may, someday, be good leverage."

Chapter Fifty-Five

Blevins was acting rapidly. It was time for Hank to press Senator Tompkins for a meeting. He called the senator's office in Washington and got good news. Tompkins would be coming down to Columbia, South Carolina for Christmas, and he had agreed to see Hank during that visit. They met in December of 1987 at the senator's office in Columbia, and security was tight. Hank passed through metal detectors and was frisked by guards. After he produced his military identification, he was finally permitted to see the senator. Tompkins's reception was cordial, especially after Hank greeted him as, "General," his former military rank in the South Carolina National Guard.

"I hope security didn't harass you," the senator said. "Sometimes they can be rough, even for combat veterans, honorably discharged. I've asked for Steve Powell to sit in with me to see you. You remember him?"

"Yes, I certainly do," Hank said. "I want him to hear what I tell you, and I understand about the extra security, General. All military installations, like Fort Jackson near here, are on special alert. They have added extra guards on all gates. Every vehicle is being stopped. Everybody in the car has to have a current I.D. The military police won't make any exceptions, even for family member of active-duty personnel. They seem to think there is going to be some sort of attack. Terrorists maybe."

"I have heard such rumors," Tompkins said, "but, what can I do for you?"

"I need some special Washington favors."

"Steve is my expert on those," Tompkins said. "What's the problem?"

Hank handed a copy of the file he and Paul had been compiling.

"What I am about to tell you is spelled out in some detail in this file," he said. "This one is for you. I hope you and Steve will take time to look at it. My attorney and I have copies. We have given copies to Agent Storm at the F.B.I. and to several other people we trust."

Hank then went over what had happened to him, his daughters, and others during the last year. He tried to show the connection of those events to Waters's death at the orphanage, the death evidently at the hand of a member of a Phoenix team during the attack. He summarized the details of the deaths of Colonel and Mrs. Manh, Gus Bean, and Bill West, all perhaps killed or directed by a man named Blevins who claimed to be an agent. Finally, he explained that he had sent a F.O.I. request to the C.I.A. months ago, asking for information about that Phoenix team at the orphanage.

"They were Elliott and McMillian, but I got nothing from the agency."

"You wouldn't," Tompkins said. "Charles McMillian is a senior officer with the agency. He is in line to be nominated to become the director."

Hank sat back, surprised. No wonder the agency had refused to talk about him.

"I understand about McMillian," he said, "but I have several other questions. The first is a need to find the identity of this Blevins who you will see is present at or at lease relevant to many events I have laid out in the file. We know he orchestrated the kidnapping of Kay and Samantha Trang in El Paso and sent obscene pictures of Kay to her father before releasing her with demands that her father work for them and someone in Vietnam. I went into Juarez with some men and rescued the other girl, Samantha, who is just thirteen years old. Here is an account of that rescue."

He gave the senator the press release he and Paul had produced in El Paso and said, "I regret that we had to kill one of the kidnappers during that rescue."

Senator Tompkins sat back, shook his head, and stared at Hank.

Powell sputtered and finally asked in amazement, "Are you saying you took men across an international border and killed a kidnapper during an attack?"

"I did," Hank said. "The shooting was self-defense, and the thirteen-year-old made it home safely. In my defense, I have been investigated and released by the El Paso police."

"If you went into Mexico," Powell said after glancing at the press release, "with some men and killed someone, you are in one big pile of serious difficulty, a difficulty that has international implications. Neither our state department nor the Mexicans can tolerate an American going into Mexico and committing a felony. If this ever gets out, the state department might come after you and demand a federal indictment."

"That's exactly what the El Paso police thought," Hank said. "They questioned me and my attorney. We gave that press release to the El Paso police and the local news media. Some reporters tried to question us, but my attorney objected. Then the captain told me I was a person of interest and released me without bail. I have not been indicted."

"Not yet," Tompkins said. "But as Steve pointed out, the feds will be very angry at this, no matter what the El Paso district attorney thinks."

"I understand," Hank said, "but I have another matter to discuss. Believe it or not, the matter is much more important because it involves nuclear weapons and Saudi Arabia."

Senator Tompkins involuntarily stiffened and glanced at Powell, whose eyes widened. Then they both recovered and tried to look as normal as possible.

"Nuclear weapons?" Tompkins asked, as if he had not heard Hank.

Hank had seen the reaction. He had no doubt it had occurred. As well as the attempt to act as if nothing had happened.

"Yes," he said. "As you will see in the file, the idea of a theft of such weapons is a common theme that started when I visited Colonel Manh in El Paso last January. At first, I thought it was a fantasy made up by a drunk, Manuel Orzon, a retired Filipino officer. The story was that two nukes were stolen from West Germany and taken to Saudi Arabia. Then when Blevins brought it up, I asked F.B.I. Agent Storm to look into it. And a short time ago, he confirmed everything, including the fact that one of those weapons was recently set off in the Empty Quarter of Saudi Arabia. So the story has to be true."

"If so," Senator Tompkins asked, "how can I help?"

"I want to know, who this guy Blevins is and if the C.I.A. knows anything about the theft of nukes and their transfer to Saudi Arabia."

"First, I have a question of my own; a while ago I saw your name on a list of current intelligence operations. This one was code titled, 'Three Colonels.' The other two colonels were Manh and Orzon. What can you tell us about that operation?"

Hank sat back and thought about the senator's obvious attempt to make a quick change of subject. Was the senator hiding something? Why did he react sharply to the mere mention of nuclear weapons?

"I know absolutely nothing about such an operation," he said. "But Manh was the Vietnamese colonel I visited in El Paso, and Orzon was the Filipino colonel who visited Manh some ten years ago, the one who, after more than a few drinks, told Manh that the two nuclear weapons had been stolen from an American depot in West Germany. When Manh first told me about that, I said the story had to be non-sense because I worked with those weapons and would have known if there had such a theft. Manh claimed there was a cover up, but both he and Orzon are now dead. I hope I'm not the third colonel to die."

"Maybe that 'Three Colonels' operation the senator saw," Steve said, "was why you and your family were stopped and questioned by those agents."

"I suppose that could be true."

"Steve," the senator said, "I've known Colonel Kean for a long time, and I trust him when he says he wasn't involved with anything illegal or with that Three Colonels operation. I want to find out what's going on. Give this high priority. If a government agency is involved, I want to find out who and why. Make sure Clemson University knows that I want them to protect Kean's daughter at school there. Keep me and Colonel Kean informed."

"Yes, sir," Powell said.

"And Colonel Kean," the senator said, "I will do everything in my power to assist you. Keep me up to date. Copy me with anything you learn. And when Steve has some answers, I want you to come to Washington and discuss them with me. Thanks again for your service."

He then got up, shook hands, and left the office.

Hank thanked Powell and went back to Hilton Head feeling much better. The skies had brightened. He had an important ally. Once home, he called Bev and told her about Senator Tompkins, Powell, and his successful meeting with them.

"Thank God," she said. "I was really worried. I'm sure they'll help you. But you still need to stay out of trouble."

Fat chance.

CHAPTER FIFTY-SIX

Three weeks later, Powell called from Washington. "Somebody up here doesn't like you."

"How can you tell?" Hank asked.

"They cursed when I pressed them for the information you wanted. At first, they said they had nothing they could reveal. In fact, if Senator Tompkins hadn't been requesting this stuff, I doubt if I'd have gotten zilch. But they finally, reluctantly, came through. I have replies from State and C.I.A. Various tidbits. I'll send a package."

"Can you summarize it?"

"The C.I.A. confirmed that Phoenix employees, McMillian and Elliott, were in Hau Nghia Province during April of 1968. They said that McMillian is still with the agency but Elliott died in Vietnam in 1968, possibly by enemy fire. The C.I.A. also said that it has files on a Colonel and Mrs. Manh and their adopted son, Le Trang. The family was questioned by the agency more than ten years ago. They were asked about connections with North Vietnam or the Viet Cong, but there is no derogatory information about them in C.I.A. records. State said U.S.A.I.D. records showed the hire of a Randy Walter in the early sixties and his being assigned to Khiem Cuong City in Hau Nghia Province in 1967. They included several of his performance reports as Director at the orphanage before he was killed in a Viet Cong attack during Tet. The cause of death was listed as enemy fire, but there were no details. Nobody at state or treasury has ever contacted anybody in your family. Senator Tompkins wants you to look at these data and then come up here to brief him. He sees major political implications, because Charley McMillian, the Phoenix agent who was there when Waters was killed, is in line to be nominated by the president to be the deputy director of the C.I.A.

That's important because whoever becomes the deputy will most likely soon become the director. My full report is in the mail to you."

When he received the report, Hank called Paul and summarized it. "Interesting," Paul said. "Is there anything about Elliott's death?" "The report just says, 'enemy action,' like Waters."

"But Waters's death might not really have been enemy action," Paul said. "And the deaths of Manh, Orzon, Bean, and West tell me that enemy action may not have killed Elliott. But more important is the fact that all those government agencies deny that any of them ever contacted you guys. If they are telling the truth, it means that somebody like the Pentagon or the C.I.A. is doing this. Whoever is involved is powerful and ruthless, just the kind of person capable of running the C.I.A. And if Tompkins is correct when he says that McMillian is in line to become the deputy director, I worry about that. Because the director is in daily contact with the president, briefing him on worldwide intelligence matters. That includes data coming out of Vietnam and matters concerning nuclear weapons. If information comes to light that indicates McMillian is not fit for the deputy job, it may derail the nomination and embarrass the president. Half-truths and sensational allegations could be used by the democrats. That may be what Powell meant when he told me that people up in Washington don't like you. It is also conformation that everything in Washington is political."

"The names Waters and McMillian have stirred up some memories," Hank said, "bad memories I'd just a soon forget, flashbacks from fifty years ago. Things happened when I was just a kid, and I barely remember them, don't really want to. I need to think about them."

He decided to call his father. To see if Hank had correctly remembered what had happened and if his father remembered anything more, something Hank might have forgotten.

"Hello, Dad," Hank started with. "How are things in Clearwater?" "Florida is always nice in the winter," his father said, "but hot as hell in the summer. As I remember, Hilton Head was just about the same. I'm fine, but your mother is having problems with memory. Pray for her. What can I do for you?"

"First, tell Mom I love her. But I really want information about what happened to Charley McMillian and me in the woods behind Schofield Barracks in Hawaii just before the Korean War started. Something has come up that I kind of remember, but it's important that I get it right. It has to do with an incident involving an army deserter named Waters who attacked Charley in those woods. I kind of remember seeing Waters attacking Charley before I ran home in panic to get you. I led you and some soldiers to the place where I had seen Waters attacking Charley. Waters had said he was a scout in training, but I thought he was a deserter. I'm pretty vague about the exact details, and I need to get it right. Do you remember anything?"

"That's something I have never been able to forget," his father said. "It was nasty stuff and we didn't want you boys to have to testify at a court-martial. So the McMillians asked the court to reduce the charges against Waters to desertion and assault. He pled guilty to both and was sentenced to fifteen years. I thought that was too easy on him. By the time the trial was over, the Korean War had started. I wanted him to be sent to Korea and be made the point man on nightly patrols into North Korean lines until he caught a bullet, but I could not persuade anybody to agree with me. So the judge sent him to safety in prison at Fort Leavenworth."

"He served ten years," Hank verified. "Then he got out on parole, went to Vietnam, and died under fire there in 1968 in War Zone C. I was with him when he died. But one thing I need to know more about, what happened to Charley McMillian later on?"

"The army quickly sent McMillian family home to the mainland as a medical emergency. I stayed in touch with his father, and he said Charley was in really bad shape, had to undergo extensive treatment, mental and physical. I'm told that a person never really recovers from an experience like what Waters did to him, never. That's why if I had been the court's president, Waters would have been executed."

"He may have been executed in Vietnam during Tet."

Hank then told his father the story of the V.C. attack on the orphanage, Waters's injury, and his subsequent death on Hank's chopper.

"I have vivid memories of his death, but I wanted to be very clear about Charley as a result of Waters. What happened to him after medical treatments back in the States?"

"His family retired in McLean. We corresponded with them now and then, Xmas cards and such. As I remember, Charley eventually graduated from Georgetown University in the district. Then he disappeared into the C.I.A."

It was true. Charley McMillian was the Phoenix agent that might have shot Waters during that V.C. attack. And now, according to Senator Tompkins, he was being considered for director of the C.I.A. It was unthinkable; a mentally disturbed killer in close contact with the president of the United States. It had to be stopped. Too much was wrong. Charley had to be stopped. The C.I.A. had to be stopped, had to find another way to thwart the Chinese, had to eliminate Charley from the picture. Hank was exposed.

CHAPTER FIFTY-SEVEN

After talking to his father and writing down a time line, Hank was convinced the Central Intelligence Agency was the mysterious, powerful organization Detective Geaches had described as being behind the El Paso kidnappings. The agency might also have been responsible for the murder of Ahn Manh, maybe even Nung Manh's death. And the several appearances of Blevins since Hank first met him made him Hank's candidate as an agency agent masterminding those crimes. Finally, after Hank had shot his agent and rescued Sam, Blevins had warned that he would retaliate. After that, Gus and Bill died.

Hank called Paul and laid out the details of Waters's assault on young Charley McMillian and subsequent hire by the agency.

"Charley killed Waters. What's more, I believe Charley was somehow involved in the theft of those weapons from West Germany and delivered to Saudi Arabia. I can't see the connection, but I think it's there. And here's something else for you to think about; I was talking to Senator Tompkins about McMillian and mentioned the theft of those weapons and the fact that one of them had been set off in Saudi Arabia. You should have seen Tompkins's kneejerk reaction; he couldn't cover it up. His eyes got wide and he glanced quickly at Steve Powell, who showed a similar response. I had hit a nerve. Both were startled. They quickly recovered, but it was there; McMillian is connected to the nuclear theft, and Tompkins knows more than he admits about that. It may explain why he called me down to Washington in seventy-four after I had written my thesis at the war college about Saudi Arabia. He wanted to know more than my thesis about how things are done in Saudi Arabia and who controls everything there. I explained a few things for him."

"That may be true," Paul said, "but it makes no difference as far as you are concerned. I agree that McMillian may be important, and must be on the table, but you are still the one who is in danger of becoming Blevins's next victim. That is what you need to concentrate on."

Paul was right, but it looked like there was nothing more Hank could do immediately. He had to be patient. Maybe Senator Tompkins could find out if Blevins was with the agency. Maybe Powell could put pressure on the El Paso district attorney and force him to exhume Nung's body. Maybe the Worchester police would listen to Mrs. Bean about Gus's death. Maybe Mrs. West's attorney would dig up something about Bill's murder. Hank had to wait, hang on, and hope. To feel better, he phoned Bev again to suggest they go to Riley's for drinks and supper at the same table where they met. She agreed.

They went at five and with great hope he led her to their booth. Riley's hadn't changed. At the bar, under loud music, a boisterous crowd of studs and young gals mixed, drank, and looked for a hook up. At their booth away from the loud crowd, Bev and Hank had burgers and cocktails, relaxed, and reminisced about how awkward they had been the first time they had met. He ordered a second round. She seemed happy. He didn't remember much after that, except they left arm in arm and were together in bed. The rest of the evening was a blur. He was still groggy when he awoke the next morning, alone in his apartment. When he called her later, she put him off. Said she didn't feel right. But the memory was enough, and he heard his mother's voice, "Under the happy white clouds, he was new again."

It didn't last. After a week he and Bev received large, brown envelopes in the mail. Inside were vivid pictures of the two of them unconscious on an un-made bed in some motel. Both of them were nude and wrapped around each other in various suggestive positions, spooned and intertwined sexually. They looked like fake dummies arranged by a lecherous producer. A note said that copies had been sent to Faith and Hope, and added, "Watch out, because the next time we will do much more than just take pictures."

Bev did not answer his calls and voice mails. After several days, he went to see her, but she did not answer the door. He called Paul and told him about the pictures.

"Face it." Paul said. "They have you under constant observation. How else could they have been at the club to slip you knockout drops? They did this to demonstrate their power. But they made a mistake; they showed they had the ability to do whatever they wanted, but they did not kill you. That was an error, because when they had you helpless and under their power, they could have killed you, just as they killed West and Bean. Because they did not, we now know something very valuable; they want you alive. Why that is, I do not know but my guess is that you have something they want. Remember how they ransacked our places. They were looking for something. And the fact that they took the hard drives of our computers, tells me they were looking for your file, the one we are keeping on them. You must have data they fear. I don't know why that is, but I know that file gives you leverage. My guess is that they will come at you again and soon. When they do, remember to use that leverage."

CHAPTER FIFTY-EIGHT

The bad guys were out there watching and waiting. The next targets could be Faith or Hope. The situation was evolving, and something was going to happen. Then Le Trang called, and the puzzle started to unravel.

"Colonel Thuc Quan just contacted me," Le said. "He's still in Hau Nghia Province. When he led the attack on the orphanage, during the Tet Offensive, he was a major, but his rank today was that of a colonel. He's evidently in a position of authority, obviously more than just a colonel in the Viet Cong."

"He must have survived the war and risen in the post-war government," Hank said. "I wonder why he never went back north. He may now be the province commander and have clout. What did he want?"

"He wants to talk to you. He didn't say why or what about, but my guess is that this may be the connection with Vietnam that Kay told us the kidnappers wanted me to set up. This may what he wants, and he says there will be no more violence if you talk to him."

"Is he going to call me?"

"No. He wants you to come to Vietnam."

Hank was shocked and Paul was negative. They met and talked about the idea. Paul related it to the fact the Hank was not killed when Blevins drugged him, but had let him live. Hank didn't want to go back to Vietnam, but Paul claimed that there would be little risk if the bad guys really needed Hank alive for some reason. If that was so, there would be much to gain if Hank met with Colonel Quan. Paul asked if Hank could really trust Le Trang.

"I don't know about that, but we better find out why wants me in Vietnam."

"Okay, let's have Trang send the colonel a wire and tell him that a trip to Vietnam would be expensive and time consuming, perhaps not even permitted by our state department. Visas would be required by both countries. Say it seems out of the question."

Quan's answer came back quickly.

"He says that you will be his guest in Vietnam," Le said. "He will pay your expenses in country. In addition, he will assemble a number of very wealthy investors for you address in a seminar. Many such Vietnamese are doing well now because of their Chinese contacts, and they want to put their new wealth to work. Quan points out that your firm would be excellent way for them to get started. He promises to set up a meeting at the new Sheraton in Ho Chi Minh City. He attached a dozen names of potential investors. He says his government will be very receptive if you apply for a visa."

"Why would a financial seminar be important to Quan?" Hank asked Paul. "I think the seminar idea us just an excuse. Quan must want to talk about something else. I don't know what that could be, but if talking to him will stop these killings, I think I might go there, much as I hate that place. I wonder if Quan had anything to do with Waters's and the Manhs's deaths or the Phoenix team at the orphanage. Now that we know McMillian is still with the agency, he might be Quan's connection. But I wonder if Le is working with Quan. He may be more involved that I thought. It occurs to me that maybe Colonel Quan really wants me to come there, so he can act out his anger and kill me."

A sober thought, but possible. In spite of that danger and as much as Hank hated Vietnam, he was willing to return if it would clear up the mess of the past year. Could he get a visa? Where would he find the money for trip expenses? He didn't know, but he went ahead and asked his firm expenses and applied for a visa.

The money problem disappeared. Hank's superiors quickly agreed to fund the trip. Contact with the Vietnamese millionaires listed in Quan's message evidently pleased them. His manager thought it was a great opportunity to reach Chinese money through them.

He needed that visa, but the White House and Congress had tight travel restrictions. The state department was faced with many confusing new rules and regulations. Requests like Hank's were taking months. A new wave of hysteria filled Washington over airliners flying there from Europe, the Middle East, and Asia, with suicide bombers aboard. He didn't have much hope. But something strange was going on, because Washington and Vietnam approved the visa requests in less than a month. He went to Paul and made out a will providing for Bev, Faith, and Hope. And he told Paul to push Ted Storm to find out what was going on with the stolen nuclear weapons in Saudi Arabia.

Bev answered him. She was not happy. "This is a worse idea than you going into Juarez. You'll be far away from us, in a land where we fought a war. Anything could happen."

Her reaction seemed to show she cared for him, and he tried to reassure her. He wasn't as confident as he sounded. The darkness around him was so deep that he saw none of those dingle stars above Hilton Head. He had never seen any in Vietnam.

He was headed for a country he hated.

CHAPTER FIFTY-NINE

Hank was in his office doing last-minute chores before he left for Vietnam, when his phone rang. Thinking his secretary had put a client on the line, he answered, "This is Hank Kean. How may I help you?"

"You can shut up and listen carefully," Onorato said. "I don't have much time, so I want you to get out a yellow pad and take notes. This call is important."

"Hello to you, too."

"I told you to shut up and listen, and I meant it this call can save your life. Just pay attention and take notes. You have to understand that I have been promoted. I now have an office very high up, so high it has a window from which I can see the Potomac River. I run a department that listens to phone calls and tapes messages. Both may be illegal, and that is why I did not want this job. I enjoyed running agents and did not want to stop. That didn't make any difference. The highest mucky-monk said that if I refused the promotion, I would be let out to pasture. So I took the job, with one proviso—I would be allowed to continue as a handler with one agent; you. I know you are headed for Vietnam to talk to Colonel Quan. I tried to stop that, because he plans to kill you. Bur some nuts higher than me blocked my efforts and approved your trip. I need you alive, so I am about to tell you two things that may stop Quan from killing you. Put them in your memory. When Quan looks like he is about to pull the trigger, you tell him you have a file that will be published if you die. If that happens, Quan knows his dream of McMillian as director of the C.I.A. will be derailed. Quan has been working with McMillian since before the attack that killed Director Waters. He believes that if McMillian becomes director, he will have direct access to the president, access he needs in order to stop China in the South China Sea. If McMillian's nomination is derailed, Quan will fail. Here are the two points you raise before Quan kills you. First, McMillian worked with Quan to organize the attack on the orphanage and kill Waters. McMillian was the one that pulled the trigger and killed him. If your file is published with that in it, Quan's dreams are finished. Point number two; with McMillian's knowledge, Quan was the one who recruited Colonel Orzon to hire the Sayyaf terrorists to steal those two nukes from that depot in Germany. Another individual whose name I cannot tell you masterminded the operation. But he funded the whole thing, hired Pakistani scientists to create the dummy nukes that the Sayyaf substituted for the stolen ones, and sent the stolen nukes to Saudi Arabia. His name is top secret on a need-to-know basis, and you don't need to know. Tell Quan that if you are killed, his role in the theft will be published and end any hopes he has for access to the president. I hope these two facts will save your life because I need you. A war with Saddam Hussein is heating up, and the fight between Iran and Saudi Arabia will be front burner. Your knowledge of Saudi Arabia will be vitally important. If you return alive from Vietnam, we will talk. I say if you return, because Quan is a violent man. If you kill his hopes of influencing the president, he may kill you out of pure spite. I do not think he will, but you never know. Good luck."

Chapter Sixty

Hank told Paul that Onorato had called about the Vietnam trip and had given him two ways to avoid Quan's danger. Paul pointed out that Blevins had never attacked Hank directly, and both had seemed to reinforce the idea that Hank was not in any kind of personal jeopardy. Paul recommended Hank proceed and offered to act as his home base during the trip. Both of them were hopeful that a face-to-face meeting with Quan might stop the bad happenings, so they resolved to continue. But late at night, as Hank tossed and turned, he had wild dreams about returning to a country he hated and facing a man Onorato had called violent and vindictive.

Hank's firm exercised a modicum of fiscal restraint by disapproving first-class tickets and giving him business-class round- trip tickets to Hong Kong. Quan had specified that Hank go to the Hong Kong Hilton and wait, but the colonel said he would pick up all costs in Hong Kong and Vietnam. Hank's flight to Hong Kong was loud, uncomfortable, long, and tiring. On the other hand, the taxi trip from the airport over the hills to the Hilton on the Hong Kong was a memorable experience. The narrow road twisted and turned through spectacular mountains and revealed magnificent views before dipping into manicured polo fields. The driver took the turns a bit faster than Hank appreciated and then laughed when he saw an alarmed look on Hank's face. All during the swerving, skidding trip, the man smiled and delivered a well-practiced travelogue about the history of Hong Kong. His skill was as good as his monologue, and Hank arrived safely at the Hilton, where he was welcomed with Oriental courtesy.

"Please sign in, Colonel Kean," the manager said. "Enjoy your stay."

"How long will I be here?" Hank asked.

"I do not know, but until Colonel Quan contacts you, please be our guest."

Hank's comfortable room had a very large picture window that looked west at Hong Kong's magnificent harbor and the setting sun. The harbor was a wide expanse of sparkling blue water full of Chinese junks, pleasure boats, fishing craft, and the air-cushioned ferries to Macao. To his left were the hills he had just passed through. On his right was the shoreline of China, now controlling much of the city's affairs. Beautiful hills and sparkling water contrasted with the looming dark Peoples Republic. Again and again, his eyes returned to the grand harbor spread out before him. Arguably the most scenic he had ever enjoyed, it dwarfed San Francisco and recalled Kipling's road to Mandalay.

On his coffee table, he found a basket of fresh fruit in an exquisite oriental black and gold lacquered basket. Opposite the picture window was a wide-screen television showing a European golf tournament and the king-sized bed looked especially welcome after his long journey. The Hilton was as luxurious as Delta's business- class seats had been cramped. He lay back, stretched out his legs, and watched the magnificent water scene before him. Life was looking better and much in contrast to his memory of the Vietnamese jungles.

He sent a wire to Paul telling him of the tiring trip and safe arrival. He tried to describe the magnificent Hong Kong harbor but soon realized that words were inadequate, so he simply told Paul about the excellent hotel and the splendid water scene. He didn't paint too grand a picture for fear of increasing Paul's suspicions of a Quan trap.

For the next three days, he enjoyed the sights and sounds of the great, historic city. The Chinese turned out to be excellent stewards, and the rewards of their brand of semi-capitalism were apparent everywhere. Each morning, hundreds of people gathered on the boardwalk below the hotel for Tai Chi exercises. During the day, traffic jammed the city streets and people filled the stores. Every business he entered was stocked with quality goods. Apparently, the Chinese had not erected any impediment to commerce. He never saw a

Chinese soldier, and the police presence was discrete. The restaurants were crowded and the considerable costs of those at the Hilton were covered by Colonel Quan. Hank used the well-equipped hotel spa, swimming pool, and exercise room to make up for his generous samplings of the bourbon and international cuisine. He needed to be ready for his visit to the mysterious Colonel Quan.

He checked at the hotel front desk each morning and night for messages and word from his Vietnamese host. On the third day, the clerk handed him a brown envelope that contained plane tickets for the following day on Vietnam Airlines. He had a noon departure for the short flight to Ho Chi Minh City. Accompanying instructions indicated that at his destination, he was to show the officials at customs an enclosed letter from Colonel Quan that apparently would speed him through. He was then to find a cab and show the driver another card from the colonel. The driver would take him to his hotel, the Sheraton, where reservations had been made in his name. A generous supply of South Vietnamese currency was enclosed.

Hank remembered an Intercontinental Hotel in war torn Saigon, but not a Sheraton. If this was a new hotel as luxurious as the Hong Kong Hilton, he was in for a treat. Saigon, now Ho Chi Minh City, must be thriving. He wanted to see the changes that communism had brought to South Vietnam. He looked forward to the trip, and he was committed now. Still, he could not shake his wonder at why Quan had asked him to return. Would he die at Quan's hand?

The Hilton's cab swiftly took Hank to the Hong Cong airport, where the staff provided him with an escort who shepherded him efficiently to the departure lounge. Colonel Quan's letter seemed to arouse immediate responses, and when boarding call came, Hank was the first to board. When he was seated, an attractive Vietnamese stewardess offered him a glass of wine and *hors d'oeuvre*. Seeking to be alert and aware, he declined both.

The flight took about an hour. A sparkling new airport greeted him at Ho Chi Minh City, with wide runways much improved from what he had known some thirty years earlier. The airport was larger than he remembered, and the ubiquitous gun emplacements were gone. The sparkling clean terminal indicated capitalism was thriving, not the decay of communism.

When Hank produced Colonel Quan's letter at customs, it worked wonders. He was ushered to a reception lounge and offered a beverage while he waited for processing. His baggage soon appeared and he was guided quickly to a cab. He showed the driver Quan's note, and the man whisked him through crowded streets to the sparkling new Sheraton, where he was warmly greeted and taken to the front desk. The place looked more like a major Washington hotel than the embattled Saigon establishments of the war years.

At the front desk, he found a message from Colonel Quan asking him to meet in the lounge at five o'clock. Once in his clean, well apportioned room, Hank had plenty of time to use the modern shower and close his eyes on the wide, comfortable bed. His trip had been well done, and he did not feel threatened. The sun was shining. Life was better than he had thought it would be.

Chapter Sixty-One

At five p.m., rested and refreshed, he went to the lounge, where he inquired if a Colonel Quan was present. Directed to a spacious rear booth, he found a trim, uniformed officer who rose to offer a firm handshake. The former enemy uniform put Hank back a few years, but the man did not look like a killer. He was gracious, had white hair, and looked to be in his fifties.

"I am Colonel Quan," he said with a nod. "Welcome back." "Thanks," Hank said. "The airport, city, and this hotel look better than I remembered."

"Peace has been good for Vietnam, as has retirement for you." Over drinks, bourbon for Hank, wine for Quan, Hank unwound.

Small plates of snacks arrived from time to time, and he sampled a few, finding them excellent. Soon, all remnants of his apprehension and fatigue caused by his long trip from Atlanta had disappeared. He even looked forward to visiting the province in which he had fought.

"Let me tell you about your seminar tomorrow," Quan said. "Fifteen investors will arrive at ten and meet you in the conference room. After our supper here, I will take you to that room to see if it is suitable for your seminar. I have reserved it for two hours, although I suggest you speak for less and leave time for questions. The attendees are quite wealthy and eager to invest. In your room, you will find data on each. For the conference, an interpreter will be available."

"I won't need a mike," Hank said, "but I would like the hotel to make copies of some handouts and an attendee questionnaire. I would hope that the handouts could be done on glossy paper in full color. I want a blackboard. Would these be a problem?"

"Not at all. Give the questionnaires to me after supper and I will have them in the conference room in the morning. I will provide

"

your blackboard. You will find the interpreter to be excellent. Is there anything else I can tell you?"

"Tell me what you have planned for the rest of my time in your country?"

"The day after tomorrow, we will drive to Hau Nghia Province. We will spend a full day there and return here the following day. You are scheduled to fly home the next day."

"Le Trang indicated that you wanted me to come to Vietnam because you had to discuss something very important, something you needed to say face to face. May I know what that something is?"

"China, but we will talk about that later."

China? No mention had been made of China before this. How did that nation fit into the picture? What concern did Hank have there? He sent a wire to Paul that brought him up to date. In it, he asked Paul to try to find a Chinese connection. Maybe Ted Storm or Onorato could shed some light.

In his dreams that night, he fought a nuclear-armed Chinese dragon.

Chapter Sixty-Two

Fifteen investors showed up for the seminar. Questionnaires and handouts were waiting for them as they took their seats in three rows before Hank. Whiting pads and pencils were at each place, a blackboard was ready, and a translator stood by. When they had settled down, a stern looking Colonel Quan in an immaculate uniform introduced Hank in Vietnamese.

Hank spoke for fifty minutes, taking his time to allow his translated words to sink in. He used the blackboard to construct a "financial pyramid." Conservative investments like insurance and annuities were at the base of the pyramid. Real estate was on the next level, and above that were stocks and bonds. At the speculative top were options and commodities. Backing up the pyramid and anchoring it were retirement plans. He used the handouts to clarify each of the subjects. He then explained that he would spend the afternoon meeting with anyone who wished. After that, Hank opened the seminar for questions. The attendees were interested enough to ask questions for about thirty minutes.

Colonel Quan acted as coordinator through lunch and the afternoon individual sessions. When the last of those was over and the investors were gone, Quan gave instructions, "Be ready to leave the hotel at eight in the morning," he said. "Bring only a small overnight bag. Leave everything, except your valuables, in your hotel room. Management will put your valuables in the hotel safe."

Then he turned abruptly and disappeared without further comment.

When Hank emerged from the hotel in the morning, the colonel was waiting in the back of a new Renault sedan. In the front were a driver and a uniformed aide who opened the back door for Hank.

Without ceremony, the car pulled away from the hotel and headed west.

Colonel Quan was silent until Hank spoke. "Thanks for setting up that seminar," he said. "It was very successful. I was quite pleased. I have prepared a package of information about the attendees, and I hope you will arrange for it to be mailed home. During individual sessions, the investors seemed happy. All in all, I thought it was well done. What did you think of it?"

"I was disgusted," Quan said. "You were discussing something completely foreign to the principles under which Chairman Ho built our country. You were talking about money and how it can be used to control people. The chairman did not believe in using money to control his people. Money is the tool of your failed capitalism. People must not be controlled by financial means. They should be the real owners of the country. Everything that is of value in a society, especially one like ours, belongs to the peasants and the workers. The peasants must control the land, and the workers must control the factories. Nothing else creates value. What you were talking about was a return to the failed French colonial-capitalist system that we rejected because we hated everything about it. I did not like that system and your ideas about it, and that is why I did not enjoy the seminar. Those rich pigs that attended wanted only to make more money. I hated them, but you need not worry, I will fulfill my obligations to you."

Gone was the affable, friendly gentleman Hank had met the first day. In its place was a fanatic, an unpredictable man not to be trusted or believed. Hank was in danger. He took a deep breath and a chance.

"With all due respect," Hank said, "what you say about farmers and workers may have been true a century ago, but today, farms and factories aren't enough. The world has become interdependent, and a country like yours needs international capital to succeed. Think about Indochina before the French, a backward region unable to control its future. The French brought money, engineers, and a banking center. Soon, they had built the irrigation system, dikes, and financial structure that transformed southern Indochina into the rice basket of Southeast Asia and made it powerful again. You need to do that today on an international level. You need an advanced financial system, one that is capitalist, not socialist. China is well on its way to becoming one of the financial giants of the world. If you remain a rural land of peasants and workers, China will swallow you."

Colonel Quan stiffened, turned, and stared at him. Then he lectured, "You are wrong when you say that this country was nothing before the French came. The emperor at Hue ruled Annam in central Vietnam and controlled both Tonkin in the north and Cochin China in the south. We were a powerful regional country then, and we will be again. If the Chinese try to swallow us, we will defeat them again, as we always have."

Quan was a soldier, apparently fixated on war and physical combat. Hank was talking about other means. He needed to shift the emphasis, "But the weapons of this fight will not be guns. They will be more capital intensive. You need to understand how capital can be used to make you strong. You need friends on the world stage that can give you access to that capital and the goods you require. The investors I spoke to yesterday seemed to understand that. They appeared to be happy with what they heard. Many told me that they were looking forward to working with me and my firm. They wanted to be friends again with America."

This apparently angered Quan even more. He paused, then spoke louder and more stridently, glaring at Hank, "Vietnam does not need friends, only allies of convenience. The Chinese were our friends during the Indochina War. We needed the Chinese then to defeat first the French and then the United States. We defeated both the French and you. As soon as you left, however, the Chinese attacked us, as they have many times in the past. We defeated them once again, I repeat, as we always have. If they attack again, we will beat them again. You are correct when you say that the Chinese are growing ever more powerful. That is why I asked you to come to Vietnam. Our future is very important, and China will be a part of it. We will talk about that tomorrow. I did not kill you before when I had a chance. I let you live because I was convinced you could be helpful to Vietnam. When you cease to be helpful, our relationship will change."

Quan then turned away, signaling that the conversation was over.

Hank didn't like the ominous sound of that. Onorato was right. The shadows of Vietnam deepened. Bev was correct to tell him not to return. Not for the first time, Hank had serious questions about what was going to happen to him in the next few days. Was Colonel Quan taking him to Hau Nghia Province to kill him? He was far from support and he had no way out. He mentally thanked Onorato for the phone call warning. He put Onorato's ammunition foremost in his mind. Would it be enough? He had been right to complete his will and arrange his affairs with Paul.

As a slight rain began to fall, Hank shivered. He was not going into a good and gentle night. Sleep would not come easily that evening. If anyone came for him tonight, it would not be Jamila, the beautiful Bedouin gal offering a gentle massage.

He was alone again.

Chapter Sixty-Three

A silent hour passed as Hank watched his world go by. Route One leading west through Tay Ninh to Cambodia had changed. Gone were the narrow, pot-holed roads Hank remembered from the war. In their place was a recently paved, clearly marked highway with substantial shoulders. The always considerable traffic had also changed from beat-up, ancient cars and overloaded small trucks to late model automobiles and sleek large trucks. New taxis, motor scooters, and bicycles darted through the mass without fear. No holes in the road, no mines had been set by the Viet Cong. They came to the Hoc Mon Bridge, a place that in the war had been one of constant danger for American soldiers from frequent insurgent attacks. The bridge had been a choke point, which the American military had to traverse. The V.C. had concentrated in the area. Many attacks occurred there and resulted in numbers of Americans being killed or wounded. But this bridge was new and the adjacent village held thriving businesses.

"The bridge was a wreck when I was here," Hank said. "This place was dangerous. We had to increase our security and add armored vehicles wherever we crossed."

Quan waited before replying, "We knew that your trucks had to pass through here to reach the capitol. So we stationed a battalion nearby and ordered mining and ambushes. They did well, creating much damage to your convoys."

They passed the road to Cu Chi, Hank's former base. The new road heading north was wide and welcoming. "What's at Cu Chi now?"

"A museum. People go there to see the tunnels. We preserved those tunnels because they were a triumph. At the end of the war, we had almost as many men living under your feet as you had on the surface, and you never knew it."

Hank shuddered at the thought, and not long after, they came to the left turn toward Khiem Cuong and the orphanage. The road was not the dirt and gravel one that Hank remembered, but wide, paved, and newly painted.

"For the first time in fifty years," Quan said, "our people here are at peace."

"Hau Nghia Province used to be hotly contested," Hank said. "What happened to the people? Is there no resistance to communism?"

"None. All traitors have repented, been killed, or fled."

As they passed the orphanage from which Hank had taken Waters, Hank saw no barbed wire and bunkers. The jungle to the west was cleared, and the place looked like a peaceful school.

When they arrived at the house where they were to spend the night, Hank saw that it was not a bamboo hut, but a large building with stucco walls, a red-tiled roof, and an impressive garden. The sprawling one-story building spoke of quality and in its rear was a spacious open room that bordered a wide deck next to the softly flowing Oriental River. Across the river, a thick jungle reminded that this was Vietnam.

"Is this the kind of housing that communism brings?" Hank asked. "Of course not," Quan said. "This place was built by a French banker and the South Vietnamese government as a residence for a capitalist fat cat. When the Americans came, it housed your province advisor, with a staff and security force. I considered attacking it but I did not, because I had several of my men on the staff and they gave me good intelligence."

That afternoon, they had cocktails on a wide, square, new deck and sitting around a table by the water. Hank relaxed and watched the little fishing skiffs drifting over still water. Quan was no longer the fanatic.

"Your baggage and room will be readied by a hostess," he said. "She will give you a massage before you sleep."

"I'll skip the massage, but I note that you are living better," Hank said. "You used to share a cave with the Viet Cong. When did you come south?"

"Chairman Ho knew we would have to fight the French again because your President Truman let the French return and the colonial system resurface. When we defeated the French once more, the Americans betrayed us at Geneva. So, Chairman Ho began building his trail to the south. When it was ready, he ordered me to go down. I went willingly, because everyone in my country is a soldier, men and women. We have always had to fight to be free. Nothing has changed. That is a fact of life for everyone in my country. By age sixteen, I had reached the south, and I was one of the first to make the journey. I walked most of the way and the trip took four months. I am still here. That is my history. What is yours?"

"My father was an army officer," Hank said. "He was injured when the Japanese attacked Pearl Harbor, and he had to retire with only a small pension. He became a mechanic, and we had little money. I joined the army, so I had a job and could marry my girlfriend. The army tested me and offered a long-term contract that sent me to college. They gave me an advanced degree to study Arabic and the Middle East. I even studied nuclear weapons."

At that last remark, Quan sat up sharply and stared at Hank. Then he stood and began pacing, nodding and talking to himself. Hank had touched a nerve, like when he mentioned nukes to Senator Tompkins. The puzzle had surfaced again. Then a servant brought crab cakes, egg rolls, and another drink. Finally, the colonel stopped pacing, calmed, and sat back down.

Hank tried again, "At first, I didn't understand why they wanted me to study nuclear weapons, but they told me I was headed for the Middle East, and that nuclear weapons were becoming a problem for the region. They said I had important work to do in Saudi Arabia and I would be serving my country in many ways."

Silent for a moment, Colonel Quan asked who had given Hank those orders.

"Good men," Hank said. "People trying to do the right thing. I trusted them because they seemed honest and sincere. That was what I like about the army; there is little corruption. And whatever we were doing, we were in it together. A military unit is much like a family. Even today, when I think about the men, I served with over the years, I have good memories about them, much different from my bad memories of Vietnam itself. Too many died here, on both sides, partly because America fought the war badly. It turned out to be what the author Mark Twain called a quagmire."

"A quagmire?" Quan asked. "That is an interesting word. I would like to know more about it, but I have things I must do now. Let us meet again in two hours. We will have a pleasant supper and I will answer your questions. You can tell me about your quagmires."

Cleaning up for the evening meal, Hank was pensive. He was far from support, alone under Quan's control. Nobody could come to his rescue. Whether he would ever see Bev, Faith, or Hope again was entirely up to his adversary, a violent enemy soldier.

It was a bad time to be on a lonely patrol in a hostile country. He needed allies, someone who would help him. He had to survive, if only to find the truth. He yearned to be free from this entanglement. He needed Senator Tompkins. He wanted Bev.

CHAPTER SIXTY-FOUR

Supper on the deck consisted of a noodle soup, followed by a baked pork, roast, and rice. A light white wine accompanied the meal, and the dessert was fruit. The delicious servings were sufficient, but not excessive. Afterwards, Hank questioned Quan, "After the war, why did you not go back north to your home?"

"South Vietnam was my home. The only ones that went back north were the wounded. By the time the Americans withdrew, many of us had been fighting here for years. In contrast, each American soldier stayed in Vietnam for just a year. That was your President Johnson's idea. It was political. By limiting a soldier's time here to just a year, he hoped to reduce American opposition to the war. But by doing that, he made the fighting much easier for us. We came to know the terrain well, but in contrast, the Americans were like raw recruits. By the time they had learned the terrain and how to fight in it and against us, they went home and new recruits arrived to be trained all over again. We were always fighting against inexperienced soldiers and that gave us an advantage."

"Why did you attack civilians?"

"We attacked only traitors who aided the Americans. But earlier you said that the Americans fought the war badly, that quagmire idea. You said Mark Twain coined it."

"Yes, he used it to describe the Philippines, where we fought after the Spanish-American War. He thought America would be trapped in the quicksand of the Far East. He was right. Asia has too much land and too many soldiers. And we did not learn from French mistakes. We sent massive numbers of ground combat units. By not using our strength, the air force and the navy, we played to your strength, manpower. It was wrong,"

"That brings me to the reason I wanted to talk to you. Your president has been getting bad advice about the Far East. I want to correct that."

In a way, Quan was right about several American presidents getting bad advice. Hank's father had been adamant on that, lecturing Hank often about it. He started with Truman immediately recognizing Israel in 1948, in spite of General Marshall, his Secretary of State recommending against it. Then the president had sided with the French and allowed them to return to Indochina, ostensibly to gain French support in Europe. And after the French were defeated again here, President Eisenhower sent American advisors to support a corrupt regime in the south. President Kennedy subsequently added to that support by sending fifteen thousand military advisors and helicopters. President Johnson then introduced American combat units and President Nixon sent more soldiers until we had more than 500,000 in Vietnam. In this debacle, 58,000 American soldiers died, as did millions of Vietnamese. Hank's father blamed the bad advice that five American presidents had received.

"You may be right about the bad advice," Hank said, "but President Johnson actually got good advice that he did not follow; his generals wanted to use America's strengths; air and naval power. The generals wanted to blockade the North Vietnam coast and bomb Hanoi to rubble. But his secretary of defense believed that if we bombed Hanoi and mined the harbors, the Chinese would enter the war. Because he didn't want to fight China, he advised restricting American forces to South Vietnam, far from China. The president decided to do it his way. From a military point of view, it was a bad decision."

Quan laughed.

"It would have made no difference," he said, "if President Johnson had done what his generals wanted. The outcome would have been the same. If you had blockaded our coast and destroyed Hanoi, we would have retreated into the hills or crossed the border into China to continue the war. We were always prepared to suffer far longer than you were prepared to fight. We would never have given up, but after a few years of massive killing of our women and children, world and American public opinion would have risen against you and forced you to quit. But enough of the past, let us talk about Saudi Arabia. That region has become far more important now. And as for the nuclear weapons you studied, Israel has them and both Iran and Saudi Arabia want them. One will have them first, but which one?"

God forbid. Hank asked Quan why the mention of Colonel Manh and the theft of nuclear weapons bothered him. Quan countered by asking if Hank had found nuclear weapons while in Saudi Arabia. Neither would answer, although they parried for more than two hours until it was time to retire.

A beautiful Oriental woman waited to soothe him into sleep. Memories of Jamila again, in Asir Province. Like Jamila, the woman was alluring, but Hank sent her away. Bev was all he needed, and he wanted to think about Quan's questions concerning nuclear weapons in the Middle East. He found no answers and spent a restless night wondering what would happen in the morning. The weather and his future did not seem as bright as they had just a short time ago. ong Kong.

Chapter Sixty-Five

In the morning, the mist had turned to rain. The jungle across from Quan's place was swarming with red ants and snakes. This was the Vietnam Hank remembered, and it was not a good place. He went to breakfast groggy and concerned.

Over a light breakfast of fruit and pastries, Colonel Quan outlined the day ahead.

"First we will visit the orphanage, and you will see that it is now a fine school. Day students are bussed there from the city. As you recall, we attacked it with mortars and came through the fence from the west. I will explain the attack and show you how and why we did it."

At the orphanage, Quan insisted that he had not wanted to harm the children or kill the South Vietnamese soldiers; only to kill Waters. "Today, I will show you why he had to die," Quan said. "The Phoenix agent, McMillian, was working with me. He helped plan the attack and insisted that he had to be the one to kill Waters. So I let him do it."

"Since you admit Agent McMillian was working with you," Hank said, "I will add him to the file I have been assembling on you and the nukes."

"I know about your file. Originally, when I tasked Le Trang to persuade you to come back to Vietnam, the orphanage was to be the place where I would kill you because of that file. I believed you were starting to interfere with some important matters, but my superiors said that if I killed you, there would be a damaging investigation, and I was not to do it. I still might disobey and plead combat necessity. But we must proceed now. I will tell you more about McMillian later, after I show you the site we will now visit."

From the school, they drove west into dense jungle, where Quan led Hank, on foot, along a narrow path lined with armed soldiers. With each step, the jungle grew darker and Hank's apprehension increased. Finally, they came to a clearing that contained two well- maintained gravestones. The names on the graves were Vinh and Hoc. Hank's worries increased. His hopes of survival darkened as the light rain increased.

"These are the graves of two children from the orphanage," Quan said. "A member of the Phoenix team, Jack Elliott, led us to this place and told us that Waters had killed these boys and buried them to hide the bodies. We dug them up and verified their identities. We then gave them a proper burial and added the gravestones. We now take good care of the site."

"How did Elliott know that Waters had killed them?"

"He said the orphanage cook had told him, and we confirmed it with the cook. Elliott also said other boys had been similarly victimized, but he did not give us proof. Elliott deserted when he found that McMillian planned to kill him, because he had been a witness to Waters's murder. I tell you these things, so you understand why we let McMillian execute Waters, an evil person who had to die. McMillian thus performed a useful service. Since then, McMillian has become very important to me and my country. Now we must leave these boys in peace. I will clarify McMillian's role and my apprehension about China during supper."

CHAPTER SIXTY-SIX

Since Quan evidently did not intend to add Hank to the little graveyard, at least until after supper, he decided to probe the relationship between Quan and McMillian. Somehow, it was keeping him alive. He also wanted to press Quan on Colonel Orzon and the theft of nuclear weapons. Not having died under the cloudy skies in the graveyard, he felt better as he went to the evening meal. The weather had improved, and a thousand stars twinkled above.

Supper was to be on the deck. He found Quan relaxing above the gently flowing river, and without preamble, the colonel began, "In World War Two, your O.S.S. assisted us by arming and supplying our army, and we were friends because of our mutual goal; to defeat Japan. We welcomed American aid because Chairman Ho was convinced that after the war, America would give us freedom. Unfortunately, President Truman betrayed us and sided with France. That allowed the French Foreign Legion to return, and we had to fight again against the French. That was the greatest disappointment of Chairman Ho's life, because he really believed that America meant freedom."

Quan's brief account was close to the truth, but it omitted the important role France had in forming N.A.T.O. America needed the French, even if Truman had to agree to allow France to return to Indochina.

"It is true that we needed France's help in Europe," Hank said, "but why are you giving me these history lessons?"

"Because Truman and four other American presidents were given poor information and made poor foreign-policy decisions. Truman supported France. Eisenhower supported corrupt leaders in South Vietnam. Kennedy sent Saigon helicopters and thousands of military advisors. Johnson added major American army combat units. Nixon escalated your involvement to five hundred thousand soldiers. Each of those decisions was based on bad advice."

"That is your view of history, but how does that affect me?"

"It affects your treatment of McMillian and the possibility that he could become director of the C.I.A. Your presidents rely on foreign intelligence primarily from one source; the C.I.A. The agency director prepares and presents a daily briefing to your president primarily on foreign affairs. No person has more influence in such things than the director. The state department and the National Security Council also have great influence, but neither of those is first to brief the president each morning. Initially because I thought you were standing in the way of McMillian becoming director, I brought you here to kill you. I was told to let you live, however, so you could help us against our worst enemy, China. Whether in Taiwan, nuclear proliferation, or economic dominance, China is also your enemy. Vietnam's concern is the fact that we are China's neighbors and have been fighting them far longer than you have, so the Chinese are a major problem for us. But China is a growing threat to both our countries every day. I was told to let you live so that we can work together to help McMillian become director. Over the years that I have worked with him, his value has continually increased. I now believe he and I can work effectively against China. In order to do that, I want to make sure your president receives the best intelligence about our mutual enemy. If McMillian becomes the director and briefs your president daily, he would be effective in providing the best possible information about China. But if McMillian is accused of murder in that orphanage, even though it was a justified killing that happened in a combat theater a long time ago, his enemies will use it against him. The president could not then select him as director. Surely, you can see that accusations against McMillian must not surface."

Because Quan was obsessed with China, he was missing the point. Colonel and Mrs. Manh were dead. The Trang girls had been kidnapped. Gus Bean and Bill West had been killed. If McMillian was involved in those, he needed to be jailed, not nominated.

"If McMillian was involved in murder," Hank said, "he must be brought to justice."

"Non-sense. If he were brought before a court, there would be doubt as to his guilt. But a trial would still derail his nomination. That must not happen, because China has become more aggressive than ever by trying to control the South China Sea. If China is successful in this new aggression, both of our countries will suffer. In spite of that, your state department is acting on bad intelligence and aiding the Chinese. The South China Sea carries one-third of all nautical cargo worldwide. Freedom of navigable waters is an international issue. America must be our ally to stop China. That is why I have let you live, to help McMillian become director."

"I will not help him in anything."

"You may find that you have no choice. But sleep well tonight, because we must rise early, so I can provide you with more evidence to help you decide."

CHAPTER SIXTY-SEVEN

No beautiful woman came to Hank's bed that evening, and he spent a restless night thinking about McMillian becoming director of the C.I.A. Throughout the night, he wondered if he would live to see the dawn and he prepared to defend himself from any approaching killer. After such a worrisome night, he was still tired and half asleep as he arose the following cloudy morning. He and Quan drove without conversation toward Ho Chi Minh City. In the villages they passed, the shops were crowded, the people seemingly carefree and without fear of ambush. Route 1, newly widened and freshly painted was crowded with the same overloaded buses, motor scooters, and business trucks. In the small villages, the streets were narrow, and Quan's driver had to proceed slowly through carts, rickshaws, shoppers, and over-loaded small tucks. Men and women packed the shops, sidewalks, and roadways. They smiled and chatted, seemingly happy and prosperous. In two hours, they reached Cholon.

"This is still the Chinese section of Ho Chi Minh City," Quan said. "It was the center of the most black-market activity during the war, the largest in South Vietnam."

"I wouldn't know," Hank said. "I was never here. The closest I ever came to Saigon during the war was coming and going through the military airport at Long Binh."

"You may not have come here, but many Americans and other foreign soldiers did. It was a gigantic market in Southeast Asia, and the Chinese ran it well. You could buy anything you wanted here. That is not the case now. We have outlawed the more harmful activities, and we constantly police what goes on."

"But Cholon is not the way to the airport, and I don't need souvenirs."

"I want you to meet a woman. She employs many lovely, young women who know how to please visitors. During the war, her mother was a bar girl on Dong Khoi Street in District One, where her best customers were the Americans. We did not like her pleasing the Americans, and several times we considered killing her because she was a collaborator, taking American money and giving them pleasure. We let her live, however, because she listened to the soldiers she serviced and remembered what they said. She then passed much valuable information to us. Her name was Phuong and her daughter, Ly, was raised in her trade. Ly is beautiful and quite skilled. She has information for you. You will find that there is something very special about her. Stay a while and enjoy spending some time with her. I promise she would give you something positive to remember about Vietnam today."

"No thanks. Not interested."

When Hank met Ly, however, she took his breath away. What Quan had said was true, she was indeed special. Her father must have been a foreigner, for she was taller than most Vietnamese women. She was dressed in a transparent Au Dai, through which were revealed her flimsy bra and almost non-existent thong. Her firm breasts were larger than any he had seen in Vietnam during the war. When she extended her small hand, she gazed at him and smiled in a way that caused a stirring he did not like. Her touch sent a volt of electricity through his groin, and he knew he had to get out of there before he did something he would regret. Ly was surrounded by lovely, semi-naked Oriental girls eager to arouse men. They were just the supporting cast, however, because Ly Phuong was the star.

She seemed nervous in Quan's presence, and after a short tour, he ordered her to take them to a more private room. She hastily complied. They sat on cushions while Ly served tea that Hank hoped was not drugged. As usual, Quan was direct and wasted no time, "Tell Colonel Kean what you know about Director Waters."

"I was a child when he came to see my mother," Ly said, "and we knew he was the director of the Hau Nghia orphanage. He began coming to the bar in the mid-sixties, well before the Tet Offensive. Mother was his favorite because she was young, attractive, and skilled.

He drank beer and used hash. Sometimes, when he fell asleep, she looked in his billfold and that was how we knew his name and who he was. Then, after more than a year, the last time he came here he got very drunk. Instead of falling asleep, he asked mother to find him a sex child. I was afraid he might mean me, but I was not what he wanted. He asked for a young boy. When mother told him that was not normal and she would not help him in such a thing, he became very angry and stormed out. He never came back. I was happy to see him go."

Ly was so beautiful and Hank was so mesmerized by her that he had mixed feelings when Quan said that the session was over and it was time to leave.

As she brushed his cheek with a soft kiss of goodbye, Ly whispered, "I want to come to America and be with you forever."

Only with great effort did he free himself and hurry out.

"As you can see," Quan said after they were back on the road to the airport, "Waters was filthy, a truly bad person. And he did more than just defile young boys, he killed them. There is no doubt that he deserved to die and McMillian should not be punished for being the instrument that made it happen. He had to kill that pedophile."

"He should have brought Waters to trial," Hank said. "Not killed." "You and I have killed many."

"But I never murdered anyone." "Some might dispute that."

As they headed back across the great city to the airport, Quan's driver once more had to drive carefully through the crowded streets. Colonel Quan lapsed into a stern silence and made no further attempts at conversation. Hank was left to observe the busy, peaceful avenues along the way, much different from what he remembered of the war. These city people looked like those of any prosperous Oriental metropolis. Crowded small buses, darting motor scooters, overloaded Renaults, and hurrying shoppers swarmed the scene. The people were smiling at each other and chatting happily. The shops looked full of goods meant for wealthy people. The sidewalks and shops were full. The end of hostilities had been good for these people. The scene was in sharp contrast with the forecasts of communist slavery that had been regular fodder of American politicians during the war. These people did not look like slaves to him. But the bustling city scenes, meant these people were the survivors. They weren't the million boat people who had fled. They weren't the ones who died in the indoctrination camps. They had neither escaped nor resisted. They were the collaborators.

Hank's father might have been correct in saying that the many, disparate decisions of the president's advisors had resulted in American soldiers being foolishly being sent to Vietnam. Too many had died, and the war had turned out badly. Why had we fought? Acheson and Marshall may have pushed President Truman in that direction, but was it because of bad intelligence? Or a valid hatred of communism? Dulles persuaded President Eisenhower to increase our involvement in Vietnam, but who told President Kennedy he needed to add thousands of advisors and helicopter units? Why did McNamara persuade Johnson to escalate the ground war in the south instead of attacking Hanoi in North Vietnam? Maybe Quan had a point; several presidents had been given some very bad advice and led America into Twain's quagmire. Quan said he wanted to make sure future presidents would receive better intelligence about China, a country that was indeed America's adversary in Asia, as it was Vietnam's. Did it make sense for McMillian to become the director? Quan was probably correct that Hank could easily torpedo that nomination. That potential might have been what had kept him alive so far.

"Join us in stopping China," Quan said at the airport. "I need to think," Hank said.

"You will have a long flight home in which to do so. Do not waste your time. Many lives depend on you. Think carefully, because much will depend on what you do."

Hank sent a wire to Paul, saying he was headed home.

On the plane, he felt very much alone, more than he had ever felt in the darkness of a night patrol in the deepest Vietnamese jungle. He had to make all this go away. He thought about Bev and how much he needed her. Ly had stirred that loneliness into a sharp ache. Would Ly really come to America? Quan must have put her up to suggesting that. Pity. The colonel was using her. Quan must have sensed Hank's need and thought he could use Ly to control him. If Quan's scheme had worked, Hank would have never been the same.

Chapter Sixty-Eight

Hank made some decisions; his first goal was to get an update from Ted or Paul on what they knew about the stolen nukes and Saudi Arabia exploding one in the Empty Quarter. Quan's reaction to the explosion simply added to that of Senator Tompkins and made it really clear; the nukes were key. Hank needed to look again carefully at Quan, McMillian, China, and the Sayyaf and find a common thread that held them together. More and more, it looked like the nukes were the glue. Paul had made no mention of Blevins. Had he struck again? Hank half remembered his mother's words, "I never cared when I was young where time would take me out of the shadows as the moon was rising."

Hank's time had taken him out of the shadows in Washington and was sending him to face the ones who had started this. The killings had to end, and he had to face McMillian. As Quan had said, it was a long flight home.

Paul met him at the Savannah airport. As they drove to Hilton Head, Hank gave Paul a quick summary of what had happened in Vietnam, omitting his encounter with Ly in Cholon. He emphasized his increasing belief that nuclear weapons were behind all this, and that the relationship between Quan and McMillian would prove that. Quan had made it clear; they were working together. The file Paul was assembling was more important than ever.

"I made detailed notes," Hank said, "for the file, and I will amplify them. For the next several days, however, I will be really busy briefing my firm about the investors I met in Vietnam and following up on each one. But we can't wait too long. We need to meet soon, maybe next week. Try to bring Storm here. Tell him to bring everything he has about the nukes. And see if he can find out what Saudi

Arabia is doing with the second bomb. We need to find out how the Saudis plan to use it. Focus on that weapon. It's decision time."

"I'll have him here," Paul said.

Hank called Bev, and she immediately invited him over. When she opened the door, she was smiling with his bourbon in her hand.

"To your safe return and better days," she said. "I was really worried. You were gone so long. Tell me everything that happened. You didn't want to ever go back there. Was it really bad?"

"There were moments when I had doubts, I would get out of Vietnam alive," he said, "but the thought of you kept me going, and I survived, at least for now."

"That's sweet," she said, moving a bit closer. "What was Quan like?"

"A hard man," he said and he told her about the colonel, describing Quan's reaction to the investors and their meeting at the Sheraton. He stressed how dedicated and violent the man was and how strongly he believed in communism and Vietnam's future.

"I don't like that guy. Why did he want you to come to Vietnam?"

Hank told her how Quan claimed that McMillian helped organize the attack that killed Waters. He described how Quan had taken him down that dark lane between rows of soldiers to the little grave-yard where Hank thought he would die. Quan told him what Waters had done to the boys and ended by saying that Waters was so evil that Quan thought that McMillian was justified in killing him. He explained how Quan wanted Hank to help McMillian become direc-tor of the C.I.A. and put McMillian, a mentally disturbed killer, in daily direct contact with the president. And Quan had attempted to justify McMillian by citing the threat China posed in the South China Sea. He did not mention Le Phuong and Cholon.

"What are you going to do now?" she asked.

Hank told her his plan; to get the latest information from Paul and Strom about the nukes and Saudi Arabia, and look at the data on China's push to control the South China Sea.

"When I have the ducks in order," he said, "I'm going to Washington to meet Charley face to face, look him in the eye, and talk some sense into him."

"I doubt even you could do that," she said. "He's a dangerous killer."

"Do you care?"

She moved to him and they took up where they had laid off.

In the morning as she kissed him goodbye, she admonished him, "If you shoot any more federal agents, you will not be welcome here."

The night had relaxed him and given him the incentive to resolve the situation. He left with optimism growing, with glowing hopes for the future.

Chapter Sixty-Nine

When a week later they met in Paul's office, Strom began with an update on the nuclear weapons.

"We now know that the Sayyaf were recruited by Colonel Orzon. In Germany, they compromised the sergeant in charge of the depot igloos, took advantage of a lazy colonel on site, and distracted the general in command. They built two fake weapons that looked exactly like the real things, weighed the same, and had the same serial numbers. They built small compartments under a maintenance truck and during scheduled cleaning, with the well-paid igloo sergeant as a lookout, they substituted the fake weapons and put the real ones under their truck. The fakes were so good that when they arrived at their new depot in the states, they passed every test, except one; they had the wrong radioactive signature. Alerted by that discrepancy, the receiving team undertook an extensive and detailed examination of the fakes. That revealed the substitution, and a full court press quickly found the guilty parties. Not wanting to alarm the nation, the administration swore the sergeant to silence and warned him that he would go to jail if he ever said anything to anybody about the theft. He was then allowed to retire. The colonel and general also retired, at lower ranks, after signing documents that would also put them in jail for a long time if they ever revealed what had happened. The investigation also discovered that a well-paid Colonel Orzon was the one who arranged the transfer of the two weapons to Saudi Arabia."

"What a debacle," Hank said. "How could a bunch of Filipino terrorists gain access to the ammunition depot without arousing suspicion?"

"Evidently, the guy in charge looked and talked like an American, with light brown hair, blue eyes, and fair skin. He was persuasive and had impressive credentials that granted him clearance to classified areas. He vouched for his men, and the depot commander accepted him and his money. The sergeant in charge of the igloo then allowed the Sayyaf team to work in the igloo while they were supposed to be cleaning it. The whole operation was smooth and well organized. The guy in charge wasn't actually an American, just the result of a liaison left over from the Philippine Insurrection. Nobody has found him yet. He is either dead or protected by the people that arranged the theft."

"Arranged?" Paul asked. "Do we know who did that?"

"Someone in the United States organized the whole thing and used the sergeant, colonel, and general as fall guys. Colonel Orzon was not the mastermind. He was just a contractor, very well paid, we think by the Saudis. We also think we know why this whole thing was set up."

To prove that, Storm then gave them documents to examine. They were complex, but the nut of it all was that someone wanted to give Saudi Arabia small nuclear weapons, assuming they would use them to force Iran to stop its weapons program.

"That's absurd," Hank said. "If the Saudis had such weapons, they might use them against Israel rather than Iran. Or even New York. When I was with bin Laden in a Nomad camp back in sixty-six, he said the king would use extreme measures like nukes against anyone who had supported Israel and let the Israelis seize the Dome of the Rock."

"But we don't know the really important things," Paul said. "Who set this up? Was McMillian involved? Why did your comments about nuclear weapons set off Senator Tompkins and Colonel Quan?"

"Well, I know one thing at least," Hank said, "McMillian must be indicted for murder."

"Evidence against him does not support indictment," Paul said. "Most of it is rumor or hearsay. With Nung and Ahn Minh gone, the witnesses who could testify about Waters are either dead or under Quan's control, and he would never make them available for a McMillian trial. As for the two young boys, their graves and deaths could have been fakes. It seems to me that a grand jury would not indict and even if it did, a D.A. might refuse to bring charges."

Spoken like a lawyer. Well, he had Senator Tompkins in his corner. He'd give Tompkins the data on McMillian and a copy of the updated file. But he wondered if Paul was correct that McMillian couldn't be indicted. If Paul was right, what was the point in trying? We'd infuriate Quan and provoke him into harming Faith or Hope. He couldn't risk that. But he had to stop McMillian from becoming director of the C.I.A. Think of the damage he could do.

"I agree that McMillian can't be trusted," Paul continued. "But I am not convinced he is guilty of the deaths you cite. Unless you know more than I have seen, I believe you need to hold off on those accusations."

"I do have more," Hank said. "Quan admitted he was in on the thefts and that McMillian was his contact. I think Quan might retaliate if we pursue an indictment of McMillian."

"I am inclined to disagree," Paul said. "I believe Colonel Quan would conclude that using McMillian would then be a closed matter. He would not want to stir up resentment in American political, business, or intelligence circles by actions that would prevent an alliance with the United States against China in the future. I think he would salvage what he could and simply move on. That would be the Oriental way."

That might be right, but Quan could react in some other way, not just drop the whole matter. He had a lot invested. He said he wanted to kill anyone who got in his way. That might mean Bev, Faith, or Hope. As Quan stood beside those two little graves in Vietnam, he said someone had ordered Quan to let him live. Who could that be? The only one he could think of was McMillian. Did McMillian organize the theft of the nukes? That made sense because McMillian was a killer, too. The two of them might take revenge in spite of what Paul thought. Thank God, he had Senator Tompkins on his side. He needed to go to Washington, update the senator, and urge him to go public if Hank was killed.

"Is it possible that McMillian might simply withdraw his name if he's threatened with exposure?" he asked Paul. "You seem to think that if McMillian were to step aside, Quan might not retaliate. If so, that would solve my concerns."

"Perhaps," Paul said. "But McMillian has worked a lifetime to become director and I can't see him quitting easily. Even if he did, there would still be people in the agency who have worked for many years with him, people who may have lost a friend in your Juarez attack. I doubt they would ignore you. You need to take steps to protect yourself and your girls, not only from Quan, but also from whoever is behind the plan to steal those weapons and give them to the Saudis. That might indeed be McMillian. If so, killers could come after you and yours from any direction. Vietnam, Saudi Arabia, or the agency."

Hank didn't like the sound of that. He had to see the senator as soon as possible.

CHAPTER SEVENTY

Hank called Steve Powell and asked for an urgent immediate appointment with the senator, saying he had new information and wanted to bring the senator up to date.

"What do you mean by up to date?" Steve asked.

"I have additional information about the deaths of Colonels Bean, West, and Manh. I went to Vietnam to meet with Colonel Quan, a senior Viet Cong leader who worked with McMillian when Charley was a Phoenix agent during the war. I want to talk to the senator about Quan."

Powell paused for a moment and then replied, "Send your file to me for review. The senator will discuss it when you come. But give me a short summary now."

"Okay. The El Paso district attorney still refuses to exhume Colonel Manh's body, but he has not moved to indict me. He lists the killing of Mrs. Manh as unsolved. Colonel Quan wants Le Trang to set up a computer link with him in Vietnam. Quan wants to strengthen communication between Vietnam and the United States in reaction to China's growing threat in the South China Sea. Quan asked for my assistance in helping Charles McMillian be nominated to become the director of the C.I.A. He thinks that McMillian would be very helpful for Vietnam with the growing threat of China, and he was worried that I might do something to derail McMillian's nomination. Quan knows I am concerned about that selection, and I want to talk to the senator about that. As for the deaths I mentioned, my attorney has asked El Paso several times to exhume Colonel Manh's body, but they are stonewalling. The police list Mrs. Manh's death as an open case. There has been no action against me concerning the death of an American in Juarez when Sam Trang was rescued. It remains only the subject of occasional media speculation. There have been no developments in the death of Colonel Bean, but it looks like murder. Mrs. West's attorney is tenacious. He will not give up. He continually badgers various Washington newspapers about West's killing and writes an occasional op-ed piece about the murder. He has asked for a special task force to investigate. Finally, to me, the major problem remains the story of how nuclear weapons came into the hands of Saudi Arabia."

"You haven't mentioned anything about Colonel Orzon."

"I don't have much concrete about Orzon. I have a report from the F.B.I. that alleges he was the one that organized the theft of the two weapons from West Germany, and the timing of his recent death in the Philippines seems suspicious. My attorney and I are trying to find out who funded Orzon's operation. I can tell you that when I asked Quan about Colonel Orzon, the question set him off. I thought he was going to attack me then and there. Even after he calmed down, he still threatened harm to me and my family. I have thought about that and asked myself why Orzon is so important to Quan. I know that he was involved in the theft, and McMillian was his agency contact. I know that those stolen weapons ended up in Saudi Arabia, because the Saudis just set one of them off. That proved the story about a theft was true. We know what happened, but not who masterminded and funded it, nor how deeply McMillian and Quan were involved. What my F.B.I. contact did tell me was that Iran went bonkers after the explosion. The Middle East is in an uproar about the possibility that Saudi Arabia has acquired nuclear weapons. Nothing there is going to be the same. The details of all this are in the file I want the senator to read."

"I don't think the senator can help you with Colonel Orzon or those nuclear weapons," Powell said. "But I will brief him after I look at your file. If he's agreeable and has time, I'll make an appointment for you. Now that a war appears to be starting with Iraq and Saddam Hussein, Washington is pretty busy these days, so don't expect a quick reply."

Steve sounded cautious, different, almost as if he wanted Hank to go away. That concerned Hank because he needed the senator's help, clout, and protection. Without those, Hank would have to walk away. He had to see the senator.

Hank briefed Paul and told Bev he would be going to Washington. She wanted to go with him, said she worried about him when he went on his trips. A week later, Powell called back with an appointment two weeks away. Hank was elated, but everything fell apart a week later when Desert Storm broke out.

He was called back to active duty as a colonel, ordered to report to the American command element in Saudi Arabia, with an interim visit with Onorato in Washington.

"Can they do that?" Bev asked.

"Unfortunately, they can," Hank said. "I signed a binding, open- ended contract."

He called Powell to cancel his appointment, but said he would be in Washington soon and would call to set up a visit then.

"All the senator's appointments have been cancelled because of the war," Powell said. "Wait until all this is over. Then call us, and we'll see what we can do."

He sounded relieved that the senator would not have to deal with Hank.

CHAPTER SEVENTY-ONE

Before heading for Saudi Arabia, Hank had to report to Onorato at defense intelligence. The handler explained, "Your cover in Saudi Arabia will be the intelligence section of the American command. Your cover job with that section will be mapping, but your primary mission is to contact Bakr bin Laden and find out what the Saudis are doing with that second bomb, the one they didn't set off. Where is it? What are they doing with it?"

It was a daunting assignment, complicated by the fact that since Bakr had taken over his father's company, he had become extremely secretive and difficult to reach. Hank wasn't even sure Bakr would agree to talk to him, much less meet, but when he arrived, he put out feelers, telling several Saudi contacts he needed to speak to Bakr. To his surprise, in two weeks, an invitation arrived. He was to come alone to a well-known Jeddah restaurant overlooking the flowing Red Sea. When he arrived, he found the door locked and guarded by scowling armed men. When he gave his name and produced his invitation, however, he was quickly ushered in. The restaurant was empty, except for Bakr sitting alone at a table with armed guards standing by. Bakr rose and greeted Hank courteously, speaking excellent English. It was almost like twenty years ago with Bakr and his father. He and Bakr laughed about Miami and the Virginia Tech Hokies, and spoke fondly about the father. Bakr gave no hint that Hank might still be suspected in his father's death. Over an excellent meal of lamb, rice, fruit, and iced tea, Bakr asked about Hank's military role in the current operation against Saddam Hussein's threat to the Saudi oilfields and to the holy cities.

"Our country is grateful to America for its help," he said. "Once again, we owe you."

After Hank explained that his task was to plan the intelligence and produce the maps needed to facilitate an imminent offensive that would drive between Kuwait and Iraq, protect the Saudi oil field, and free Kuwait, Bakr nodded happily.

"I am pleased more than ever that you have returned," Bakr said, "and I would like to help. What may I do for you?"

"You might be able to clear up a very important rumor," Hank said. "Some powerful people in Washington are spreading a story that your country obtained some suitcase nukes stolen from a depot in West Germany and might be trying to replicate them. What can you tell me?"

Bakr pulled back from the table, stood, and stared down at Hank. He waved his arms as he talked to himself, exclaiming, "La," (no) and, "Na'am," (yes) several times. He appeared to be debating himself. This continued for several minutes. Then he quieted, sat back down, and said, "If you were anyone else, I would leave without responding. But my father asked me to assist you whenever I could, and the king supported him. What I am about to tell you will satisfy that obligation and end our relationship. After this, we will not meet again, and I will forever deny what I am about to tell you. Do you understand?"

"I do," Hank said.

"Then listen carefully," Bakr said, motioning the bodyguards away and leaning forward, his voice now cold, "for I will not repeat myself. We purchased two weapons from the Sayyaf. We are now replicating them with the goal of producing ten of our own weapons. Pakistan has been persuaded by someone in Washington to supply the nuclear fuel and scientists to assist in the replication. We exploded one of the stolen weapons in The Empty Quarter to verify its power and show Iran that we have these bombs. Then we told them covertly that we will use such weapons in their cities if they continue to build a nuclear weapon. We intend to push back the current Iranian expansion in the Persian Gulf and regain dominance over Iran. We will eliminate the threat the Shiites pose to us. As a result, neither your country nor Israel will have to attack Iran. No Third World War will be started in the Middle East. The Iranians have ceased their production of such weapons. That is all I will tell you, all you need to know."

"The Iranians may respond by attacking you," Hank protested.

"If they do," Bakr answered, "America has signed a defense treaty with us and will come to our defense again. World opinion would support you for doing so."

Hank sat back, closed his eyes, and considered that idea. Then he answered, "You were with me when your father said the king might use such weapons against Israel, or even America. The mere possibility terrifies me. Could that ever happen?"

"I am not privy to such decisions," Bakr said, "but I remind you that at the same meeting, my father also said that nothing of importance can happen in the kingdom without the knowledge and approval of the king. He will decide whether, when, and who we will attack."

Bakr then rose, looked down at Hank, and continued, "I will say nothing more. But I warn you to be careful how you use this information. If you act rashly, we both will be in great danger. As far as I am concerned, this conversation never happened."

Then Bakr turned and left. The guards then escorted Hank from the restaurant.

Hank reported the discussion to Onorato, and was ordered to return to the Pentagon.

CHAPTER SEVENTY-TWO

On the long flight from Dhahran to Dulles international, Hank had plenty of time to think about the connection between the theft of nuclear weapons and Blevins, Quan, or McMillian. Bakr had said the operation had been orchestrated by someone in Washington. That someone had to be McMillian. Neither Blevins nor Quan were in a position to do it alone, but either or both of them could have been activated and controlled by McMillian and the C.I.A. He reported his conclusions to Onorato.

"That is absurd," Onorato said. "Why would the C.I.A. have done this?"

"For two reasons," Hank said. "First, to have McMillian become the director and act with Vietnam against China in the South China Sea. Second, to use Saudi Arabia against Iran to stop the Iranian nuclear program. Even if McMillian doesn't become director, and I'm convinced he should not, the second objective has succeeded; the Iranians have already responded to the idea of Saudi Arabia having nukes by stopping their own program. In other words, the whole crazy idea of giving the Saudis nuclear weapons worked. Think about it."

"I think you're nuts," Onorato said. "We're going to release you from active duty, with no more obligation. You will not be recalled. Go back to Hilton Head and forget this."

Onorato would not listen to anything more, so Hank headed for a reunion with Bev, Faith, and Hope. They were happy to have him home safely from combat. Bev was overjoyed. Over cocktails, she wanted to know everything that had happened, from Bakr to Onorato.

When he finished the summary, she asked, "Is it over? Are we through with retaliations?"

"Almost," he said. "I just need to tie up some loose ends. I'll update my file to include what Bakr said about the Saudis copying the American weapon for use against Iran. Then I'll take the file to Washington and discuss it with Senator Tompkins. Finally, I'll confront McMillian. If he refuses to stop the non-sense in Saudi Arabia and the killings here, I'll release the file to the media. He knows that would destroy him, so I'm positive he will agree."

She tried to stop him from confronting McMillian, a proven killer, but he was adamant. She then wanted to go with him, but he refused, telling her the trip had to be all business. When she protested about the danger, he told her he would take his Glock.

"Don't worry," he said. "I'll be back in a week and we'll be rid of McMillian, Blevins, and Quan. When I'm gone, lock the doors and turn on the alarm. Stay in touch with Paul and the police. This will be over soon. We'll start a new life."

Before leaving, he went to Paul, summarized what Bakr had said and asked for advice.

"Ask the senator to pressure the agency," Paul said. "Make sure Tompkins has a copy of your file just in case anything happens to you. The senator looks like your last best hope."

"I agree," Hank said. "I'll brief him before I confront McMillian, but before then, you need to add Bakr's comments to our file and my conclusions about the C.I.A. I'm convinced this will be over once I show Charley the updates."

Chapter Seventy-Three

Paul urged Hank not to start a fight, but fighting had always been what Hank did best, so he made an appointment with Powell to see Tompkins and was grim, determined, and ready for a confrontation when he reached McLean. He put the Glock in the motel safe and took the Metro commute to the Hart Building. There, he found metal detectors and several guards who eyed him suspiciously as he approached.

"Photo identification?" one asked curtly as the others stood on alert.

Hank handed over his driver's license and his military identification. Seeing the latter, the guards seemed to relax a bit.

"What are you here for, Colonel?" one asked, courteously. "Senator Tompkins at eleven o'clock," Hank said.

Another guard checked an appointment schedule and nodded. "Empty your pockets into this tray," he said. "Your watch and belt, too. And step slowly through the detector."

When Hank passed those tests, a guard gave him back his things while another went through his briefcase.

"What's in the large envelope?" the guard asked.

"A document I intend to give the senator," Hank said. "It's neither sealed, nor classified. You can look at the contents if you want."

The man opened the envelope and went through everything thoroughly. "Looks okay," he finally said to the other guards and returned the briefcase.

"I'll take you to the senator's office," the senior guard then said. "When you're done, his gal will call for an escort to take you out. Security is tight nowadays. You cannot wander around this building without an escort."

He then led Hank to an elevator and a suite of corner offices on the second floor. Senator Tompkins's name was prominently displayed on a brass plaque next to the large, dark-wood, double doors. Inside, Steve Powell was waiting.

"Welcome," he said with his typically firm handshake. "Was security rough?"

"Almost as bad as the airport," Hank said. "At Savannah, a very ugly man patted me down more intimately than he had to."

"He's clean," the guard said.

"Thanks," Powell said. "We'll call when we're done."

Steve led Hank to a small office and explained that when Senator Tompkins was free, he would send for them.

"What are you going to ask the senator?" he then asked.

"The question of the stolen nukes has cleared up," Hank said. "I have laid out my conclusion that McMillian was behind everything, from the nuke theft to the killings. It started a long time ago, with Waters in Vietnam. Everything is in this file for the senator to study and keep."

"Why did McMillian kill Waters?" Powell asked.

"That, too, is in the file," Hank said. "Waters raped young McMillian a long time ago in Hawaii. Waters was convicted of child abuse and sent to Leavenworth. After he served time, he volunteered for C.O.O.R.D.S. and in 1965, he went to that orphanage in Vietnam. McMillian then joined the Phoenix program, went to Vietnam, and killed him."

"That's a pretty strong accusation."

"In the file I have a letter from the wife of a Vietnamese colonel who was at the orphanage when Waters died. I also have details supplied by Colonel Quan, the North Vietnamese officer who led the attack that killed Waters. The accounts agree. I also spoke with Bakr bin Laden who told me enough to prove that McMillian and the C.I.A. supplied nuclear weapons to Saudi Arabia for an attack on Iran. These data are enough to disqualify McMillian from becoming the C.I.A. deputy director. Media scrutiny of these notes would derail his nomination. A man like McMillian should not be anywhere near the president. In addition, he may have been involved in several kidnappings and the murders of Colonel and Mrs. Manh. I believe he arranged the deaths of Colonels Bean and West. He threatened me and my daughters. He's given the Arabs nuclear weapons. He's crazy."

"Okay," Powell said. "What do you want from the senator?"

"I want to brief him about this file and ask him to publicize it if I am harmed. And I especially want him to question the agency about the stolen nuclear weapons."

Steve shook his head negatively at the mention of nuclear weapons. He seemed to want to dismiss that subject, and that added to Hank's concern. Washington was an even darker place. Then Tompkins's secretary leaned in and said the senator was ready to see them.

"Are there other copies of this file?" Tompkins asked after Hank had briefed him.

"Yes," Hank said. "I have one. My attorney has another and has given one to an F.B.I. agent. I intend to give McMillian one. There are others held in secure locations. I'd like you to review the file and publicize it if I am killed."

"Steve tells me that you make serious allegations against McMillian," the senator said. "But he also says you lack proof. That there is reasonable doubt."

"I have no doubts about McMillian," Hank said. "I have facts about two kidnappings, six murders, and a foreign conspiracy."

"There are some facts in this file," Powell admitted. "Coincidences that lead to McMillian. And I agree with Colonel Kean that if the media saw this, McMillian's nomination would be over. The mere suggestion that he might have been involved with foreign powers in American politics would kill any nomination for him. In the file, the nuclear-weapons story has been clarified, and it is a real problem."

The senator rose and paced the room quietly thinking. Then he stopped and said, "I'll review your file and release its contents if anything happens to you. Steve, I want you to support Colonel Kean in every way you legally can."

"But, Senator," Hank said, "one development is most important; the Saudis may be trying to replicate these weapons for use against Iran. I hope you will look into that."

"Nuclear weapons are a concern," the senator said.

"When the senator has time," Steve said, "I will brief him more fully about that. But now he is due on the floor for a vote."

In the outer office, Powell did not offer to continue discussion. He simply told Hank that after the senator reviewed the file, he might want Steve to look into it. If so, Steve would be in touch. Then he called for an escort to let Hank out.

Back at Tyson's Corner after making notes on his visit with the senator, he called McMillian's office and asked for a meeting. He was put on hold for a considerable time before he was told to meet at Charley's Georgetown home after supper.

CHAPTER SEVENTY-FOUR

He called Paul to fill him in on the session with Tompkins and the fact that he was going to confront McMillan. e then called.

"I have to make Charley back off," he said. "Tompkins agreed to publicize our file if I am attacked. I made a special pitch for him to look into the status of the Saudi nukes and the idea the Saudis might replicate them."

When he called Bev to tell her he would be meeting McMillian, she began to cry.

"What's wrong?" he asked.

"I just wish you wouldn't confront him," she said. "He's a killer, and I don't know what I would do if you were hurt. But whatever happens, whatever you are told, whatever you hear, I want you to know that I'm very much in love with you."

Then she abruptly hung up and would not answer his repeated return calls. He was mystified, but he had to make preparations to meet McMillian, so he stopped trying to reach her.

After a light snack, he put his pistol in the briefcase together with a copy of the file to give McMillian and headed for the metro. Forty-five minutes later, he rang McMillian's doorbell, and a fit-looking man answered. He led Hank to a waiting room, and they sat in silence until, to Hank's amazement, McMillian and Blevins came in.

Hank jumped up and tried to move toward Blevins, but the guards stopped him.

"He's carrying," one said, "but not bugged." "Take his piece," McMillian said.

He and Blevins watched warily as the guard opened Hank's briefcase and removed the Glock. Only then did McMillian come over to shake hands.

"It's been a long time," he said. "Many eventful years. I see you recognize Steve Blevins, the leader of the detail with me tonight. Knowing you, I asked for the best. What can I do for you?"

"I have some information for you," Hank said, handing McMillian the envelope. "It's all summarized in this file. I'd like you to read it and think about what it says. I've been keeping it ever since I met Blevins in El Paso three years ago. The file includes the history of Randy Waters; what happened in Hawaii in 1949, his trial and imprisonment at Leavenworth, and his later hire by the state department for assignment to Vietnam. I have included statements given by Colonels Manh and Quan as to how Waters died. I quote Colonel Quan about his long relationship with you, starting with your involvement in the attack on the orphanage. Quan admitted he planned the theft of two nukes from the American depot and claimed you were his contact for that operation. At his request, I recently visited him in Vietnam and went with him to the graves of two children Waters killed. During that visit, he talked about your wish to become the agency director. I have described the kidnapping of the Trang daughters and the deaths of Colonel and Mrs. Manh, Gus Bean, and Bill West. Recently, I met with Bakr bin Laden in Jeddah, and the file summarizes the meeting, during which he laid out how the Saudis plan to use the weapons you helped Quan and Orzon steal. If you don't resign from the agency, I'll release the file to the media, and you will be ruined. If I am harmed, Senator Tompkins will release the file for me."

"How many copies of this trash are there?" McMillian asked. "Senator Tompkins has one. I retained one. My attorney has one.

The F.B.I. has another, and any of these people may have made additional copies for other people they trust."

McMillian sat back and stared at Hank a long time with his eyes half closed.

"You realize that all this is baloney," he finally said. "It would never stand up in court. Waters's death was justifiable homicide, done in a fit of rage."

Hank had anticipated such a claim, and he was prepared to answer, "That's pure non-sense. The killing was premeditated. You volunteered for Phoenix duty in Vietnam to find Waters. You collaborated with Quan to attack the orphanage, so you could kill him. Quan's statement is quite clear on the fact that you wanted to be the one who killed Waters."

McMillian turned red in the face and almost choked with anger.

"I went to that orphanage to protect the children," he finally sputtered. "But when I saw that obscene individual, I was overcome with rage. I could not stop myself and so I shot him, making sure the bullet hit him right between his legs where it should have. I didn't mean to kill him, just to destroy that part of him that had attacked me and so many others. He was a pedophile, evil incarnate. You saw what he did to me."

"Vengeance is for the court and God, not you."

"Your slander would not even merit an indictment," McMillian continued. "Any reasonable judge would throw it out because it is based on the testimony of a dead man and a colonel in an enemy army. If it went to trial, a jury would declare me innocent."

Paul had made that possibility clear, but it made no difference to Hank. "Maybe so," he said, "But the media and your opposition might see it differently. There are too many facts. And even if you went to trial and were acquitted, the publicity would end your career, an ugly end to your long service. The details in this file would embarrass the agency. You would be branded a serial killer and a traitor. You would never be free. But because of our childhood friendship, I'll make you an offer. If you resign, I will change this file to present the case against the Saudis having nukes, not your involvement in that or the various deaths and the kidnappings."

"I cannot do that," McMillian said. "You are threatening me."

"I have no choice," Hank said. "You are a killer working with a foreign government in a conspiracy that could endanger the United States. Senator Tompkins promised that if anything happens to me, he would not only to release this file, but also demand a congressional investigation. That alone would derail your nomination. Colonel Quan would not want his country's reputation being brought out in such a way. He would respond, most likely, against you, not me."

"You are wrong about that," McMillian said as he turned to the guard. "Get him out of here. Keep his weapon."

Discouraged, Hank went back to his motel and called Paul. "McMillian listened to me," he said, "But he threw me out and scoffed at the idea that I might release the report, said everybody would just laugh at it. He called it bullshit, but I survived and did what I intended. I looked him in the eye and told him to resign."

"Knock on wood," Paul said. "You're alive."

"Alive but saddened," Hank said. "I'll be home tomorrow."

Hank's long, long journey was over. He had tried everything he had, but the damn thing was still unsolved. It was beyond him. He had to acknowledge defeat. Too bad. He had given it all he had. The whole thing was too much.

Chapter Seventy-Five

The next morning as Hank prepared to leave for Dulles, the phone rang.

"I read your report," McMillian said. "We ought to find a compromise. Let's try. We can meet at nine o'clock tonight at the tennis courts in the Montrose section of Rock Creek Park. The courts are open and lighted. The meeting will be worthwhile. I'll return your gun. We can have a full discussion. If you're worried, bring Steve Powell for security."

Hank called Powell and asked if he thought the meeting was a good idea. If so, would he come? Powell not only said the meeting was a good idea, but he offered to drive. Hank then called Paul and said he and Powell would meet McMillian that evening.

"You're crazy," Paul said. "He'll be coming at you with your own pistol. He'll stage your suicide. Don't risk it. It's not worth it."

"Steve Powell will be with me," Hank said. "I'll be okay."

On the way to the park, Powell said he had more information about the Saudi development of nuclear weapons, maybe a solution to the problem. He asked Hank to come by the senator's office in the morning.

When they arrived at the tennis complex, the courts were almost empty. McMillian was there, of course, with three bodyguards, one of whom was Blevins. In wasn't a great night for tennis. A light mist had fallen and made the park gloomy. Just one couple was on court, playing bad tennis, occasionally slipping and almost falling on the wet surface.

"Those two are going to break something," Hank said.

"They're not worth watching," McMillian said. "I don't like it here.

Let's go someplace where we can stay dry and talk."

The guards led them to a darkened and more secluded area away from the lighted tennis complex. With Blevins in front, a second guard following, and the third back with Steve, the group walked about a hundred yards down an ever-darker lane. Agreeing to meet McMillian was a mistake. Paul was right. This was a suicidal mission. With each step, his apprehension grew; it was as if he was back with Quan on the path between rows of armed soldiers to that small graveyard in the wet jungles of Vietnam. He should not have come. When McMillian finally stopped, Hank saw that the guards had put on gloves and drawn pistols. Steve Powell was not going to be able to provide enough security. That was when Hank knew he would never see Bev, Faith, and Hope again.

"I've thought this over," McMillian said. "We can end this fight right now. I've read your brief, and you've made your point. But more killing won't stop anything. We need to find a way to compromise. Here's my offer. If you can walk away and keep quiet about the past, I will guarantee that nothing more will happen to you, your family, or any of your friends. You have a good supporter in Senator Tompkins. He will publicize your file if he decides I am not living up to my commitment. If you walk away, I promise you that there will be no more killings. That should be acceptable to you, because all this is your fault. You started it back in Hawaii a long time ago. When we first saw Waters in his tent camp, I wanted to run away, but you insisted on talking to him, finding out what he doing out there in the woods. So we went in to talk to him, and that started everything. We are at the end of a path you initiated."

That was baloney, just an excuse to shift blame. He couldn't accept it. Too many people had died. Their families and friends deserved closure, and walking away from the problem wouldn't solve anything. Above all, McMillian was a madman, a threat to the country. He couldn't be allowed near the president.

"It would be a shame," McMillian continued, "if you reject my offer. This story would end badly for you or yours. That need not happen."

"You could survive a trial, you know," Hank said. "You'd have a good lawyer and many supporters. At trial, you might win. If you continue on the path you have started, however, you will be the one to end badly."

"I can't take that chance," McMillian said. Then seeing no agreement from Hank he turned to Blevins and commanded, "Take him out."

"If you kill me, Senator Tompkins will come after you."

"You're a fool, Hank Kean. Senator Tompkins is the one who orchestrated all this; the theft of the nukes, the Saudi involvement, Orzon story, and your involvement. He persuaded Colonel Manh to feed you rumors about drugs to divert you from the nukes. He knew from his time with you after the war college that you were the kind of man that would take the bait and run with it. The idea was to confuse you and keep the nuke story away from him. It worked."

"I don't believe you. How could he make Manh lie about Orzon?" "It was easy. All he had to do was promise a lucrative government computer contract for the kid's business. And he knew that if you heard the rumors about drugs and the Manhs, you would run with the story and keep it alive. He was right. You did a good job, so well done that Tompkins even had me believing this was all about drugs. When I checked it out, however, I uncovered the scheme. You see, after Tompkins planted the story with Manh and persuaded him to write you, all he had to do was sit back and watch it unfold. He just had to help it along now and then, and that was what tipped me off."

"How did he help it along?" Hank asked.

"He got you that quick visa to Vietnam. He funneled bits of information to us so we would suspect you and your family about drugs. He knew that if we pestered you, we would tick you off and keep you angry and confused. And you wouldn't suspect him. You even asked for his help and furnished him with updates. You never suspected he was the mastermind of the theft of those nuclear weapons."

"Is Bakr bin Laden's story about the Saudis replicating nukes true?"

"Absolutely. Tompkins arranged the theft and then sent the Saudis the two weapons. They couldn't believe their luck. So they set one off, to see if it actually worked and then threatened to use the other against Iran if it continued building a bomb. And the damn scheme worked. Can you believe it? Iran has stopped its nuclear program, at least for now. The Saudis had a temporary problem in replicating the one bomb they had left. They wanted to build their own weapons, but they had neither the expertise nor the nuclear fuel. So Tompkins arranged for Pakistan to supply fuel and scientific expertise. And now the Saudis are on their way to replication. The Pakistanis were the same people that built the fake ones used in the depot when the Sayyaf stole the weapons."

"How do you know all these things?" "Your girlfriend works for us."

Hank lunged at McMillian, but Blevins and another guard stopped him.

McMillian glared at Hank for a moment and then commanded, "Take him out."

Hank involuntarily ducked as he heard a sputtered soft pop. Then realizing, he had not been hurt, he straightened and saw McMillian on the ground with Blevins bending over him. The other two agents stood beside Hank, while Steve was behind him with the two fake agency tennis players. Blevins put something in McMillian's coat pocket.

"McMillian was a traitor working with a foreign government," Blevins said. "He was an affront to the agency. He had to go. What I just put in his pocket was a picture of you with that hair dresser from Hilton Head. That will confuse the police and divert them from us, send them in your direction, giving us more time to get out of here. My compliments, sir. You've got good taste in women. The original photo is in Charley's house, in the safe. We will now tell Colonel Quan how his C.I.A. contact died, and Quan will be very unhappy. The Vietnamese had plans for McMillian. Too bad. All that is over, so there will have to be changes. I am confident that if you live tonight, you will not be indicted, especially if you claim some rogue agents killed him and make sure the police note that there is no gun powder residue on your hand or jacket. But Colonel Quan may be a problem for you. He won't like what has happened. He may blame you. So, get your gun back. You may need it. Quan is a violent man with a long memory. In Vietnam we heard you tell him that memories are the stuff of dreams. If that's true, I expect you're in for some really bad ones."

He had no doubt about that. Stunned by Blevins revelations, he didn't know what would come next. What would happen?

CHAPTER SEVENTY-SIX

"Colonel Quan may be in your future for quite some time," Blevins then said, "if you have one. But what I must decide now, before the police arrive, is how to deal with you."

Then two agents took Hank by his arms, and Steve Powell and the fake tennis players came forward to stand beside Blevins. The stage was set.

"I might easily stage a murder-suicide scene," Blevins said. "One of my men could sap you with a club. Then I would take your pistol, the one that just killed McMillian, stick its barrel in your mouth, and make your finger pull the trigger. That would stand police scrutiny. You would be out of circulation and out of my hair. I liked that idea, but you can relax. Our team leader has ordered me to let you live."

"Your team leader?" Hank asked. "What team? The C.I.A.?"

"No, not the agency. Our team is called Three Colonels. That's right, the same Three Colonels operation Senator Tompkins asked you about when he met you in Columbia this last December. Two of the three colonels, Manh and Orzon, are already dead, and I wanted to make you join them. Our team leader, your long-time handler, Onorato, ordered instead that you should join our team; Ted Storm, Steve Powell, and the five C.I.A. agents with us here tonight. That's right, Storm and Powell. They joined our operation because they believe, as you and I do, that to furnish Saudi Arabia with nuclear weapons would be insane, suicide for America or Israel. The five C.I.A. agents with us here are also committed to stopping Tompkins's crazy idea. You have already met two of them, the tennis players. They were in Juarez when you took Samantha Trang from them. They are Tom and Sharon Moore, the real estate prospects Bill West took to Rappahannock County. The other two, Ron and

Jim, took care of Gus Bean up in Massachusetts. The mission of our operation is to prevent Senator Tompkins from arming Saudi Arabia with the small nuclear weapons they are attempting to build in that factory Mohammad bin Laden built for King Faisal in northwest Saudi Arabia."

Hank stared in disbelief first at Blevins and then at Powell. These people had killed Gus, Bill, and probably the Manhs, to stop the Saudis from getting a bomb. They thought their ends justified their means. They were wrong.

"We joined Onorato's team," Blevins said, "because every one of us believes very strongly, as you emphasized to Onorato, that to arm Saudi Arabia with such weapons would be a colossal mistake. You reported what Bakr bin Laden told you if the Saudis had such weapons, they would very likely use them against Israel or New York. We cannot allow even the possibility of that happening. That is why the Three Colonels operation was formed."

"That's correct," Powell said. "When I read your file, I imme-diately saw the danger to Israel and America, obvious danger that Senator Tompkins ignored. I went to Onorato with my concerns, and he contacted Ted Storm for verification. That was when Storm joined us. Onorato is our leader because as a long-time official in defense intelligence, he has the clout to get things done in Washington. He has compiled a file that is better than yours because it concentrates solely on stopping the Saudi operation, not on peripheral things such as the deaths of Bean and West. We are nearing the end of all this, thank God."

"Why are those deaths of Gus and Bill mere peripheral?" Hank asked. "They were good men, combat veterans. Their deaths are rel-evant. You have to pay for killing them."

"Their deaths are not in Onorato's file," Blevins said, "because Tompkins had nothing to do with them. Those deaths were not involved in this nuclear mess. Their deaths were entirely my idea, acting on my own out of anger at your killing David, a good man and friend. You and I may hash out that later. Now we have to focus on our objective; to thwart Senator Tompkins and end the Saudi nuclear threat. I really wanted to kill you, as did Colonel Quan when you were under his control in Vietnam, but Onorato overruled both of us.

Because he saved you, he asks that you cooperate with Operation Three Colonels."

"I won't be much help if I am in jail for the murder of McMillian."

"You will not be indicted. Just remember when the police arrive to show them where I threw your pistol. Tell them that rogue C.I.A. agents killed him. Insist they test you immediately for powder residue on you or your clothes. They will find none and will believe your story. If they don't, just call on your attorney, Paul Ruth. The district police will quickly let you go."

"Before the police arrive, I want to tell you the remaining plans for our operation. In a few days, Onorato will meet Senator Tompkins and Steve Powell. Onorato will show his file to the senator. When Tompkins fully understands what that file contains, Onorato will demand that the good senator announce his immediate resignation, promising to never again run for an elective office. Instead, he will leave Washington and reside in his Hilton Head condominium, to spend the rest of his days writing his memoirs and fishing for mackerel in the Atlantic waters off the island coast. He will cancel his deal with Pakistan to provide nuclear fuel and scientific support to Saudi Arabia. At Hilton Head, you and Paul Ruth will watch Tompkins at all times, and Onorato will monitor his phone and computer. If Tompkins does not agree to our demands and live up to our demands, Onorato will release his file to the media. You will then also release your file as additional proof. Steve Powell is confident the senator will take the deal rather than risk humiliation and a trial that would put him in jail."

Powell nodded.

"I can't ignore your killing Bean and West," Hank said. "When will we meet?"

"Not for a very long time," Blevins said. "My team and I are going to disappear as only C.I.A. agents know how. You will never find us. But rest assured, we will be watching to ensure Tompkins does not renege on his agreement. We will know he has done that if the Saudis set off another bomb in the Empty Quarter with a nuclear signature that is not that of the bomb stolen from Germany. A different signature would indicate they had developed one of their own. If that happens, Tompkins's boat will explode the next time he goes fishing. He knows that."

"Now, please, listen carefully, for I have just one final very important item for you: McMillian lied when he said that your girlfriend worked for him. I tried to enlist her, but to her credit, she refused. She's a good one. Now, my team and I must leave before the police come."

With that, the five of them disappeared into the darkness, and Steve Powell came to Hank, held out his hand, and asked, "Deal?"

Hank thought for a moment. Then he asked Powell, "Do you realize what that crazy nut you work for actually did? Think about just a second; the Iranians have stopped building nuclear weapons. They're afraid the Saudi program will explode a bomb in Tehran. They don't know that the Saudis can't build a bomb. All they know is the Saudis exploded one and are saying they will explode the next in Iran. It worked, and your fruitcake boss made it happen. Talk about unexpected consequences. I will find a way to avenge Gus and Bill. Warn Blevins about that."

Hank shook his head. Then he nodded and stuck out his hand. "Deal," he said.

Powell ran for his car, and Hank was alone with McMillian's body. Hearing the dismal howl of approaching police sirens, he looked up and realized that the mist had disappeared. He was alive. A thousand stars twinkled above. It was a dingle night.